"DON'T PLAY DUMB WITH ME."

"I know what's going on. I saw you take Garland and Hattie aside, and I saw the fire trucks in front of the house. You want to see what's left of her house, don't you? You want to see if her little secret gets buried with her, so to speak."

My frozen ears stood at attention. So did Greg's.

She sniffed. "You're not exactly Columbo, are you?"

"No ma'am, I'm not." Greg had managed to sound enough like Columbo for me to pick up on it, but apparently Amy had not.

She sniffed again. "Columbo would know that it's not the damn furniture everyone is after, or Lottie Bell, or the house—but a secret that goes with the furniture."

Den of Antiquity Mysteries by
Tamar Myers
from Avon Books

GILT BY ASSOCIATION

A DEN OF ANTIQUITY MYSTERY

TAMAR MYERS

AVON BOOKS
An Imprint of HarperCollinsPublishers

This is a work of fiction. Names, characters, places, and incidents are products of the author's imagination or are used fictitiously and are not to be construed as real. Any resemblance to actual events, locales, organizations, or persons, living or dead, is entirely coincidental.

AVON BOOKS
An Imprint of HarperCollins*Publishers*
10 East 53rd Street
New York, New York 10022-5299

Copyright © 1996 by Tamar Myers
Library of Congress Catalog Card Number: 96-96487
ISBN: 0-380-78237-5
www.avonmystery.com

First Avon twilight printing: March 1999
First Avon books printing: December 1996

Avon Trademark Reg. U.S. Pat. Off. and in Other Countries, Marca Registrada, Hecho en U.S.A.
HarperCollins® is a trademark of HarperCollins Publishers Inc.

Printed in the U.S.A.

10 9 8 7

For my husband, Jeff

I would like to acknowledge my editor, Carrie Feron; her assistant, Ann McKay Thoroman; and my agent, Nancy Yost. In addition to these ladies in the publishing business, I owe a debt of gratitude to Page Hendrix at the York County Library in Rock Hill, South Carolina.

And, of course, to all you antique dealers out there.

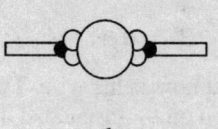

1

The invoice from the estate auction read as follows:

one Louis XV armoire
one Louis XV desk
one small Louis XV table
one carved and gilded mirror

It said nothing about a body. I read the invoice one more time just to be sure. *No body.*

I sat down rather heavily on a sturdy Victorian side chair. Finding a corpse in a closet is not a daily occurrence at the Den of Antiquity. One should excuse me then for stopping to catch my breath before I called the Charlotte police. I'm sure you will understand as well when I tell you that it took me several minutes to catch that breath.

My name is Abigail Timberlake, and the Den of Antiquity is all that I have. Three years ago I was a happily married woman, mother of two almost grown children, library volunteer, and president of the Episcopal Church Women. I even had a dog, Scruffles, and a cat, Dmitri. But that was then, and this is now, as my children used to say.

Buford Timberlake changed all that. As ex-husbands go, Buford is the sludge at the bottom of the pond. Timberlake the Timber Snake, I call him. Of course some of the credit should go to the blond puffball who used to be

1

his secretary and now is his wife. Tweetie Byrd—her real name, I kid you not—insinuated herself into my husband's lap, and then his life, with the rapidity of a striking snake, so maybe she's part reptile, too. At any rate, Tweetie is now mistress of the manor, and stepmother to my son, Charlie. Thank God, my daughter, Susan, had already flown the nest when The Byrd took over.

That Buford had been awarded custody of everything near and dear to me (with the exception of my shadow) has nothing to do with my competence or moral track record. It is simply because Buford is a lawyer. A damn good lawyer. Maybe the best. Buford is capable of convicting Pollyanna of a bad attitude, and once he decided to go for Tweetie, who was twenty, and cast me aside, it was all over except for the pain.

I am lucky to have escaped with my antique shop. I can only guess that Tweetie presumed the Den of Antiquity was a geriatric sex club, and being so consumed with Buford, hadn't enough energy left over to take that on as well. I would like to think that the shop would have remained mine no matter what, since I started it from scratch. Of course I started my children from scratch as well, but that didn't stop Tweetie Byrd from taking over my nest and stealing my remaining fledgling.

None of that has anything to do with the price of antique silk in China, or what I'm about to tell you. I just wanted you to know that I didn't have it "made in the shade"—to quote The Byrd—and I still don't. The fact that my dearly departed Aunt Eulonia (herself a murder victim) left me a considerable estate last year, and I finally have some financial stability, is none of Tweetie's business. The point I'm trying to make is that my shop has come to fill a tremendous void in my life. Outside of my loved ones, it is my life.

So I hope you can understand how it was that finding a corpse in a closet was threatening, to say the least. I realize now how callous this must sound to you. How shocked you probably are that I didn't immediately respond to the corpse as a person. But I was in shock myself, you see. After all the stress I'd been under, something had simply shorted out in my brain. Even now I cringe when I say this, but I was far more concerned about what the body would do to my business than about the body itself. I wish now that I had felt differently.

I also wish that I had called 911. Unfortunately, someone else beat me to the punch.

"Well, well, what have we here?"

I jumped several inches off the chair. There are eight sleigh bells attached to my front door, but I was so distraught I had not heard anyone enter. In my frame of mind, it could well have been the corpse conversing. I whirled and faced the speaker, a middle-aged police officer in a blue uniform.

"He isn't on my invoice," I said stupidly.

"Ma'am?" Charlotte police are invariably polite.

"He wasn't part of the lot. I only bid on the desk, the table, the mirror, and that!" I pointed to the armoire, in which the body sat, slumped in a heap.

"Name?"

"I don't know his name!" I wailed.

"No ma'am, your name."

"I have a right to remain silent, and refuse to answer questions," I began. "I have a right to call an attorney. If I—"

"I'm not arresting you, ma'am," said the man in blue. "I just want to ask you a few questions. We can do that here, or down at the station. Take your pick."

That was like asking me to choose between liver and boiled turnips. Following Aunt Eulonia's murder, I spent more than my fair share of time hanging around the police station. For the record, allow me to stress that all of my hanging around was in front of the bars, not behind them.

Still, police stations give me the heebie-jeebies. On the other hand, I had been dating—on and off—a very handsome police detective named Greg Washburn who had recently been promoted (demoted, he claims) to a desk job downtown. Unfortunately our relationship was now in its "off" stage, and until Greg came up with a satisfactory explanation for why I saw him at Hooters in the company of a redhead with humongous hooters of her own, I didn't want to see him. Reluctantly I chose the boiled turnips.

I stood up. I've seen newborn foals with sturdier legs. "I'll go to the station."

"Then excuse me, ma'am," the officer said, and he began talking into his cellular phone.

There was a lot of static, and he conducted his business several paces away, but I still managed to hear words like "victim" and "perpetrator." My blood ran cold. It was clear to me that there were two victims in the shop right then, and no perpetrator. Unless I could convince him otherwise, I would have to kiss my career as an antique dealer good-bye. After all I'd already been through, I didn't think I had it in me to fight my way through the jungle that is our justice system.

Faced with fight or flight, I fleetingly considered fleeing. Frankly, it crossed my mind to fling a cranberry glass vase at him, and then make a run for it. I keep a lot of room open on my credit cards, and I had just filled my gas tank that morning. But I was never good at throwing things, and had, in fact, been passed up by the girls' softball team in college. Twice. Besides which, the cranberry glass vase was exquisite.

The officer stepped back into grabbing range. "I've called for assistance."

I took a careful step backward. "There's no need for that," I said quickly. "I'll go peacefully. I promise."

He smiled. "I was counting on that, ma'am."

This time I heard the bells and was not surprised when

a pair of men stepped in. I mean that literally. Rob Gold-burg and Bob Steuben are life-partners who own the shop next door. Ever since my Aunt Eulonia was murdered, the two of them have been clucking over me like mother hens. Rob is a handsome, robust man in his fifties with a thick head of hair just starting to gray at the temples. He has a temper. Bob is a spindly man almost twenty years younger. His face is too narrow to be handsome, and his hair is mousy. He does, however, possess a voice that could calm the Bosporus Straits.

"Everything all right?" Bob asked in that wonderful voice. "We saw the car outside. There hasn't been a rob-bery, has there?"

"Damn bastards should be shot for robbing antique stores," Rob said. "Either that or lock them up and throw away the key. No parole, that's for sure." Their shop had been robbed twice, and he meant every word.

I pointed to the armoire.

"Holy moly!" It was Bob's turn to sit on the Victorian side chair. He's not as tough as Rob, and his face had turned to white porcelain.

"What a waste of a perfectly beautiful armoire," Rob moaned. "Eighteenth-century French?" Either he was even tougher than I thought, or he was in shock as well.

"From Lula Mae Barras's estate," I said. "I bought it for a client, but now it's ruined. You don't know a good way to lift bloodstains from wood, do you?" Thinking about the armoire was much easier than thinking about the body.

"I'd try a teaspoon of baking soda with an ounce of clear ginger ale. Make sure it's mixed well and apply it with a cotton swab. They should lift right off."

"Does diet ginger ale work?"

"Excuse me," the officer said, "but this isn't home ec class. We have—"

The bells jangled again and I could see that his backup

had arrived. He intercepted his reinforcement at the door and the two officers conferred with each other. They nodded in my direction. I could feel them talking about me. Handcuff size, leg irons, that sort of thing.

"I didn't do it," I said to nobody in particular. I think I repeated it several times. No doubt I was beginning to sound like a broken record, or was that a chipped CD?

Bob got out of the chair and gave me a quick hug. "You're in shock, dear. Is there anything we can do?"

"Yes, anything," Rob said. "I could even pinch-hit for you here, as long as they remove *him*."

Bob flashed his partner a warning look. Offering to tend shop for me was going too far. The two of them are never more than an arm's reach apart, and they had their own shop to run. Despite their obvious differences, I had long since thought of them as a single unit, the "Rob-Bobs." Married couples, even newlyweds, are seldom that attached at the hip.

"Well, we could do things for you at home. You know, bring in the paper, feed the cat, that sort of thing," Rob said.

"Yes," I heard myself say. "Please bring in the paper, and the mail too. Dmitri is all out of food—I meant to buy some on my way home tonight. Would you mind terribly?"

"What kind?" Bob asked.

"Dry. Any brand. But fish-flavored."

"Consider it done," the Rob-Bobs said in unison.

"Oh, and one more thing."

"Yes?"

I spoke quickly. "Whatever you do, don't call Buford. He can't find out about this. If he does, I won't see Charlie until he's eighteen. And I can kiss this shop good-bye." I looked around sadly.

The Rob-Bobs exchanged glances. "Sweetheart," one of them said, "you positive you don't want us to call

Buford? He's bound to find out anyway. Surely he wouldn't want the mother of his children going to jail.''

I couldn't help but laugh. ''Buford would send God to jail if the Tweetie Byrd asked him. No, I swear Lake Norman will freeze over solid before I ask Buford Timberlake for any help. Whatever trouble I'm in, I'll get out of by myself.''

The Rob-Bobs nodded.

''You always did look good in stripes,'' one of them said kindly.

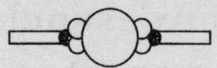

2

I composed myself for the interrogation. To be honest, I was disappointed. I suppose I had imagined a windowless room lit only by a harsh spotlight trained directly at my eyes. Behind the spotlight I would hear, but not see, a chain-smoking detective, who was undoubtedly wearing a rumpled, sweat-stained suit, and who had a voice like James Cagney.

I didn't expect to be handed a cup of well-brewed coffee, with cream and sugar. The room I was in had no windows, but the recessed fluorescent lighting was sufficiently bright for me to read the fine print on the sugar packet. The chair I was offered was contemporary and boxy, but the natural cotton upholstery looked comfortable, as well as clean. Ditto for my interrogator. It was Greg Washburn.

"Name please?"

"Abigail Louise Timberlake. But you already know that."

The Wedgwood-blue eyes blinked. "Please, Abby. This is an official interview. I have to ask these questions for the record."

"Ask away," I said. When he was through, I had a few questions of my own.

"Marital status?"

"Divorced. Three years. From Buford Timberlake. We were married twenty-three years."

Greg smiled, revealing perfect white teeth. "You like to anticipate my questions, don't you?"

"I like to be prepared," I said. "Thinking ahead means fewer surprises. And I'm forty-seven."

"Eight," he said. "Your birthday was last week."

I gave him a pointed look. "So it was."

"Place of employment?"

"The Den of Antiquity, 3629 Selwyn Avenue. I'm the proprietor."

"Want to guess what I'm going to ask next?"

"What a body was doing in my armoire?"

"Bingo."

I shook my head. "Beats me. I never saw it before in my life."

"The armoire?"

"No, the body. Or should I call it a corpse? The armoire I've seen. French, you know. Parisian. Circa 1775. The finish is in very good condition."

"How long have you had it?"

The question momentarily threw me. "Had it? Oh, you mean the armoire! I haven't! I mean, it had just arrived. It and three other pieces that I bought at auction yesterday."

Greg ran a large hand through a head of thick, almost black hair. His own hair. "Tell me about the auction."

I tore my eyes away from him and stared into my coffee cup. It was remarkably reflective and made me wish I'd backbrushed my short brown hair that day, instead of merely combing it off my face.

"The auction was at the Purvis Auction Barn down in Pineville. It started yesterday afternoon at two. The usual crowd was there."

"Usual?"

"I mean the auction was open to the public, but it

wasn't advertised, so mostly just dealers showed up. Keeps the riffraff out.''

He raised a dark eyebrow. Unlike most men I'd been dating lately, Detective Washburn had two of those.

I took a deep breath. My choice of words had been unfortunate. "What I mean is, having the general public there can complicate things.''

The other eyebrow shot up.

"Well, we don't like them to see what we pay for the goods,'' I admitted sheepishly. "They wouldn't understand our markup system.'' But there was more to it than that.

While I am happy to take my customers' money, most days I can do without their attitude. You'd be surprised at some of the things I've seen and heard during the eight years I've been in this business. Everybody wants to buy steak at hamburger prices, and just because most antique shops in the area do allow a certain amount of ''bargaining,'' that doesn't mean we are willing to give our merchandise away.

I have had customers scratch their initials in pieces of furniture and then claim that the pieces used to belong to them and were stolen. Sometimes they run car keys along the inside of a chair leg and then ask me to discount it. One lady used a nail file to mar the glaze on a Limoges platter and then had the nerve to demand I sell it to her at half-price. Yes, I know, these folks are the exception, but even many of my best customers expect me to sell them an item at cost. Where, I wonder, do they think my mortgage money is coming from, and what do they expect me to eat? Just because I received a one-time inheritance from my Aunt Eulonia, I'm not immune to the cost of living.

We dealers must make a profit to survive, just like anyone else. If we're very lucky we are occasionally offered first crack at someone's estate *before* they die. Folks moving into nursing homes or retirement centers obviously can't take it all with them. Sometimes after a death, relatives will invite me over to the deceased's house and ask me to make an offer. But I don't have the connections Purnell Purvis does, and most Monday afternoons will find me down at Purvis Auction Barn, bidding on pieces that I think will sell well in my shop.

I must confess that until recently the Den of Antiquity has housed an eclectic collection of middle-of-the-road items that date from the early eighteen hundreds through the Great Depression. The fine pieces from the Barras estate would have been out of my reach, had it not been for the windfall of Aunt Eulonia's estate. But I must emphasize that I cannot afford to *keep* such expensive items in stock. I must turn them around, and soon, if I expect to remain in business.

At any rate, the antique community in the greater Charlotte area is a close knit one. We are like family. Sometimes we love one another, sometimes we hate one another. Monday afternoons at Purvis Auction Barn is our family reunion, and we don't cotton much to outsiders. Old Purvis only lets them into the barn because they have money. But as I said, he doesn't advertise, so thankfully the outsiders are few and far between.

"It's basically an auction among friends," I added.

The eyebrows came down. "You said before that yesterday was *mostly* just dealers. Were there other folks there as well?"

I shrugged. "There might have been. Every now and then one of the public wanders in, and if they look like they can rub two nickels together, Purvis lets them stay. But we're a big group, and things can get really hopping. So I can't say for sure if there were any drop-ins yesterday."

Before he could ask me anything else, a uniformed officer walked into the room without knocking and whispered in Greg's ear. I never knew men were capable of conversing so softly. When the interloper left, Greg settled back in his chair like a cat about to nap. He may have been relaxed, but my heart was pounding.

"You ever see the deceased before?" he asked.

I shook my head. "No. I never saw the body until I opened the armoire door."

The Wedgwood eyes regarded me calmly. "He has a name, you know."

I nodded. Let him try to trick me into saying a name I'd never heard. He would have to wait forever.

Greg suddenly leaned forward. "It's Arnold Ramsey." He sat back again.

The name meant nothing. However, hearing the name had a strange effect on me. Until that moment, because of shock, the body in the armoire had been just that—a body. A corpse. My concern had been my business and visitation rights to my son. The body was just a thing. A hunk of meat. It may as well have been a cow. But a name changed everything. Suddenly that was a man, a person in my newly purchased armoire. And he was dead!

I began to cry.

"There, there," Greg said, in that helpless tone men use when they encounter tears. He gallantly handed me a handkerchief.

I graciously accepted it. But to my disgust, the handkerchief, which was clearly a man's handkerchief, smelled like a woman. A woman who wore cheap perfume.

"The redhead?" I asked, immediately handing the cloth back.

He crossed his arms. "It was your idea that we cool it for a while, Abby. It was you who suggested we date other people."

I crossed my legs. "I only wanted to catch my breath, Greg. Things were moving faster than I expected. I didn't want to end up married again before I knew what hit me."

He was kind enough not to laugh, but not kind enough to suppress a huge grin. "Who said anything about marriage? I thought things were fine as they were. We were both having a great time, weren't we?"

"Were we?"

"The sex was super," he said, the grin bigger than ever.

I stood up. I am on the short side—four foot nine without heels. Unfortunately, because I had planned on unpacking my new purchases, I was wearing a pair of old flats. A good pair of spikes can push me up to five feet and do wonders for my self-esteem, not to mention the respect I get.

"We never *had* sex, buster. You must have me confused with Silicone Sally."

"Her name is Deena," he said. "And we're just friends. I was only kidding about the sex."

I forced a big grin of my own. "No, you were right the first time. We did have sex. Only it was so mediocre I must have blocked it out."

He glanced around nervously. No doubt our conversation was being monitored, if not taped. It had been stupid and unprofessional of him to forget that.   .

"Very funny," he said softly.

"Yes, sex with you was often very funny," I said loudly. "Remember the time we traded clothes—"

"Abby!"

I relented and backed off, for old time's sake, if for nothing else. Greg had always been a gentleman, and I mean that as a compliment. And even though I was furious at him for dating Deena, there was no point in burning bridges. A little grovelling and a dozen yellow roses can go a long way with this gal.

"Well, back to my business," I said briskly.

He pointed soberly at the chair, and I sat back down. "Yes?"

"Did you know those two guys who delivered your armoire?"

"Jimbo and Skeet?"

He shrugged. "You tell me."

"Well, I don't know their last names, if that's what you want. I just know that they called each other Jimbo and Skeet. So yes, I have seen them before, but I don't really know them. I just know that they've worked for old Purvis for years."

He glanced down at a tablet in his lap. "And what can you tell me about Purnell Purvis?"

I sighed. "The old coot's a tyrant," I said charitably. "He can turn honey into vinegar just by looking at it. Still, Purvis would never do anything like that. Force someone into an armoire and then kill them."

"How do you know that?"

"I just do. He might be as mean as a knotted-up snake, but he has principles. Ask anyone."

"No, what I meant was, how do you know that Mr. Ramsey was forced into the armoire and *then* killed? How do you know it wasn't the other way around?"

"Well, that should be fairly obvious to anyone who has seen the armoire."

"Yes, but pretend for a moment that I haven't seen the armoire. If I looked at it through your eyes, what would I see?"

"Well, I mean, right there on the back wall of the armoire there is a message written in blood. A dead man can't write, can he?"

I had never seen Greg more attentive. If only finding dead bodies wasn't so stressful, it could sure put the life back into a relationship.

"A message? What did it say?"

"You mean *you* didn't see it?"

"Ah, of course I did. But I'm interested in your interpretation."

I knew he was bluffing, and it's frightening when you see things that a trained police investigator misses. Maybe all that training to look for hairs and dust molecules out of place has left them blind to the handwriting on the wall.

"Of course, it wasn't a whole message," I said. "Just the letter 'B,' but you can bet it stood for something important. I know I wouldn't waste my time or blood writing meaningless graffiti if I were dying. Say, you wouldn't happen to know a surefire way to remove bloodstains, would you?"

"I'll ask the lab," he said. He was scribbling furiously on his pad.

I waited patiently, content for the moment just to watch him. Greg Washburn is easy on the eyes. No, make that the most handsome man I have ever met. I know that beauty—especially physical beauty—is subjective, but if Greg Washburn were on TV or in the movies, millions of women would fall in love with him. Yet he had picked me to date, when there had to be thousands of other Charlotteans who would jump at the chance. Perhaps I had been precipitous in reining in our relationship. Even if I lost my head entirely, there had to be worse things than waking up some morning and finding out that I was Mrs. Greg Washburn.

"Greg?"

He looked up, the Wedgwood-blue eyes half-shaded by long black lashes. "Yes?"

"I was thinking. I mean, maybe we could start over. If you know what I mean."

"You know this Arnold Ramsey after all?"

"What?"

"How well did you know him, Abby?" he asked. He wasn't kidding.

I stood up again. "Look, I told you I didn't know him. So, if you'll excuse me—" I took a small step toward the door, waiting for him to stop me.

"I'm going to have to impound the armoire," he said quietly.

I stopped. I tossed my head. Unfortunately head tossing is a gesture that is far more effective when one has long hair.

"Impound it then. Now can I go?"

He had stopped scribbling and was obviously doodling. "And I'm afraid that includes the other three pieces you bought as well."

I stared, first at the tablet, then at him. It was a remarkably good sketch of me. The man must have had art lessons somewhere along the line.

"Do what you have to do," I said as nonchalantly as I could.

"That's what I'm leading up to. Abby, I'm not doing this to be mean, honest, it's just procedure."

My children accuse me of having a warning bell in my head. Perhaps they are right, because my head was certainly buzzing.

"There's more, isn't there?"

He clipped his pen to the top of the tablet. "I'm afraid your shop is going to have to be off-limits for a while. Just until we complete the investigation," he said quickly.

"What? But you can't do that! It's only three weeks until Christmas!"

He stood up. At six feet even, he towers over me.

"It'll only be for a few days, Abby. And it's not like you sell Christmas merchandise."

I was fit to be tied. What did he know about the market? I might not sell glove and scarf sets, or bottles of cheap cologne, but I do a healthy trade at Christmas. Outside of the summer tourist season, Christmas is *the* time in the antique business. What better gift can one give than something that has been appreciated enough to have been given before?

"You can't do that! There are laws," I sputtered. In

my moment of temporary insanity I was even thinking about calling Buford. Fortunately that moment lasted only a minute. Buford had been my ally when we were dating in college, but early on in the marriage—after its consummation on our wedding night—he began his rapid metamorphism into adversary. When my insanity had safely passed, I realized that Buford would happily have me— as well as the furniture—impounded.

Greg put a huge hand on my shoulder in a clumsy attempt to calm me. I shrugged it off. If it hadn't been for my certainty that we were being watched, I would have slapped it away.

"I'm sorry, Abby," he said. He sounded sorry, too.

It was too much to take. "This will hurt me more than it will you," Mama used to say before she spanked us children. I didn't need to hear that from Greg as well.

"You *find* whoever killed Arnold Ramsey," I said. I left the room.

No one made a move to stop me. Perhaps they would have, had they known that I had no intention on waiting for them to solve the case. I wish I could say that my motives were pure, that I had a burning desire to bring Arnold Ramsey's killer—or killers—to justice. But I didn't. With just three weeks left until Christmas, and the most expensive merchandise I'd ever owned just sitting there as if it were in storage, I had one thing on my mind. It was time to liberate my shop.

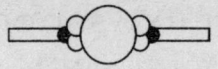

3

There was no practical reason for me to return to my shop that morning, but I had to nonetheless. When I'd left the Den of Antiquity in the care of a blue-suited officer an hour and a half earlier, I never dreamed that it would be off-limits to me for a while. I needed to say good-bye.

My timing couldn't have been worse. The folks from the *Charlotte Observer*—the city's largest newspaper—and the folks from Channel 9 and Channel 3 were out in force, and when they saw me, I may as well have been the rabbit at a greyhound race. I had already parked the car and was about a block from it when they spotted me. Unlike that bunny on a stick, I had no guarantee of outrunning my pursuers. Given my short legs it was doubtful I would have outrun any of them, except maybe for that one gal who was wearing a six-inch heel on one foot and a cast on the other. Frankly, if it wasn't for Wynnell Crawford, who owns Wooden Wonders, I would have been rabbit hash.

"Get in here!" Wynnell shouted.

I ducked into her shop and she slammed the door shut behind me, locking it with one expert stroke. The handful of customers browsing about were just going to have to be patient.

"How long have they been out there?" I huffed.

I'm pretty sure Wynnell scowled. She has eyebrows the size and shape of dwarf junipers, so sometimes it's hard to tell.

"They've been out there for at least an hour. We told them you weren't coming back for the rest of the day, but they wouldn't listen. Why are you back?"

"To say good-bye."

"They are not hauling you off to the slammer," Wynnell exclaimed.

Wynnell is my dearest friend. But outside of our mutual love of antiques, we have nothing in common. Even that's stretching things. I tend toward ornate pieces. Lots of detail. If heaven isn't furnished with gilt rococo, I'm going to be deeply disappointed. Wynnell, on the other hand, adores blocky Federal Period sofas and massive Victorian beds. I prefer to "display" my merchandise, whereas Wynnell stacks her stuff, leaving only narrow and somewhat dangerous passageways for her customers to navigate. Still, we are best buddies.

"They did, dear," I said, "but they aren't locking *me* up. It's my shop I'm talking about. They're locking it up for the next couple of days."

She gasped appropriately. "So close to Christmas?"

"What do they care? Oh Wynnell—"

There was a sharp rap at the door and much to my surprise—and dismay—Wynnell darted down one of the narrow passageways and opened it. The new arrival was not a reporter, but Jane Cox, the new owner of Feathers 'N Treasures, my aunt's old shop. In the process of letting in Jane, Wynnell expelled all her customers with the exception of one young couple who were doing unseemly things on a four-poster, rice plantation bed. Wynnell sells a lot of beds and no doubt it is at least partly due to her lenient policy of allowing her customers to try things out.

"Hey," Jane said, "I heard the news. Is there anything I can do to help?"

I bided my time, thinking carefully before answering. Jane Cox is a mere child of twenty-three, and an orphan to boot. One can't help but feel motherly toward her. On Selwyn Avenue we have already taken to affectionately calling Jane "C. J." We do it to her face, but she doesn't seem to mind at all. She thinks we are purposefully inverting her initials, like folks have to invert their names on some documents. Cox, Jane, that sort of thing. The truth is—and this is highly confidential—the C. J. in this case stands for Calamity Jane. That woman could take a freckle, turn it into a mole, turn that into melanoma, and wipe out the entire population of the United States with the world's first contagious cancer. Calamity Jane can do that in the time it takes me to put a new roll of toilet paper on my bathroom spool.

"Thank you for offering," I said with a smile. "I'll be just fine."

She paled: "They've arrested you, haven't they? First-degree murder, isn't it? I have a cousin whose brother-in-law was convicted of murder. Down in South Carolina. They gave him the death penalty. Lethal injection. Do you know what he had for his last meal? Fried okra and collard greens. Can you imagine that? Now Abby, when they ask you what you want for your last meal, order something really expensive. Lobster maybe. You won't have to pay for it. Ha! While you're at it, have something really fattening for dessert. You won't have to worry about gaining weight either. Ha!"

"I haven't been arrested," I said patiently. "They just asked me to close down my shop while they investigate."

She sucked in her breath sharply. "Ooh, I saw that in a movie once. The cops put a police tape around this woman's house—supposedly there had been a murder there—and the next thing you know a moving van pulled up and the cops robbed this woman of everything she owned. Even her grandbabies' pictures in those Kmart frames. Only they weren't cops you see, but just some very clever burglars. Well, don't worry. If they clean you out, I've got some stuff in my storeroom that I just don't have floor room for. I could let you have it real cheap." Calamity Jane was nothing if not generous.

I patted her arm gratefully. She usually goes on much longer than that.

"Thanks for your offer, dear, but would you mind awfully if I spoke to Wynnell alone? It's strictly business," I added, so she wouldn't get hurt.

Calamity Jane slapped her hands to her cheeks. "Oh, I'm so sorry! My Uncle Maynard had to file for bankruptcy too. It was awful. The poor man—"

"Please," I cried, clapping my hands over my ears.

Wynnell, bless her, grabbed one of C. J.'s elbows and steered her over to the door. By then the couple on the rice plantation bed were eager to exit as well. *Buying* a bed was the farthest thing from their minds.

"Lordy, she wasn't on to something, was she?"

"No, dear," I assured her. "You wouldn't happen to have an aspirin, would you?"

She found two in her desk drawer. I took them without water, chewing them thoroughly instead. It's an acquired taste, but the drug enters your bloodstream a lot faster that way.

"You know, I've been thinking," Wynnell said.

"Yes?"

"Your killer is a Yankee."

I should have known. Wynnell smells a Yankee behind every nefarious deed ever committed. She once tried to talk me into believing—unsuccessfully, I might add—that Hitler's maternal grandmother was originally from Massachusetts.

"Okay, I bite," I said tiredly. "Why do you think the person who killed Arnold Ramsey was a Yankee?"

Her mouth had opened wide enough for Sherman and

all his troops to enter—side by side. "Arnold Ramsey?" she finally asked.

"You know him?"

"Well, I know *an* Arnold Ramsey. It might not be the same one."

"Tell me about the one you know," I said. "I can't just sit on my hands. I'm going to talk to *anyone* who might have even the slightest connection to this horrible thing."

Wynnell looked worried. "Be careful, Abby."

"Tell me about Arnold Ramsey," I said, perhaps a wee bit impatiently.

"Well, he's just a kid who was once married to my niece, Mary Beth. The day after their divorce he married a floozy named Norma. She's a waitress down at Bubba's China Gourmet."

I knew the place; it's on a back road between Pineville and Matthews. At one point the building used to be a Baptist church, so the architecture is anything but Chinese. The cuisine can best be described as Southern Chinese. *Not* food from southern China, but Chinese food with a Southern accent. It has an unusually expensive fixed menu, but it serves a very reasonably priced buffet. This is what attracts most of its business. I hear that some interesting things show up in the buffet from time to time, but I am loath to eat at a Chinese restaurant—even a Southern Chinese restaurant—that has a salad bar, replete with iceberg lettuce and Jell-O. There, I've praised something I hate so I've done my charitable deed for the day.

"I'm sure Norma Ramsey has too much on her plate to talk to me," I said. "Got any other ideas?"

"There's always old Purvis. He's the one who shipped the stuff." As she spoke, Wynnell tugged dangerously at a loose thread on her purple and pink plaid pants.

Having done my good deed for the day, and because I am genuinely fond of her, I feel the need to describe Wynnell in more detail. Unfortunately the hedgerow eyebrows are not the first thing one notices about her. It is her clothes that scream loudest for attention, and you can almost hear their anguished cries. While Wynnell fancies herself a seamstress, she couldn't sew a straight line if her life depended on it. She also refuses to use patterns for the garish materials she rescues from the bargain bins at area fabric stores. Her originals are often so makeshift that even she has trouble putting them on.

I prayed that the purple and pink plaid pants wouldn't pull apart, revealing more than I cared to see. I had only heard about the fiasco when her skirt got caught in a revolving door in downtown Charlotte, but I'm told it left not a few eyewitnesses traumatized. Wynnell, it seems, does not always wear panties.

"Purnell Purvis is on my list, too," I said. "Can you think of anyone else?"

The hedges merged. "Those pieces you bought were from the Barras estate, weren't they? You might want to try talking to the family."

"That's a brilliant idea!" I gave Wynnell a hug. "You don't happen to know them, do you?"

"Ha! Not hardly. They are strictly la-dee-da. I read about them on the society page, same as you do, but that's it. Maybe your mama knows them."

I would ask Mama. My mother is not la-dee-da, but she is cultured and refined (alas, qualities she failed to pass on to me), and knows a good many influential people across the South. Pat Conroy once made her crabcakes for breakfast, or so she says.

I sneaked out the back door of Wynnell's storeroom and headed for Pineville to chat up old Purvis, but it was getting on to lunchtime and my car seemed to be driven by my stomach. That is to say, every turn I took somehow edged me closer to Bubba's China Gourmet. Clearly I was in need of an MSG fix, with a little grease thrown in.

The parking lot was full—thanks to that low-priced buffet—so I had to park across the road, in front of the carpet remnant store. I was nearly run over by a semi, two pickups, and a slew of cars—most of them bearing Ohio plates—before I made it across. The second I opened the door a melange of confusing aromas swirled about me. They were almost tangible.

"How many?" the hostess asked. She was a big Caucasian girl in a long, exotic dress. Something you might buy at Pier One Imports.

"Just one," I said. "Nonsmoking."

"We don't have a nonsmoking section," she said, accenting each stressed syllable with a loud crack of her gum.

I foolishly followed her to a red Naugahyde booth. There was a red-and-white-check tablecloth on the table, and an old Chianti bottle stuffed with silk flowers. The seats were a patchwork of fried noodle crumbs and duct tape. I took my time sitting down.

"Would you like to order from the menu, or try our generous buffet?" She sounded bored.

"Well—"

"Today we have several special items in our buffet," she said, and looked at me inquiringly.

"Do tell," I said.

"Today, in addition to the usual selections, our chefs have prepared stir-fried collard greens, sweet and sour okra, and moo goo gai grits." She said it with a straight face.

"You don't say!" I said kindly. "Perhaps I'll take a look at the menu."

She handed me a bright red menu with a gold-embossed dragon on it. It was then that I noticed her name tag said Norma.

"I see your name is Norma," I said pleasantly. "Two Normas in the same restaurant, isn't that something!"

She rolled her large, pale gray eyes. "So you're a Norma, too."

"My name is Abigail. I'm talking about Norma Ramsey, the waitress."

The gum popped loudly. "I'm Norma Ramsey."

I put down the menu. "You?"

She took a step back. "Am I supposed to know you, lady?"

I picked up the menu casually. "Well, no, you're not. Clearly I've made a mistake. The Norma Ramsey I'm talking about just lost her husband."

"So?"

"I mean, her husband just died. Like today—or maybe yesterday."

"Yeah, someone finally did Arnie in," she said. "Are you a cop or something? 'Cause I already talked to the cops."

I was having trouble believing my ears. "*You're* Norma Ramsey, the widow of Arnold Ramsey?"

She was a talented girl and produced a staccato burst of pops from the gum before answering. "What about it? Look, lady, I gotta get back to the door. If Bubba sees me talking to you this long, I'm out of here."

I fumbled in my purse for some money. It may not buy happiness, but now and then it can buy cooperation. All I could find, besides two twenties, were three ones. I put the singles in her hand.

"You're a comedian, right?"

I snatched back the singles and gave her one of the twenties.

"Oops, I can barely open my mouth," she said. "I think I got lockjaw."

I gave her the second twenty. "Speak, sister, or I shout for Bubba."

"Hey, Sally," she said to a pretty Oriental girl, "cover my post, will you?"

Sally mumbled something but headed for the door. Norma Ramsey slid into the booth opposite me.

"Like I said, I already talked to the cops. I don't have anything more to say."

I smiled pleasantly. "I'm not a cop, Norma. I'm an antique dealer. Your husband's body was found in an antique clothes cupboard. The armoire in question belonged to me."

"Oh," she said, and smiled.

"That's funny?" I asked.

"Yeah, it's a hoot. Arnie suffered from claustrophobia. It's kind of—now, what is that word—"

"Ironic?"

"Yeah. Arnie hated tight spaces. It made him crazy just to shower." She actually chuckled.

I swallowed back several things I could have said. "You don't seem all that broken up," I said calmly.

"Who me? Look, lady, Arnold Dewayne Ramsey was the meanest son of a bitch to walk this earth. When he was drunk he had a backhand like a tennis player, and he was always drunk."

I stared at her for a moment, and the large, pale gray eyes stared back. I finally figured it out.

"You mean he hit you?"

"Just about every day until I moved out. Lady, I haven't lived with that scum-sucking S.O.B. for over a year. Anything else you'd like to ask?"

I was taken aback. My script had called for a grieving widow, crying her eyes out at home. I wasn't prepared for a tough-talking young woman with a wad of gum in her mouth as big as an egg.

"What can you tell me about your—well, Arnold Ramsey—besides that he was an abusive husband?"

"He was a lousy lay." She laughed and had to clamp a hand over her mouth to keep the gum in.

"Where did he work?" I asked with dignity.

This time the gum came out but she caught it and popped it right back in. "You are a comedian! Arnie liked to lie around all day and watch them talk shows. He kept trying to get us on Ricki Lake. Said they hadn't heard nothing yet, till they heard our story. He was right about that."

"I'm sorry," I said.

"Hell, don't be sorry. The son of a bitch is dead, isn't he?"

"Very," I said quietly. "So you supported him?"

"Yeah, well most of the time." She paused. "But don't you go giving me this bullshit about why didn't I leave him then if it was me who was bringing in the money. I did leave, remember? It just took me longer than it might could have. Anyway, Arnie did work sometimes. It just wasn't steady work."

"I understand. What kind of work was it?"

She shrugged. "Odd jobs. Things he'd read about in the paper."

I had a brilliant idea. "You wouldn't happen to have a picture of him, would you?"

"Of Arnie? Hell no, I ripped them suckers up a long time ago. But let me tell you, he was mean-looking. Like a big rat that had rabies. I don't know what I ever saw in him."

As a mother of a nineteen-year-old I could easily answer that. Without a doubt Norma's mother had disapproved of Arnold Ramsey. More often than not, that's all it takes.

She slid out of the booth and stood up. "You married?"

"Divorced."

She nodded sympathetically. "Here's a tip that won't cost you nothing. Never sign any papers for a man, no matter how much he sweet-talks you."

"Gotcha."

"Hey, you gonna order? I can take it back for you."

I glanced at the menu. The Hunan hush puppies were the most appealing thing I could see.

"I think I'll pass dear. I forgot that this was a religious fast day for me."

"Yeah?" she said, and walked off without another word.

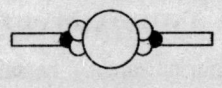

4

Purnell Purvis is a pudgy man, with a paunch, and pink cheeks that suggest a preference for Pernod over Perrier. He's on the shady side of fifty (depending on your point of view), bald as a cue ball, and dresses nattily. By that I mean Purvis is fond of wearing suits and very flashy ties. I have never seen him wear the same tie twice.

I found Purvis in the barn, which was very lucky, come to think of it. Monday is the only day you can count on him being there. The rest of the time Purvis is out roaming around looking for estates to buy, or—and this is strictly rumor, and not to be repeated—passed out in some bar or another.

I'm sure that over the years I've poured thousands of dollars of profit into Purvis's pocket. Normally he greets me—and the other female dealers—with a hug and a kiss. This manner of greeting between acquaintances is customary in the South, but it seems to shock Yankees. At any rate, this particular Tuesday Purvis didn't seem at all glad to see me. The yellow Happy Face on his black tie was in a far better mood.

"I've been in business for thirty years," he said, without greeting me first, "and this is the first time something like this has happened."

"Trust me, it's never happened to me before either."

"It's a goddamn nuisance," he said. A more sensitive soul than I might have thought, his tone was slightly accusing.

"I'll say. They shut you down, too?"

"Say what?"

"I can't even get into my shop until they complete their investigation."

"You don't say!" He was softening.

"So you see, I'm really in a jam here. I was hoping that maybe you could help me out."

Mama always says that it's easier to catch flies with honey than with vinegar. If you heard Mama try and talk her way through a difficult situation, you'd think she had a whole jar full of the pesky things.

"What kind of help?"

"Just some information," I said pleasantly.

"Yeah? Like what?"

Out of the corner of one eye I could see Jimbo and Skeet. They were standing on either side of a Victorian Turkish platform rocker. Presumably they were supposed to be doing something with it, but it didn't take a genius to figure out that their attention was on us.

"Is there somewhere we could go to talk? Somewhere private?"

"Sure thing, little lady." Purvis is not easily perturbed, but it was obvious something was bothering him. Still, I am a valued customer, and he was doing his best to be gracious.

He led the way through a maze of antiques, some in crates, others calling seductively to me in all their glory. Our final destination was his office, a mere cubicle next to the men's toilet. A length of dusty green velvet served as the door. An exquisite Wooton desk almost filled the room, leaving just enough room for two chairs. I took the smaller chair. It was contemporary and poorly made.

"Care for a drink, little lady?" He reached inside the

desk and pulled out the bottle of Pernod. There were about two sips left in it.

"No thanks. Purvis"—we all call him by his last name—"I know that the police have already talked to you, and I wouldn't be bothering you, except that this is very important to me. You see—"

He hushed me with an outstretched hand. "Ask away, little darling."

I took the plunge. "Did you happen to know the deceased, a man named Arnold Ramsey?"

It might have been my imagination, but Purvis's cheeks seemed to grow pinker. "Never heard of him until the cops came this morning. Is that all you wanted?"

"No, I have a few more questions, if that's all right."

He considered that while he sipped from the bottle. "I don't have all day, little lady. Can you make it quick?"

"Sure thing. Did you see or hear anything unusual yesterday—after the auction?"

He drained the Pernod and put the empty bottle back in the drawer. He did it solemnly, as if it were part of a religious rite, as if he were preparing to say Mass. I tried to imagine Purvis killing a man half his age. It was perhaps possible, but not plausible. His hands were barely bigger than mine, and he was certainly in poorer shape. The only thing Purvis had going for him was his weight, and paunches are more likely to be lethal to their wearers than to others.

"Nope," Purvis said. "I didn't see anything unusual after the auction."

"Before?"

"Nope. I don't exactly keep an eye out for murderers." He opened a different drawer and took out a new bottle of Pernod. "You sure you don't want a little sip? It's almost teatime."

"How can you drink that stuff?" I asked. "It rots your teeth."

It wasn't even two o'clock. Purnell Purvis had a problem.

He took a swig. "Picked up a taste for this in France."

"Army?"

"Nope. I studied in France for a year. The Sorbonne. The scholarship kids drank table wine. This"—he waved the bottle—"was the hip thing for the rich kids."

I felt my eyebrows rise of their own volition. "You were rich?"

"Nope. Not me, my parents. My granddaddy and his brothers owned one of the biggest department store chains in the Southeast. Biggest in North Carolina, that's for sure."

I tried to remember a department store chain named Purvis but couldn't. He read my mind.

"The family sold it after World War II. New owners changed the name and it went public. I could tell you which one it was, but you wouldn't believe it."

"Try me, dear."

He took another swig, perhaps to fortify himself for my shocked response, but then got distracted. "You ever been to Paris, little lady?"

"Only in my dreams."

"There's nothing like the Seine on an August morning. The light! Did you know Paris is called the City of Light?"

It was time to steer him back to my original agenda, but I wanted to make a short detour first. "Do you know the Barras family socially?"

He snorted, spraying me with Pernod. "Who the hell would want to? They're all snobs," he said. "La-dee-das. But you know what? They're all losers. Every last one of them."

"Is that a no?"

For reasons known only to him, he put that particular

bottle away and brought out a third. What a waste of the magnificent Wooton desk.

"Of course I know them. Lottie Bell Barras Bowman is a rich old bitch who once had my mama blackballed from the Charlotte Women's Club. The stuff you bought belonged to her sister-in-law, Lula Mae. Anyway, Lottie Bell's kids, Bobby and Hattie—twins—were in my class at the academy. Stuck-up little shits, the both of them. Pardon my French." He laughed.

"Go on."

"Garland and Toxie are a couple of years younger, but I knew them. Noses always in the air. Squire—well, he's dead now. But he was the only one of the bunch who would give you the time of day. Everyone at school hated them. Do you know what we kids used to call them in school?"

"No, but could we get back to the auction?" I asked quickly.

"*Bare ass*, that's what!"

I smiled to appease him. "Do you mind if I talk to Jimbo and Skeet?" I asked pleasantly.

"Only Lula Mae was different," he said. He had the tenacity of a teenager trying to borrow the family car. "She was a friend of Mama's. I used to go along with my mama to Lula Mae's sometimes when I was a little kid. Believe it or not that's when I first got interested in the business. Antiques, I mean.

"My mama had expensive furniture, but it was all new. That blond, bland, postwar stuff. Expensive junk, all of it. Thank God most of that stuff just gets thrown out. It's just like the postwar architecture. They're tearing down a lot of those buildings now from the fifties and sixties. They just don't age."

He had a point. Fortunately the humans from my generation don't have to suffer the same fate. What with miracle creams and laser rays, my generation can maintain their facades deep into their dotage.

"So," I said, "you don't mind if I talk to Jimbo and Skeet?"

"Excuse me, little lady."

He got up from his chair by the desk and exited the cubicle. He was gone only a minute, but when he returned he seemed considerably more relaxed.

"Too late, little lady. Seems they've already left on their next delivery." I could feel his eyes give me a quick once-over. "Say, you wouldn't be free for lunch, would you?"

I politely reminded him that since, by his own reckoning, it was already teatime, lunch had to be a thing of the past. He took my refusal graciously and gave me the customary hug and a peck. No doubt as soon as I left Purvis promptly pursued the Pernod.

Think me crazy, but the next person on my list to see was eighty-seven-year-old Lottie Bell Barras Bowman. No, I didn't for a minute think she was physically capable of killing a young man in his twenties and stuffing him into an armoire. But she *did* have three names that began with the letter "B" and, according to Purvis, plenty of doh-re-mi. She could have hired a killer—assuming such things are done in Charlotte, of course. It was beyond me just why an elderly woman would want to have someone killed, but it seemed a worthwhile thing to check out. If the world is indeed going to hell in a handbasket, as Mama claims, there is no reason Charlotte should be exempt.

They say that old money can afford to present a shabby side to the world. It has nothing to prove. By this measuring stick the Barras family made its fortune when God was still a child. The magnificent Greek Revival mansion of Lottie Bell Barras Bowman is all but hidden behind a tangle of overgrown camellias, azaleas, and aucuba. From above, the house is screened by a canopy of immense laurel oaks. Monkeys and parrots would not have seemed out of place in this setting.

Perhaps the jungle was meant to discourage casual visitors. As it was, I tripped twice on vinca major that was crowding the cracked, tilted squares of the front walk. I snagged my pantyhose on a dead branch poking out of a monstrous aucuba. I was swatted in the face by a branch hanging from one of the tree-sized camellias. Had I been there to push a religion, I'm quite sure I would have turned around and set my sights on some tropical jungle where the natives are more forthright in their persecution. A large pot over a cannibal cookfire gets right to the point.

I should have done the polite thing and called first, but Lottie Bell Barras Bowman does not list her number in the book. Fortunately among us dealers it was common knowledge where the old money lives. You never know what you might find in the curbside trash outside some of those homes.

Much to my surprise, Mrs. Bowman herself answered the door. I don't mean this unkindly, but she appeared older than her garden. Perhaps she did know God when he was a boy.

"Mrs. Bowman?"

She stared at me with eyes that had once been blue, but which time had faded to a pale, watery gray. I had no doubt she was Lottie Bell Barras Bowman because I had seen her picture on numerous occasions in the society write-ups. And since she was wearing a cashmere sweater, an English wool tweed skirt, and a triple strand of eight-millimeter cultured pearls, there was no mistaking her for an elderly housekeeper. Old money, as you know, insists on uniforms.

I extended my hand. "I'm Abigail Timberlake, Miss Bowman."

Her hand was like ice, but her smile was as warm as a June day. "Come on in, dear. You'll catch your death of cold standing out there."

I accepted her invitation gratefully, although it was a typical Charlotte December day, sunny and sixty degrees. It was fierce wild beasts that might be lurking in the underbrush that worried me.

Perhaps I should be ashamed to admit this, but the contents of Mrs. Bowman's house made my mouth water. I pointed to the carpet in the foyer.

"Ooh, I love this carpet," I gushed. "Hadji Jallili Tabriz?"

"I beg your pardon?"

I repeated my question.

She gave me an odd look. "The rug belonged to Granny Barras. It's old, so don't mind the worn spots."

She led down a long, portrait-hung hallway. Her ancestors smiled at us from elaborate gilt frames. Eventually we turned left into a magnificently appointed parlor. The drapes covering the windows were almost thick enough to supply extra support for the ceiling. It would have been dark as a tomb in there, had it not been for the chandelier. When I saw it, I gasped.

"And that chandelier! Irish Waterford, right? Circa 1800?"

"Would you mind speaking a little louder, dear?"

I repeated my question, while she stared at my lips.

"Granny Neely, Mama's mama, brought that over from England. I had to have it wired myself. Even Mama was afraid of electricity. Whenever there was a storm she couldn't wait for the power to fail so she could light the hurricane lamps. Your ever lived through a hurricane?"

"Hugo," I said, careful to look at her.

"Lordy, that *was* a storm."

There were tea things laid out on a low mahogany table with claw feet. English, I thought. The tea set was Tiffany silver in the Japanesque style, circa 1870. The teapot was silver, with copper, gold, and ivory accents.

"You really didn't have to go to all this trouble," I protested. "After all, I invited myself."

"Nonsense, dear. Do you prefer lemon or cream?"

"Cream, please," I said, and I knew it would be the real stuff.

As she was pouring I noticed for the first time a huge blue stone on the ring finger of her right hand. The stone—rock, really—was a true cornflower-blue, and as clear as the Caribbean on a windless day.

"That's a lovely ring," I couldn't help but say, when I had her attention again. "A sapphire?"

She glanced down at her hand. "I suppose it is. Daddy picked it up on one of his travels. India, I think. No, Kashmir."

I gulped. Kashmir sapphires were discovered only in 1888. By 1925 the mines had been all but exhausted. In the last twenty years, no major stone claiming this provenance has appeared on the market.

Allow me to explain that Kashmir sapphires are hands-down the finest in the world. They are not inky-blue like most Australian stones, they lack the telltale green tints of the many Thai stones, and their velvety color is even richer than that of their closest contenders in Sri Lanka. Carat for carat, a true Kashmiri sapphire of exceptional quality will cost far more than a diamond. Fifty thousand dollars per carat is not unheard of, and the stone Lottie Bell was so casually wearing had to be well over ten carats.

"Have you had that appraised, dear?"

Her thin penciled eyebrows arched innocently. "Whatever for? Daddy was always bringing home trinkets, but he hated spending his money. I'm sure it isn't worth much."

I nodded vigorously. "But—"

She had a dry, raspy laugh. My son, Charlie, once owned an iguana that hissed like that.

"Anyway, I never take it off, you see. Sugar?"

I asked for four lumps. After the cream, it was in for the penny, in for the pound.

"It was very good of you to see me on such short notice," I said.

She laughed again. "Goodness child, you wrote that letter at least a month ago. I hardly call that short notice."

I took a sip of my sweet, white tea. It was ambrosia.

"What letter was that, ma'am?" I asked politely.

"Why, the one you sent along with your application from the agency. You suggested a time that suited you, and I agreed."

"Ma'am?"

"Come, child, I'm the one who's supposed to be losing my memory."

I took another quick sip of the tea, just in case it was my last. "I'm afraid there has been a mistake, Mrs. Bowman," I said, tilting my chin up so she could read my lips clearly, if not loudly. "I never sent you a letter."

She shook her head. "No mistake, dear. I have the letter somewhere here. Althea Terwiliger from Charleston, isn't that right? Recent graduate of Miss Emma Bromley's School of Lady Companions?"

"I beg your pardon?"

The old woman got up and sifted through a stack of letters on top of an ivory-inlay secretary.

"Here it is. It says you were to arrive—oh no, you're not due until *next* week!"

I shook my head. "I'm not a lady's companion, Mrs. Bowman. I'm Abigail Timberlake from Charlotte. Originally from Rock Hill. Proud owner and manager of the Den of Antiquity."

I had to say it twice, and I could tell she heard me

when the hand wearing the enormous rock began to tremble. "You're *not* a lady's companion?"

"Not normally," I said as casually as I could. "I'm an antique dealer."

Her mouth tightened into a thin line. She was far too much of a lady to make a big stink—not without grave provocation—and I am just enough of a lady not to provoke her that far.

I smiled. "The tea was delicious."

She smiled back. A couple more of those smiles and I would have to thaw out under a hot shower when I got home.

"Let me show you to the door." It was an order, not an offer.

I trotted along obediently behind her. In the hallway the ancestors' smiles had turned into frowns. A few were glowering.

"I didn't come here to buy or sell anything," I practically shouted.

She ignored me. At the front door she graciously read my lips one last time.

"I didn't come here on business," I said. I moved my lips carefully. "I was hoping for some clue that might help the police solve the murder."

She blinked. "What murder?"

"The murder of Arnold Ramsey. He was found dead in your sister-in-law's armoire."

She gasped and then fainted. She did it all at once. Not like in the movies, where the heroine sags and then crumples like a stiff pair of dirty blue jeans. Lottie Bell Barras Bowman was fully conscious one second, and in the next instant headed for the floor like a ton of bricks. In all modesty I must report that I caught her, and prevented her from suffering any serious injury.

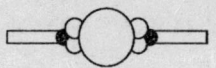

5

Unfortunately my life seldom imitates the movies. I was quite unable to carry Lottie Bell Barras Bowman to one of her luxuriously upholstered couches. She was as unwieldy as a fifty-pound bag of potatoes and twice as heavy. It was all I could do to drag her away from the door and prop her up against the foyer wall. I had no idea where she kept her smelling salts (I wouldn't have known how to use them, anyway), but I did manage to find a cluster of ostrich plumes stuck in a vase on a marble-topped table halfway down the hall. A couple of light passes under her nose, and Lottie Bell came to with a sneeze.

"Bless you," I said kindly.

She was either an Episcopalian or a Catholic, because she was up on her knees and then standing before she could say Jack Daniels—which, by the way, were the next words she said.

"Ma'am?"

"I said, Jack Daniels, child. It's in the decanter on my desk in the library. Be a dear and fetch it for me."

Of course I hesitated. One doesn't normally abandon an octogenarian who has just passed out.

She struggled free of my supporting grip and leaned against the wall. "Are you deaf, child? I said, bring me my dear friend Jack."

I was brought up to mind my elders so I obediently trotted off in search of Lottie Bell Barras Bowman's best buddy. I found the library easily enough. There had to be at least a thousand books in there—many of them leather-bound—and the stacks, which lined all four walls, towered to the ceiling. There was even a rolling stairs, and I was sorely tempted to climb it, just for the fun of it. But I stuck to business and retrieved the Jack Daniels.

Before I could ask her where to find a glass—there had been none in the library—Lottie Bell took a swig straight from the decanter. Then, being the proper lady that she was, she patted the corners of her mouth with an embroidered handkerchief that she fished out of the recesses of her ample bosom.

"Medicinal purposes," she said.

She was studying my face, waiting for a response, so I laughed politely.

"No, I mean it. Doctor's orders. I have high blood pressure and the whiskey helps calm me down."

I nodded. It is my policy never to argue with folks who are in the final quarter of their first century.

"Let's go back and finish our tea," she said matter-of-factly.

The tea was a little too cool for my taste by then, but I drank a second cup dutifully. Between sips Lottie Bell and I chatted about innocuous subjects—the weather, where to buy the freshest shrimp, and the strange popularity of rayon. It was as if we were old, but not especially dear, friends.

"Tell me about the body," she said suddenly.

I put my cup down carefully. It was a rare Limoges pattern, and replacements must be hard to find. I certainly had never seen one like it before.

"Ah yes, that. It was gruesome."

"Cut up and all that, you mean?"

I shuddered. "Heavens no!"

She looked disappointed. "I am eighty-seven years old, child. I can take it, I assure you."

"I'm sure you could, dear," I said pointedly.

She stared at me with those faded eyes. "What? You don't possibly think—but you do, don't you?"

"Anything is possible, ma'am."

I didn't really think Lottie Bell was capable of killing a strapping young man with anything less than a gun, but that didn't mean she wasn't capable of hiring someone who *was*.

She laughed, and it was the tone of her laughter that acquitted her. Mama laughed that way once when I was a little girl playing with my dolls, and had announced that my stomach hurt because I was going to have a real live baby any minute, just like Lorrie Anderson's mama. Still, one can't be too careful.

"I am not allowed to divulge the details," I said.

She sighed. "Well, just the same, I'm sure it was horrible. And it is horrible for the Barras name, too, having a body discovered in one of our furniture pieces. I told Lula Mae not to will her things to *that* girl."

I mouthed an "Oh?" Since she was reading my lips, I didn't actually have to say my words.

"Amy. Anyway, she was married to Squire less than a year. I hardly call that a marriage."

"Squire?" I asked just by moving my lips. It was fun.

"Squire Cornelius Barras, my nephew. My brother Cyrus's only son. Lula Mae's, too, of course."

"Of course."

"When Squire killed himself—"

"Squire killed himself?"

She shrugged and took a quick nip at Jack. "Well, it's hardly news. It was in the papers, of course. And television."

"When?"

She pursed her lips as she thought, and I was struck by

the symmetry of the wrinkles that circled her mouth. It was beautiful in its own way, like the furrowed cone of a volcano.

"Let's see," she said, "it was '64 or '65. No, it had to be '65, because '64 was when Lula Mae and I took that trip together to Vegas, and Squire drove us to the airport."

That explained it. I was a high-school junior in 1965. Society suicide was not high on my list of things to remember.

Lottie Bell had fallen silent. The volcano had disappeared and her face was serene, if not smooth. I wondered if she was back in Vegas with Lula Mae playing the one-armed bandits.

"Please go on." I had to shout to get her attention.

She shook her herself and fixed her gaze on my mouth again. "Squire shot himself with a shotgun. He had made an error in judgment by acquiring another student's answers on a medical school exam. Unfortunately he was observed, and so the school was going to expel him."

I nodded. The upper class can be quite creative when it comes to coining euphemisms for their crimes. Apparently cheating is a bourgeois term.

"Anyway," she hastened to assure me, "he was always a neat boy—always so considerate—so of course he did it in the bathtub. With the shower curtain drawn. The suicide, I mean. That Amy girl found him."

"How awful!"

The pale eyes narrowed slightly. "Yes, but that was no reason for Lula Mae to will family things to a virtual stranger. No one has seen hide nor hair of her for thirty years. That wasn't fair of Lula Mae, was it?"

I bobbled my head. Politicians take note. This is a trick I learned from my children. With enough practice it's possible to indicate "yes," "no," and "maybe" all at the same time.

Apparently I was still no expert at bobbling. "Well, she wasn't even blood," Lottie Bell said indignantly. "And there were no children. It isn't right that family heirlooms should pass to a stranger. And then she sold them!"

I saw her point. That's exactly how I felt about Tweetie becoming stepmother to my children. Of course, Tweetie hasn't sold my children—yet!

"She wouldn't consider selling those pieces back to the family, before putting them up for auction?"

She shook her head vigorously. "And oh how we tried. Garland, that's my nephew—my sister Mimi's son, may she rest in peace—talked to her until he was blue in the face, but she wouldn't budge. She told Garland that since she was never treated like one of us, she didn't want to have anything to do with the family. Except to inherit our property."

"Why didn't y'all just buy them at the auction?" I asked sensibly.

Lottie Bell recoiled in horror. "Gracious, child! How would that have looked? Buying our own things back in public!"

"*Trés declassé*," I said with just a hint of sarcasm. "Did you talk to Amy yourself?"

"My blood pressure, remember? It would have gone through the roof. Pow—I might have exploded."

She laughed, and I laughed with her. I could feel the beginning of a connection.

"Those four pieces," she said, her eyes going from my mouth to my eyes, "were in the family at least five generations. I have a record of it somewhere"—she pointed in the general direction of the library—"but I can't remember exactly where. Just wait until you get to be eighty-seven."

"One of the saddest things about being in the antique business is selling other folks' heirlooms," I said.

"Those were *important* pieces," she said.

"I know, dear. That's why I bought them. That armoire, in particular, was a lovely piece."

She waved a bony hand. The skin stretched across it was as thin as an onion skin. Perhaps those lucky few who die from old age do so because their souls burst right through their skin.

"I'm not talking about the way they look, or their value. There is something about them that is truly special."

I bobbled foolishly.

"Stop that, child. My granddaddy told me something about those pieces, but I can't for the life of me remember what." She sighed, and her gaze left my face along with her thoughts.

I waited silently, as long as I dared, but when I saw that the papery skin on her cheeks was glistening with tears, I reached out and patted her hand ever so gently.

"There, there," I said stupidly.

She made a single mewing sound, and then she was with me again, staring intently at my mouth. "What did you say, child?"

I scrambled for words. "Do you have Amy's address, ma'am?"

She had me retrieve her address book, which was on her desk in the library. I was gone only a minute, but when I got back it was plain to see that Lottie Bell and Jack Daniels had strengthened the ties of their friendship. I pretended not to notice.

Lottie Bell's gnarled fingers raked clumsily through the pages of the leather-bound book. "She lives down in Rock Hill," she said. "On Grady Drive. You know where that is?"

I nodded. Mama lives in Rock Hill. I owed Mama a visit anyway.

*   *   *

I grew up in Rock Hill, which is in South Carolina, just across the border. The time was when Charlotte and Rock Hill were distinctly separated by twenty some miles of woods. Now that Rock is one of the fastest-growing urban-satellite cities in the nation, the distinction is becoming blurred. Still, Rock Hill has managed to hold on to much of its small-town charm, and I find my return visits there pleasant. And I must confess—although you may find it hard to believe—I actually enjoy time spent with my mother.

There was no point in calling Mama to tell her I was coming. Mama has unique psychic abilities that manifest themselves through her nose.

Mama was standing just inside her front door, waiting. "I could smell you coming," she said.

I sniffed my armpits quickly. They were still fine.

"And there's trouble, isn't there?"

I told her about the body in the armoire. I also apologized for not having called her the second it was discovered.

"Lord have mercy," she said several times over while she wiped her hands on the frilly white lap apron she wore.

Some time back in the late 1950s Mama entered a time warp and has yet to emerge. Her everyday uniform is a neatly tailored dress with a full circle skirt, a strand of pearls, and high heels. Of course the home version of the uniform includes an apron—Mama does her own housework. The away version has a pocketbook that matches both her shoes *and* the pillbox hat with its saucy little veil.

"Mama, everything's going to be all right," I mumbled. I was a little miffed that *I* had to be the one to comfort *her*.

Mama smoothed the apron and folded her hands in her

lap. "Well, it's obvious that you haven't heard then, have you?"

"Heard what, Mama?"

Mama took a deep breath and half-closed her eyes. "Buford's been trying to reach you all day. He and Tweetie have decided to take the kids to Disney for Christmas."

I gasped. "He can't do that! According to the settlement he gets Charlie during the school year, but I get him for vacations and holidays."

I would have custody of Charlie *all* the time, if it weren't for the fact that Buford Timberlake is not only the best lawyer in both Carolinas, but—and maybe because of that—he's plugged into the good old boy system tighter than a three-inch cork in a two-inch bottleneck.

Mama still had her eyes halfway shut. "Honey, according to Buford there's a clause in the settlement that gives him the right to take the kids—well, Charlie at any rate, because Susan's on her own now—with him when he visits special places that will benefit them educationally."

I headed for Mama's phone. "Well, we'll see about that. Disney World doesn't count. The children have both been there three times. Buford's going to have to think up something new."

Mama closed her eyes all the way. "He has. They aren't taking them to Disney World, dear, they're taking them to EuroDisney."

"France?"

Mama opened one eye. "They'll be leaving the day after school lets out for the holidays, and he promises to have them back in time for the new semester."

I let loose with a string of invectives then that would make the Whore of Babylon blush. Words came out of my mouth that most retired sailors have yet to hear. Please believe me, I don't normally swear in the presence of my mother. In fact, I normally eschew swearing altogether. But even a properly raised Southern lady has her limits. Besides, every one of those words I learned from Buford.

"You forgot to add asshole to the list," Mama said calmly.

"Asshole!" I screamed.

Mama burst out laughing and after a few seconds so did I. We laughed like schoolgirls at a slumber party, alternating between giggles and gales, the one infecting the other. We laughed until our chests hurt. For a long time it was impossible to talk.

"I bet his ears are still burning," she finally said.

"I hope there's nothing left of them but sizzling stumps," I said. "Mama, you don't suppose I stand a chance of stopping him, do you?"

Mama shook her head. She was fingering her pearls now, which was a sign that she, at least, perceived the crisis to be over. The apron she reserved for the hairiest moments.

"But Abby, honey, next time you talk to the kids— well, remember, this wasn't their idea. And try to put yourself in their place. If you were offered a trip to France when you were that age, would you have gone?"

"Not if it meant spending Christmas without you, Mama."

It was a lie, but one she needed to hear.

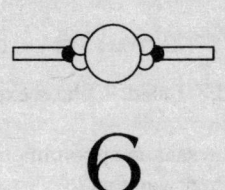

6

Grady Drive is one of Rock Hill's best-kept secrets. The street is crossed only by Selma, dead-ends into Windemere, which is itself a dead-end street. Together the three streets comprise Poplar Forest, one of the smallest but most idyllic neighborhoods in the city. I had often heard it said that Grady Drive is God's waiting room for people going to heaven. I had never been there before, but now I believe it.

Amy—Mrs. Squire Cornelius Barras—lived in a sprawling brick ranch perched on a hillside overlooking Grady Lake Two. Grady Lake One is just across the street. The two small lakes and their attendant woods give the street the feel of the country, and I could have been miles from nowhere when I stepped onto her driveway, instead of in the heart of Rock Hill. I followed a winding brick path, past a grove of palmettos, to the front door. Even the chime was charming. It sounded like Big Ben, only not quite as loud, I suppose.

"Yes?"

The woman who answered the door was a lot younger than I expected. She had a pleasant but nondescript face. She could have been twenty-five, or thirty-five, but not more. Her accent was local.

"I'm here to see Mrs. Squire Barras," I said.

"What about?"

"It's personal," I said. "She's expecting me."

"Oh, is she?"

I nodded. "She said an appointment wasn't necessary."

"She did? When was that?"

I shrugged and mumbled something about the days all running together, how that happens to people my age.

She smiled. "You're either Irish or a reporter. Or both. Now what's this really about?"

"It's about a body in an eighteenth-century French armoire."

Her smile vanished. I had a feeling she was going to slam the door.

"I'm not a reporter," I said quickly. "I'm Abigail Timberlake, the woman who bought the armoire."

The door opened wide. "Please, come in."

I followed her into the most exquisite living room I have ever been in. The walls were a rich orange-red—not as red as Chinese red—and tinged with just a hint of brown. Stepping into that room felt like being hugged.

"I like color," she said.

"Apparently you do. Ma'am, I'm here to see Mrs. Barras. Is she home?"

"I'm Amy Barras, dear. Please, have a seat."

I sat. "*You* are?"

She laughed. "Did you expect some old hag? I'm fifty-six, dear."

"Yes, well—I mean—"

"Plastic surgery, dear," she said easily. "Nothing major. Just a little snip here and there. A couple of tucks. A few stitches. There's nothing to it these days."

She made it sound as simple as my first home economics project in high school. But the apron I made for Mama had been a disaster. There were more puckers on that thing than on a platoon of lemon suckers. Not so with Amy Barras. If the time ever came when I needed a plastic surgeon, I knew who to ask for a referral.

"Mrs. Barras—"

She waved to preempt me. "I already talked with the police. And with my attorney. I can assure you that the armoire was empty when the crew from Purvis Auction Barn came to pick it up."

I nodded encouragingly.

"Well, there's really nothing left to say on the subject, is there? I mean, I didn't know this Ramsey guy. I'm afraid I can't answer your questions, Mrs. Timberlake."

I smiled patiently. "I haven't asked them yet. They are about family. Your husband's family."

She turned and looked out the large window. The palmetto trees seemed to have caught her eye.

"Oh them," she said softly. "What is it you want to know?"

"I take it you didn't get along with them?"

"I never had a chance. Squire and I met at Myrtle Beach the summer we graduated from college. He was going to go on to med school, and I was all set to start a teaching job down in Florence, South Carolina, come fall. You believe in love at first sight?"

I shrugged. I had once, but not anymore. I had been immediately attracted to Buford when I met him on a water slide at an area amusement park. Then I thought it was love. Now I see it as lust. Perhaps if Amy and Squire had been married longer than a year, she might see things differently.

"Well, it *was* love at first sight," she said, reading my mind. "We were made for each other. All our friends thought we were a perfect match. Unfortunately his parents didn't agree. I was too much of a redneck to suit them. They threatened to cut him out of their wills if he married me."

"And did they?"

"No. Squire was their only son. They couldn't afford to alienate him, so they made peace with the fact that he

was going to marry beneath him. And they did a pretty
good job of it, too. I actually grew to like them."

I raised my eyebrows and she laughed.

"Now the others, they were a piece of work. None of
them came to our wedding. Not a single soul. And Christmas—well, Mother Barras invited the entire clan over for
Christmas dinner, and again, not one of them showed up.
It about broke her heart."

"Did you stay close with your husband's parents after . . ." I paused, sure she knew what I meant.

"After what, dear?" she asked placidly.

"You know, your husband's death."

"It wasn't just a death, honey. It was suicide. Feel free
to say it. Squire, the one true love of my life, blew his
head off with a shotgun. Blam! Apparently my love
wasn't enough to see him through a sudden change in
careers." She laughed again, and this time there was a
hard edge to it.

"How awful" was all I could think to say.

She waved a hand in dismissal. "You can't imagine
the mess. At least he did it in the bathtub, with the shower
curtain pulled. I mean, what *does* one use to scrape one's
husband's brains off the floor? It was bad enough that he
plugged the drain with all those bits of—"

"Ma'am?" I interrupted. I was turning green around
the gills. I don't even like mixing meat loaf with my bare
hands.

She arranged her face in a smile. "Now, to answer your
question—yes. I did stay in touch with his parents. I
wouldn't say that we were close, but we had a certain
connection. Our mutual love of Squire bound us together
somehow."

I nodded. "There are some who might think you stayed
close to his parents in order to benefit financially."

"What a stupid thing to say," she said calmly.

"Excuse me?"

"Look, I didn't need my in-laws' money. Squire had a trust fund. It was more than enough. Anyway, I quit teaching about three years after Squire killed himself and went into business for myself."

"Oh?"

"Inside and Out, your complete home design center."

I'd heard their ads on the radio and seen them in the paper and on TV, but it seemed like I never had the time to stop in. Mama has, and she thinks the all-in-one concept is the neatest thing since toothpicks.

"So you've done all right for yourself," I said.

She smiled. "I'm not going to let you see the books, but yes, I've done all right. In fact, I don't have to go in now unless I really want. Today was one of those days I just decided to stay home and do nothing."

"I'm sorry I disturbed you," I said. "I have only one more question, if I may?"

"Ask away, dear. But first let me guess. You're wondering why an attractive eligible woman like me never remarried?"

That wasn't my question, but I was certainly interested in the answer. "You must be psychic, Mrs. Barras."

She started to respond but was interrupted by a loud honking from the back of the house. "Geese," she said. "Would you like to see?"

She led me from the living room and through a large family room—den, we call it here in South Carolina—to a redwood deck overlooking the lake. A flock of eight wild Canada geese had just landed and were still settling themselves on the water's surface. As far as I was concerned that was the answer to her question. If I lived in her house, on that lake, with wild geese as drop-in visitors, I wouldn't consider remarriage. Why mess up perfection with a man?

"Have a seat, dear." She pointed to a deck chair.

I politely accepted her offer. "Actually, Mrs. Barras,

my question had nothing to do with marriage. I just wanted to know if you are aware of any family legends connected with the furniture you sold at auction.''

It may just have been the sun skipping behind a small cloud, but I thought I saw that bland, perfect face darken for a moment.

"No," she said. "I mean, what kind of legends?"

"Well, I don't know. Like maybe it came over on the *Mayflower*. Something like that?"

She laughed loudly and a couple of the geese honked and shuffled their wings. "Really, Mrs. Timberlake. And you an antique dealer! Mother Barras's furniture was late eighteenth century. That's a hundred and fifty years or so after the *Mayflower*."

I must have blushed. "Well, that was just a rough example. So you're not aware of any particularly interesting historical notes to the furniture? Ancient family secrets, that kind of thing?"

"My, my, but aren't we nosy." She said it so casually, I didn't think she was annoyed.

"Well?"

She stood up. "Look, I already said no. Or maybe you have a hearing problem like Aunt Lottie Bell."

I stood up. I hated to, but it was clear that once again my tongue was ushering me to the door.

"Speaking of Lottie Bell," I said, "she claims that the family tried desperately to buy that furniture from you, *before* it went to auction."

She led me back through the house while she talked. "After the way they snubbed me—and Squire—I wouldn't have sold that bunch a life jacket if I'd had a concession on the *Titanic*. What else did that old bag say?"

I'm sure it was silly, but I bristled at that remark. Two cups of tea and a little Jack Daniels did not exactly a friendship make, but one should never speak disrespectfully of the elderly. Not if one hoped to join their ranks someday.

"Mrs. Bowman said that you were the one who stayed out of touch all these years," I said accusingly.

If she was still annoyed, I couldn't tell. That expensive smile of hers made a wonderful mask.

"Oh, did she now? Well, you tell her—" She turned her head and stopped speaking.

I waited for an uncomfortably long time. I was about to excuse myself and find my own way out when she turned her head again. I had the feeling she had been crying, even though there were no tears. Perhaps her tear ducts had fallen victim to those nips and tucks.

"For your information, Mrs. Timberlake, I never re-married because I meant what I said. I loved Squire with all my heart. No other man could have taken his place. And because I loved Squire so very much, I honestly tried to love his family. Even after they made it so painfully clear they wanted nothing to do with me.

"I sent the whole bunch Christmas and birthday cards for several years. And with the exception of Squire's parents, none of them responded. You ask your precious Lottie Bell why."

I felt as if I owed her an apology, but I wasn't sure what I should apologize for. Instead I thanked her for her time and admired her palmettos. She smiled, and when I drove off she waved.

I didn't have to fight the rush-hour traffic when I drove back into Charlotte because it was all coming the other way. Tega Cay, Lake Wylie, Fort Mill, York, Rock Hill— the satellite-city workers were hurrying home to their suppers. I, however, was hurrying across the state and county line to the nearest telephone. A long distance call from Rock Hill wouldn't have dented my piggy bank, much less broken it, and Mama is very generous with her phone, but I have principles. I have never understood how it can be that long distance calling time costs more to nearby cities than it does across the country. Why is it that I can call Tokyo, Japan, for less money than it takes to call Rock Hill from Charlotte? Not that I have much reason to call Tokyo, mind you.

Fortunately there is a North Carolina Welcome Station just across the border. I waited patiently while a man from Michigan explained to his wife that his business trip was going to take at least a day longer. While he lied, I was busy giving the blond tart on his arm the evil eye. Finally the phone was mine.

"Hello?" said another blond tart. It was Tweetie, Buford's new wife.

"This is Abigail," I said pleasantly, "is Charlie there?"

"Buford isn't here," she chirped, and hung up.

I called back. "I asked to speak to my son, dear," I said kindly. Not all of the bulbs in Tweetie's chandelier burn at the same time, if you get my drift.

"Please, Abigail, we don't want any trouble. Buford has a right to take his children on a special trip like this, as long as he notifies you first."

Mama is surprised that I don't hate Tweetie. Frankly so am I. Until she jiggled her way into our lives everything was just fine. At least I thought it was. But Buford must have felt otherwise, because things went from hunky-dory to hanky-panky pretty fast. Perhaps it is because Tweetie is a few sandwiches short of a picnic, or maybe it's her tender age (three years older than our daughter, Susan), but I find it easier to blame Buford. He had it all—*me*—and he chose her.

"Tweetie, honey, I have no intention of making trouble for you. I simply want to speak to my son."

There was a long silence and Charlie got on the phone. "Mama?"

"Charlie, baby, what's new?" I tried to sound cheerful.

"They told you, didn't they, Mama? About Dad taking us to France for Christmas?"

"Yeah, they told me. It sounds like fun." I couldn't believe I said that.

"You aren't mad at me, Mama, are you?"

"No dear, of course not." It was the truth.

"I could stay home, Mama. I don't mind, really. It's just that I'm taking French in school you know, and Miss Wells—"

"You go ahead and go, honey. I'll spend Christmas with Grandma."

"You sure?"

"I'm sure."

There was a distinct pause. "I love you, Mama."

"I love you too, dear."

Charlie had given me my Christmas present early.

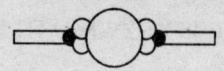

7

Despite what my critics say (Buford in particular), I am not a haphazard nitwit who flops along through life without a plan. I do sometimes have a plan. My plan then was to systematically talk to every single one of the Barras clan and find out what they knew about my new furniture. In retrospect this was a nitwit plan—there was no reason for me to suspect a Barras was involved, but it was a place to start. And I had to do *something*.

My next victim, as Mama began to call them, was Dr. Robert Barras Bowman. He is a prominent Charlotte heart surgeon, who once made national news when it was revealed that he had been charged with exposing himself to elderly cardiac patients of both sexes. Dr. Bowman, the tabloids claimed, was directly responsible for three of his patients' heart attacks. At his trial it was revealed that he had also slept with thirteen area prostitutes (who knew there were that many?!). Dr. Sex—the tabloids dubbed him that—got off scot-free. Who do you think his defense attorney was? None other than Buford Timberlake.

By the time I was done talking to Charlie it was too late to catch Dr. Bowman at his office, and since it was Tuesday, and not his golf day, I decided to chance it on catching him at home. I know, it is terribly rude to just drop in on folks as I'd been doing, but it is also terribly rude to kill somebody and stash him in someone else's armoire. As far as I was concerned, everybody I planned to talk to was possibly the murderer.

Dr. Bowman lived in a rambling Tudor-style house in Myers Park, *the* neighborhood to live in Charlotte if you are old money. His is the kind of house that was meant for a family with children, but none are in residence. The children have long since grown and flown the coop, and his wife flew the coop as well when she found out about the thirteen prostitutes. At any rate, the shiny black Jaguar in the driveway seemed out of place.

Just as I was walking up from the street the doctor came outside and took down a large American flag that had been hanging by the front door. Although I had never met him, I had seen his picture many times in the paper. Still, I was lucky to recognize him at dusk, and without his toupee.

"Dr. Bowman, I'm Abigail Timberlake. Buford Timberlake's wife."

It was a painful lie, and a waste of words. "You mean ex-wife," he snapped. "Buf filled me in on the divorce."

In the interest of my investigation, I bit my tongue. "Do you have a few minutes to talk?" I asked politely.

He gave me a quick once-over. I felt like something in the butcher's case.

"Come on inside," he said, and turned and went in.

I followed, understandably nervous. I had no desire to see whatever it was that supposedly gave three people heart attacks. And if the man laid a hand on me, one or both of us was going to be sorry. I once took a self-defense class and know how to do unspeakable things to the soft round organs on a man's body (their eyes included), but I certainly didn't want to put my knowledge to the test.

It took only a few seconds to see that Dr. Bowman was not into antiques. The living room, which was dutifully enormous, was filled with Italian leather couches and audiovisual systems that would make a Japanese weep with envy. It was very much a man's room.

He invited me to sit and we did a brief little dance (choreographed by me) that ensured that we sat on two different couches. Mama may have raised a nitwit, but she didn't raise a fool. I made sure my couch was nearest the door. In fact, we sat on opposing couches with a naked bronze woman kneeling between us. The bronze beauty was holding a thick slab of glass in her outstretched arms, and was presumably a coffee table. Her eyes were closed and metal lips had been cast to give her a *Mona Lisa*–like smile. She appeared to be waiting for something.

"What's this about?" he asked. He was sitting with his legs crossed—ankle on knee—and I was careful not to even glance anywhere near the trouble zone.

"I'd like to ask you some questions about the furniture that belonged to your aunt, Lula Mae Barras," I said pleasantly.

He frowned. "I don't give a rat's ass about that."

"Yes, well—I bought that furniture at an auction yesterday and when it was delivered today there was a body inside."

"Some kid hiding out from the cops, eh?"

"No, a *dead* body. A murder victim."

He scratched his thigh. I studied the bronze maiden. Thanks to a lascivious sculptor, she was doomed to have erect nipples for all eternity.

"I don't see what this has to do with me," he said.

"Well, it doesn't," I hastily assured him. "I just had some questions that I hoped you might be able to answer. As a personal favor," I added dangerously.

He sized me up again. I am four foot nine and not spectacularly endowed, so it took only a few seconds. Clearly his bad reputation had left him desperate.

"Yeah?"

I took that as permission to proceed. "Your mother—

what a sweetie pie—thinks that my new furniture had special significance to the family. Unfortunately she can't remember any details. You wouldn't happen to know them, would you?"

He laughed. "Mama, a sweetie pie? You been nipping at her Jack Daniels, have you?"

"I had *tea*," I said indignantly. "And that is no way to talk about your mother."

"Maybe not, but Mama's an alcoholic, plain and simple. Anything my mother says is suspect. Just ask my sister, Hattie."

"I just might," I said. "Is that Hattie Bowman?"

"Hattie Bowman Ballard."

I forced a smile. "I don't suppose you'd mind giving me her address and phone number."

He gave me a smarmy smile in return. "I don't mind at all, but you won't need them. You can find her at the perfume counter at Belk's in South Park Mall."

I glared at him. "Not all women hang out at perfume counters, you know."

"This one does."

"How would you know, unless you hang out there, too?"

His smile had changed from smarmy to smug. "Hattie works there."

"Well" was all I could think to say. Crow is not a tasty dish.

"So go to Belk's and talk to Hattie. She'll corroborate what I said. Our mama is a lush."

"How you talk!"

"Now, I'm not saying she outright lies; the old bat probably believes the crazy things she says. But if a flying saucer hovered over her backyard on Halloween night, don't you think someone else in Charlotte would have seen it as well?"

I stood up. "You should be ashamed of yourself," I

said, "calling your mama names to a stranger."

He looked far from ashamed. More like a cat that had caught the mouse and was about to devour it for dinner.

"I've got a new CD," he purred. "*Sensual Sounds of the Twentieth Century.* There's an expanded version of 'Bolero' on it. Why don't you sit back down and I'll put it on."

"Why don't you jump into Lake Norman, you oversexed cretin," I said and darted for the door.

There are certain advantages to being small. I was able to dodge through the maze of leather sofas without getting caught, whereas he whacked his knee against the thick glass plate of the coffee table. I am fairly certain that it was he who yelped, and not the bronze lady with the *Mona Lisa* smile.

It had been a long, hard day and I was in need of a book fix. Nothing can transport me from my problems quite like a good book, unless it's food. Since both books and food can be purchased in South Park Mall, it seemed like a good time to drop in on Hattie. I picked up the latest thriller by Gwen Hunter and had a slice of pizza—pepperoni, double cheese—in the food court. I held the book with my left hand and ate with my right. I am one of those picky people who hates getting grease stains on the printed page. When I was done with the pizza I reluctantly pocketed the book and dropped by the perfume counter at Belk's.

Perfume counters in large department stores can be intimidating, even for experienced shoppers. They are invariably confusing. But those stories of country girls losing their way among the bottle-topped islands, only to be found years later, dead—but smelling rather pleasant nonetheless—are exaggerated, I'm sure. It took me only five minutes to find the sample bottle of Shalimar cologne. I found Hattie in ten.

"Mrs. Ballard?"

"Yes, ma'am. Can I help you?"

The speaker was a remarkably average woman. She stood about five feet five, had shoulder-length medium brown hair, just starting its fade into gray, and brown eyes. Her features were regular, except that the very tip of her nose was missing. It was as if a sculptor had chiseled off one small wedge too many. She was dressed in moderately expensive clothes, but all off the rack. She did not look rich enough to be Lottie Bell's daughter, or seamy enough to be Robert's sister.

"Could you please direct me to the Shalimar?"

She smiled. "Honey, I think you already found it."

I had the decency to blush. I can afford my own cologne, I assure you. But those sample bottles call to me with siren songs.

I introduced myself and told her the predicament I was in. I talked fast so that I could at least highlight everything before she tuned me out. I need not have worried.

"How terrible," she sympathized. "I once opened our hall closet to hang up my coat and Ed—that's my husband—was in there, behind the coats, with his chin resting on the bar and a flashlight shining up at his face. It about gave me a heart attack, and Ed almost died laughing. Of course that was about thirty years ago, when we were first married. Today Ed's chin couldn't fit over the bar."

"Buford's couldn't, either."

She looked me up and down.

"Okay," I said, "I couldn't get my chin over a closet bar if I tried."

We both laughed.

"I spoke with your mother this morning," I said casually.

"Oh?" For the first time she seemed wary.

"I wanted to get as much information as I could on the four pieces of furniture. I know it's a long shot, but I thought knowing something about their history might give me some clues that—''

''What kind of clues?''

I shrugged. ''Well, I don't know of course. I'd have to hear the clues first.''

''I don't know any clues,'' she said, and started rearranging a bevy of bottles that graced a silver-plated tray. I noticed that the tip of her right index finger was stained yellow.

''Your mother seems to think that the furniture has some sort of historical significance.''

She looked up. ''You used the key word, Mrs. Timberlake. 'Seems.' Mama *seems* to think. But she doesn't, not anymore. Since Daddy died—almost three years ago—Mama lets old Jack do the thinking for her.''

''Jack Daniels,'' I said knowingly. ''Your brother feels the same way.''

''That's the *only* thing Bobby and I agree on.''

''I see.''

She set a bottle of White Diamonds down with a thunk. ''Do you? I married a machinist, Mrs. Timberlake. A man who went no further than high school. Bobby took my parents' side on that one.''

''I take it none of them was very pleased.''

''Edward may not have a wall full of diplomas, or a pedigree that goes past his grandparents, but he's pure gold. I couldn't have asked for a better husband, and my children couldn't have asked for a better father. And speaking of my children, all three of them went to college, and all three of them are happily married and productive citizens.''

She took a deep breath.

''Now you take Bobby. A Harvard graduate married to a Vassar graduate. What did they produce? Three spoiled brats, two of whom couldn't hold a steady job if their lives depended on it. But then, what could one expect from the examples they were shown? Bobby—well, I'm sure you know all about Bobby. But as bad an example as he is, he doesn't hold a candle to Elise, his ex-wife.''

She paused to catch her breath.

"Do tell," I said quickly.

"Elise is a Yankee. But if my parents objected to that, they never said a word. Not to me, at any rate. That's because Elise is a blueblood, and a college graduate. And not just any college, either, but a blueblood college graduate. They didn't seem to care that Elise was—and probably still is—the biggest snob on either side of the Mason-Dixon line. She wouldn't even let her kids stay over at my house because she was afraid they would absorb middle-class values. Can you believe that?''

I reached out to pat her arm but she jerked it away. "Unfortunately I can, dear," I said. "It sounds like you have a lot in common with Amy, your cousin Squire's wife.''

She stared at me, and I stared back. Her innocuous looks had been transformed by intense emotion. She seemed bigger and brighter. The tip of her chiseled nose was a vivid red. "Don't even talk to me about *that* woman," she spat.

I nodded. It was obvious she was jealous. Amy had been accepted by her in-laws, albeit reluctantly. Edward Ballard had probably always been an outsider.

"I loved Squire since we were kids," Hattie said softly.

"What?" The woman could change subjects faster than a trapped teenager.

"Of course, we were cousins, so nothing could come of it. But Squire and I were soul mates. If I had been married to Squire"—she half-sighed, half-whimpered— "he wouldn't have done what he did. I could have stopped him.''

"There's no use beating yourself up about that," I said

firmly. "People who commit suicide are responsible for their own actions."

She shook her head. There were tears in the brown eyes. "Oh, I don't blame myself, honey. I blame Amy. She obviously wasn't there for him in the same way I would have been."

I struggled to think of something to say that wasn't critical. It was like dealing with a trapped teenager again.

"Well, about the furniture. You don't remember any family legends attached to it?"

"Nothing."

I thanked her for her time and turned to walk away.

"But I wouldn't have sold it like Amy did," she whispered to my back.

I twirled. My kids claim I can hear a mouse fart on the other side of the house.

"I beg your pardon?"

She smiled, her brown eyes apparently unafraid to meet mine. "I just meant that Aunt Lula Mae's furniture had sentimental value to me. Squire and I used to play in that armoire when we were kids."

When I said good-bye to her a second time I was thoroughly confused. If that was the case, then why hadn't she expressed dismay when I first told her about the body in the armoire? Why the silly story about her husband hiding in a closet? Although she was one of the most innocuous people I'd spoken to that day—Mama included—Hattie Bowman Ballard was also the most suspicious.

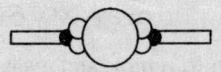

8

It had been one of the longest days of my life. My dogs were barking—Mama's expression for sore feet—and I had a migraine that reduced my vision to about forty percent. All I wanted to do was to pop back a couple of pain relievers, soak my tired tootsies, and crawl into bed. I certainly was in no mood to entertain.

"Come right on in and take a load off your feet," Rob Goldburg bellowed. "Dinner will be ready in just a few minutes."

For a second there I thought I had the wrong house. Then I saw my familiar beige furniture and cream-colored walls. The Rob-Bobs wouldn't be caught dead living in such drab surroundings. And plus which, my key had turned the lock, and that was my cat Dmitri, fast asleep on top of the home entertainment center.

"Uh—" It hurt even to smile.

"We knew you had a hard day and wanted to surprise you," Rob shouted. To be honest, he may have been speaking in a conversational tone, but with the state my head was in, even a whisper was too loud.

"That's very kind of you," I mouthed.

"Here." Rob thrust a foamy concoction at me that looked like milk. "Drink this, it will cure what ails you."

I had nothing to lose and gulped it down. It was warm and slightly bitter, but it did the trick. In a few minutes my vision began to return, and even my tootsies felt better.

"What was that?" I whispered.

"Goat's milk with a couple of aspirin dissolved in it. Bob said he learned that trick from some shepherds in Morocco."

"Did I hear my name taken in vain?" Bob appeared at the kitchen door wearing one of my bib aprons. Even though he is a slight man, the apron was far too small.

Rob smiled at his partner. "You were right. She came dragging in with one of those goddamn headaches." He turned to me. "When we came by to feed Dmitri, we had just been to the store. Rob said it was a shame to waste tonight's goodies on just the two of us. So here we are."

"You tell her the big surprise yet?" Bob asked.

"What surprise?" I demanded.

They grinned like a pair of Cheshire cats.

"Tell me now, or you can't stay for supper." Never mind that they made it. It was *my* kitchen, after all.

Rob took a deep breath. "Okay, here goes. We fixed you up with a date."

"What?"

"More goat's milk?" Bob asked kindly.

"Forget the damn goat's milk," I snapped. "What date? With whom? When?"

"With Bob's podiatrist," Rob said. He looked ready to duck. "Tomorrow evening. Dinner at the restaurant of your choice."

"I can't believe it!" I screamed. "Are you two trying to take over my life?"

"We could cancel the date," Bob said. He sounded hurt. "Arvin is a super nice guy, though. I promise. I just know you two would get along."

"And I hear he's handsome," Rob said and rolled his eyes.

"That's just what I need," I said, "a date with a handsome podiatrist. Instead of holding hands, he can rub feet." I paused. "You know, it does have some appeal at that."

"It would make Craig jealous as hell," Rob said.

"That's Greg, dear. I'll think about it."

"That's a yes," Rob said triumphantly.

My kitchen timer went off.

"Ah, my cue," Bob said. He turned to go back into the kitchen. "Supper will only be another minute, I promise. Can you wait?"

I nodded, amazed that my head no longer hurt. The truth was, I could wait all night if it meant not having to eat one of Bob's dinners. The man is supposed to be an excellent chef—or so I hear—but his cooking, like his medicinal remedies, tends to be on the exotic side.

"It's Cajun tonight," Rob said proudly.

"Oh."

"He's trying to learn how to cook Southern. You have to give him credit for that."

"Cajun is Louisiana," I said. "This is the Carolinas."

Rob shrugged. "In Toledo where he comes from, it's all the same. We'll straighten him out eventually."

Bob called us into the dining room with that deep bass voice of his, the one that could calm the Bosporus Strait. On the table was a huge pot of gumbo, bowls of rice, and a platter of boiled crawfish.

"The crawfish come first," Bob directed. "And no fair just eating the tails. We have to suck the heads."

Despite the goat's milk with aspirin, my headache was returning. "Eating shellfish is against my religion," I said.

Bob blinked in surprise. "Really?"

Rob laughed. "She's Episcopalian. I'm the Jew. But I don't think either of us are up to sucking the heads. How about we just watch?"

Bob was disappointed, but he attacked the platter of

crawfish with enough gusto for the three of us. While he ate, Rob and I talked. When I mentioned Jimbo and Skeet, Rob banged his fist down on the table hard enough to make our forks jump.

"Those snot-nosed, lazy-assed sons of bitches? What the hell were they doing delivering your merchandise?"

"They work for Purnell Purvis," I reminded him.

"They're a couple of assholes," Rob said.

Clearly there was a story there and I asked him to share it. He snorted a couple of times like a bull about to charge a matador.

"I bought a pair of life-size blackamoors from Purvis last year. Eighteenth-century, black marble and gilt. Both holding torches. Beautiful, but I paid far too much for them. Somebody kept bidding me up."

"That was me," I said. "I couldn't afford them then, but I'd never seen anything quite like them. I wanted them so bad I could taste them."

"They cost me twelve grand," Rob said. "You have expensive tastes."

"Now you're starting to sound like Buford, dear," I said gently. "Get back to Jimbo and Skeet."

"Oh, them. Well, they treated my blackamoors like they were hunks of concrete. They didn't have them wrapped. Not a single blanket around them. Nothing. As a consequence one of the pair got scratched. A good-size nick, really."

I sucked in my breath. "Ooh."

"Those lazy-assed bastards tried to claim the statue was already like that. The hell it was! I inspected both statues at the preview. They were in exceptional condition."

"I remember. Did Purvis make good on the damage?"

Rob snorted. "Hell, he gave me a goddamn rebate, but what good did that do? I wanted the pair for myself—in mint condition like I found them. I ended up selling them for a tidy profit, but that wasn't what I was after."

"Of course not. I'm surprised Purvis didn't fire those two."

"He can't," Bob said, licking his fingers. The platter of crawfish had been properly decimated.

"Oh?" I asked.

"They're his sons," Bob said. "Jimbo and Skeet Purvis."

Rob and I exchanged glances. Even though he was a newcomer, Bob knew a lot more about some of the people around us than we did. Perhaps, as a Yankee, he didn't know it was bad form to ask personal questions.

"Funny," I said, "but they don't look at all like Purvis. Or each other, for that matter."

Bob ladled gumbo over the rice in my bowl. "Different mothers, that's why. And Jimbo does sort of look like Purvis—if you put another eighty pounds on him. And a red nose."

"You're mean," I said. "But since you know so much about them, tell me this. Do you think either of them is capable of murder?"

The ladle hung, dripping, in mid-air. "We are all capable of murder, Abigail, under the *right* conditions. But if you're asking me if these two are more capable than some, I'd have to say yes."

A goose ran over my grave, as Mama is fond of saying. "Why? I mean, why especially these two?"

The ladle came down, smothering my rice with spicy gumbo. "The odds, Abigail, that's why. Pure statistics. Neither man is educated, married, or gainfully employed."

"They work for Purvis," Rob said.

The ladle came down with more goodies for my rice. "Purvis pays them shit—pardon my language, Abigail. Bob is right, they're both lazy. If they worked for anyone else but their father, they would have been fired a long time ago."

"I see," I said. I took a bite of the gumbo. It was delicious.

"Well, I don't," Rob said. "If you ask me, those two are too damn lazy to step on their own shadows, much less kill someone."

Bob shrugged. "I was just telling her my opinion."

"Well, you're scaring her," Rob said.

It was awfully sweet of Rob to be concerned on my behalf, but I wasn't afraid of Jimbo and Skeet. They didn't look like they had the energy to kill anyone. They certainly didn't have the energy to kill someone *and* drag the corpse all the way to my place.

"I was wondering if they knew the victim," I said.

"Could be," Rob said. He patted my arm needlessly. "You haven't told us the corpse's name yet. He does have one, doesn't he?"

"Arnold Ramsey."

"Holy shit!" Rob said.

"You know him?"

Rob stood up, knocking his chair backward, but he managed to catch it before it hit the floor. "No, I don't know him. But I think I heard someone cough outside. Over there by the window."

"Here? Now?" The goose that had run over my grave returned and did a quick dance.

"Shhh. Stay put," Rob said.

He tiptoed to the door, opened it as soundlessly as any cat burglar, and slipped out. The door closed behind him with only a soft hiss.

I waited, my heart thumping. I didn't notice Bob's absence until he returned from the kitchen wielding a rolling pin.

"You never know," he said sheepishly.

When Rob returned the door closed with a thud. "It's too damn dark out there," he growled, "but there was somebody there all right. He held up a cigarette butt. The tip was still glowing.

"I'm calling the police," Bob said, and was dialing before I could stop him. Not that I would have, of course, unless I'd known that it would be Greg Washburn, Investigator, who showed up.

The Rob-Bobs discreetly, and unnecessarily, took their bowls of gumbo and disappeared into the kitchen. Then even more unnecessarily, Bob sneaked back in and handed Greg a clean bowl and spoon.

"Don't mind if I do," Greg said. He sat down and tucked a napkin into his shirt, just as casually as if he were dining at home.

I thought it presumptuous of the man, and couldn't resist telling him so. He smiled.

"I've decided to break it off," he said.

"What?"

"With Deena. Seeing you again this morning made me realize I might have made a mistake."

"*Might* have?"

"All right. I screwed up. But damn it, Abby, I missed you."

Just like a man, I thought. Misses me, so he goes out with someone else. Someone with more plastic in her body than Barbie.

"You have a fine way of showing it," I snapped. "Does this Deena person know you're breaking it off with her?"

He shook his head. "I was on my way over there when Bob's call was patched through. But I plan to tell her tonight, I swear."

"Go easy on her," I said generously. Unless Deena had less heart than Barbie, she was going to be hurt.

"Does this mean things are, uh, okay between us?"

"What?" I asked incredulously.

He reached for my hand. His long dark lashes fluttered

involuntarily. Half of me wanted to jump into his arms; the other half wanted to slap him.

"Hold it right there, buster," I said in my gruffest voice. "Two and two do not make five."

"Hey, I admitted I screwed up. And I promised I'd talk to her tonight."

I pounded the table with my fist, but nothing even rattled. "You don't get it, do you? You can't turn Deena off like a faucet, and then when you turn it back on, there I am."

"You're right. I don't get it, Abby. What do you want me to do? Fall down on my hands and knees and beg?"

I sighed. "Time, Greg. That's what I want."

Those uncannily blue eyes registered confusion. "How much time? A week? A month?"

"At least until the day after tomorrow," I said. "I have a date tomorrow night."

He had the temerity to chuckle. "Yeah, right."

"A podiatrist named Arvin."

"You're a hoot, Abby."

"I'm deadly serious." I stood up. "Now about this Peeping Tom. Can you tell if it was Jimbo or Skeet?"

Greg stood up as well. Even though he was still wearing the napkin, he looked as adorable as ever. It was going to take all the willpower I could muster to keep him at arm's length just for the evening—never mind a week.

"It wasn't either of them," he said authoritatively.

"No? How can you be so sure?"

He held up the cigarette butt Rob had brought inside. "There's lipstick on this. Pink lipstick. Does that sound like your Jimbo and Skeet?"

I studied the butt without touching it. I could see a faint smudge of pink, but I wouldn't have noticed it without having it pointed out to me.

"A woman then," I said stupidly.

Greg cracked a smile and I got a fleeting glimpse of

his incredibly white teeth. "That's my guess. Any friends or neighbors who smoke?"

"None who like to do so in the bushes."

"Touché." He handed the butt to me.

"Wait," I said, afraid to touch it with more than my fingernail tips. "Don't you need this for evidence?"

I got treated to the pearly whites in all their glory. "Evidence of what? This isn't a TV show, Abby. Smoking in your bushes was certainly bad manners, and whoever did it could be found guilty of trespassing *if* we caught her in the act, and *if* she had been properly warned. My guess is it was some local teenage girl, sneaking in a quick puff."

"I see. Well, if it's that insignificant—which I don't think it is, considering a dead body was found in my shop today—why are you here? Why did you even bother to come over?"

"To see you," he said.

He tried to lock those gorgeous eyes on mine, but I turned away and studied the tan and gray abstract painting that hung innocuously on one of my cream walls. Mama had bought it as a housewarming present. She didn't like carrying coals to Newcastle, she said. No antiques for the antique dealer. The painting had become a symbol of my life then, drab and abstract. Empty without Greg. I put the antiques I'd been living with up for sale in my shop.

But now it was time to get on with my life, to reclaim the things that gave me pleasure. It was time to put some color back into my new digs. Maybe some rich vibrant red like on Amy Barras's walls. But not blue. Certainly not Wedgwood-blue.

"Well?" he asked.

"Well, what?" The beige sofas had to go, too. Maybe a cheerful yellow chintz with cabbage flowers, a la English country estate. It would fit in much better with the few antiques I hadn't taken to the shop.

"Tomorrow then?"

"Can't," I said. "I've got that date with the podiatrist, remember?"

He laughed and let himself out, and I didn't move until one of the Rob-Bobs came out of the kitchen and hugged me. Then I burst into tears.

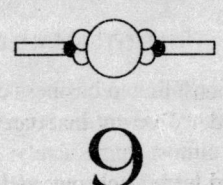

9

I did not sleep like a baby—my babies never seemed to sleep. Instead I slept like a hibernating bear, only waking up once during the night when Dmitri, who likes to sleep on my chest, inadvertently stuck a paw in my mouth. The second time I awoke it was already morning, but not quite time for my alarm. I guess I had been too tired to unplug the phone when I went to bed.

"Hello?"

There was a long pause during which my blood temperature plunged several degrees. Six-thirty in the morning is too early for those annoying sales solicitors, so it could only mean one thing. Mama, or one of my children, had suffered a calamity; appendicitis perhaps, or a fatal or near-fatal car accident. There was a lesser chance that my daughter Susan was calling to say she was pregnant. Not that I was expecting her to be pregnant, mind you, but if she turns up that way out of wedlock, you can bet I'll hear about it at an inconvenient time. But not before noon.

"Hello?" I rasped again.

"Mrs. Timberlake?"

I sat up in bed, spilling Dmitri off my chest. "Which hospital is it?"

"Huh? This is Garland Riggs, Mrs. Timberlake. I'm the owner of Broken Tree Nursery on Nations Ford Road. I want—"

"I don't take unsolicited business calls at home," I said angrily and slammed down the receiver.

It rang again almost immediately.

"Yeah?" I answered only because, with my luck, *that* would be the hospital calling."

"This isn't a business call," Garland Riggs said quickly. "Least not nursery business. This is family business."

"Susan never mentioned you," I said defensively. "And she doesn't believe in abortion, so you're going to have to pay child support."

"Huh? Mrs. Timberlake, my mama was Mimi Barras Riggs. Lula Mae Barras was my aunt. Well, my aunt through marriage."

"Oh, *that* Garland Riggs."

My predicament was slowly and uncomfortably coming back to me. I remembered that Garland was of the Barras cousins and had been on my list to contact that day. But of course a good deal later. God created breakfast, then Adam and Eve—in that order. Read your Bible if you don't believe it.

"Mrs. Timberlake—"

"It's Ms.," I said crossly. "I'm divorced now. You're not calling from another time zone, are you?"

"No, ma'am. I'm sorry if I woke you. I'm an early riser myself, and I tend to forget the rest of the world sleeps in."

"The rest of the world does not *sleep in*, Mr. Riggs, just because you get up with the chickens. What is it you want?"

"I heard about what happened yesterday. I was wondering if we might have breakfast together and talk about it. My treat, of course."

It was an odd suggestion coming from a male, and a total stranger. I probably would not have accepted his invitation, had not something in his voice reminded me of Greg.

"Breakfast would be fine," I said. "Can you give me forty-five minutes."

"Sure, forty-five minutes. How about Denny's?"

I would rather eat breakfast at Denny's than haute cuisine at the finest restaurants in Paris, but it wasn't where I wanted to eat that morning. More important than the food was the possibility that one of Greg's acquaintances might see me out with another man. Clearly Greg didn't believe that I had a date with Arvin. Well, I'd show him!

"Can we make it the Waffle House on South Boulevard?" I'd seen patrol cars parked outside that place more than once, and, as we all know, men gossip more than women.

"The Waffle House will be fine. How will I recognize you?"

"Just look down," I said blithely. No amount of pretending is going to alter the fact that my most distinguishing feature is my lack of height.

It was uncanny. The second I put the receiver down, the phone rang again.

"Yes, Mr. Riggs?" I said patiently.

"Riggs? I'm sorry, I must have dialed the wrong number," the caller said, exhibiting rare telephone manners for this day and age, even in the Carolinas.

"Wait!" I shouted.

It was too late, not that it much mattered, because Lottie Bell Barras Bowman called me right back. This time I answered with my name and she stayed on the line.

"I was wondering if you could come over this morning for tea again."

"Well, I, uh—"

"Of course, it wouldn't actually have to be *tea*."

"That's very kind of you, Mrs. Bowman but I—"

"There's something I found regarding the furniture that

I need to show you. Something in my granddaddy's diary.''

"Oh?''

"How does ten sound?''

"Ten sounds fine.''

"Tea at ten, then. Or whatever.'' She giggled girlishly and hung up.

I ignored Dmitri's demands to have his chin scratched and jumped in the shower. I was just toweling off with one of the ultra thick and terribly expensive bath towels Mama had given me for my birthday when the doorbell rang. It was Murphy's Law, of course. For what it's worth I am genetically incapable of *not* answering a bell—be it the phone or the door. Fortunately the towel was large as well as thick, and a quick tuck turned it into a rather modest sarong. Any reasonable person would have seen that.

Greg did not. "Is that how you normally answer the door?''

I gave him what I hoped was an impish smile. "This towel is a lot bigger than the one I normally wear.''

"Very funny, Abby. Can I come in, or do you want the whole world to see you like that?''

"Just a minute,'' I said. I closed the door and scampered back to my bedroom, where I put on a long-sleeved, quilted polyester housecoat—the one I bought for Susan to take with her to college. I opened the door just a few seconds past my minute.

"Hysterically funny, Abby. Remind me to laugh sometime.''

Instinct told me he was upset about a lot more than how I dressed to answer doors. I stepped aside and let him in.

"I told Deena,'' he said without further preamble.

"You what?''

"I broke it off with Deena. Just like you asked." He sounded miserable.

I glanced at the clock. It wasn't even seven yet.

"When?"

"Last night, on my way home. I was going to wait until today, but I got to thinking on my way home—"

"You spent the night at her house, didn't you?"

"Talking, Abby. That's all we did was talk."

I may not be able to spot lipstick on a cigarette butt. Collars are another story. I pointed to the offending smudges.

"Where does she think your eyes are located?"

"She was crying, Abby. She laid her head on my shoulder. I comforted her. That's all that happened, Abby. I swear."

"I see." Actually I felt like one of the blind men in the Hindu parable of the elephant. I thought I had hold of the elephant's trunk, but for all I knew it was the tail. And any time you find yourself holding a tail in your hands, watch out! You're liable to be dumped on.

He was pacing. Periodically he raked his long strong fingers through that thick, almost black hair.

"God, it was a nightmare, Abby. We'd only been out a few times. No more than five, I swear. You would have thought we'd been married for ten years. Are all women like that?"

"Like what?" Never answer a rhetorical question with a question. Like I said, it was too early in the morning for me, and I hadn't had breakfast.

"She threatened to kill herself, Abby. Can you imagine that?"

"She did?" The poor dear should have told me her plans. I might have volunteered to help her out. I am only joking of course—but just barely. People who use suicide threats to manipulate others deserve at least a serious illness.

"She said I'd led her on. She said we had an under-standing. Hell, Abby, what kind of understanding was it, if I didn't even know about it?"

I did feel for Greg. He honestly didn't have a clue. It was very much like when our puppy, Scruffles—Charlie has him now—tried to play with the birds that hung around the feeder on our deck. Scruffles would bound happily at them, not meaning to catch them, only to play, but the birds would take to the trees. Greg was like Scruffles; adorable, cuddly, and perennially confused.

"She'll get over it," I said calmly. "You know us women. We're always reading commitment into every-thing. It's in our genes. Part of the cavewoman survival thing. If we can get a caveman to share his bearskin on a permanent basis, we know our little cave babies will stand a better chance."

"What?"

"Never mind. She'll be *fine*, Greg. That's the point. She carried on like she was supposed to, and you resisted just like you were supposed to. Right?"

He waited a second too long to answer.

"*Right?*"

"Yeah. I didn't do anything. I already told you that."

I glanced at the clock on my VCR. It was five minutes until seven.

"Look, sweetie, I have a breakfast appointment I'm already late for. Why don't you stay here and catch a few winks before you go on duty? We'll talk some more later."

He nodded and headed for the sofa. Halfway there he stopped and turned around."

"Who's the appointment with? The podiatrist?"

I smiled patiently. "No, that's tonight. This morning it's with a nursery owner."

"You're a hoot,' he said and stumbled to the couch.

I hoped to hell that half of Charlotte's finest hadn't chosen to eat at the Waffle House that day.

As soon as I saw the truck, I knew that Garland hadn't left yet. It had his nursery logo painted clearly on both sides. It was what I call a monster truck. The double cab was perched precariously atop wheels large enough to land a jumbo jet. It stood head and shoulders above the other vehicles in the parking lot—to mangle a metaphor.

Garland Riggs should have described himself for me. There weren't any police officers—that I could tell—at the Waffle House at seven twenty-five when I arrived, a mere ten minutes late. The five men and one woman looked astonishingly alike, although the woman's mustache was perhaps the heaviest. Graying brown hair, plumpness, and late middle age were just a few of their common denominators. Had it not been for the blue jacket with the green logo of a broken tree on it, with the name Riggs embroidered across its branches, I would have had to resort to asking for names.

"Mr. Riggs, I presume," I said, holding out my hand.

He took it without standing up. Since he was a Southerner born and bred, that meant he was pretty angry.

"Did they give you my message about being late?" I asked pleasantly.

"Yeah." He glanced pointedly at his watch. "I have a business to run. It's Christmas tree season."

"I'm sorry, but I kept getting interrupted. First the phone, and then the doorbell. The phone was your aunt."

"Aunt Lottie Bell?"

I nodded. "She's invited me for tea this morning."

"Why would Dotty Lottie have you over for tea?"

"Don't be rude," I said. "I think she's really sweet, and clear as a bell, in spite of her fondness for Mr. Daniels. Last time, we had a fascinating conversation."

"Oh? What did she say?"

"I don't betray confidences, Mr. Riggs."

He stared at me.

I stared back calmly.

"Well, since you're going to be having tea later then I guess you won't be needing this." He tucked the plastic-coated menu behind the napkin dispenser.

I pulled it back out. "You offered me breakfast, didn't you?"

"Ma'am?"

I called the waitress over and ordered scrambled eggs with cheese, bacon, grits, and raisin toast. "And try to scare up some marmalade for the toast," I said gently.

The waitress, who looked astonishingly like her customers, sauntered off to do her thing, but not without first letting me know that the assortment of jelly packets at my table was not negotiable. If my basket didn't contain marmalade from the get-go, I was out of luck. And speaking of luck, didn't I know how lucky I was to live in a country where I could choose between grape and strawberry?

"So what's this all about?" I asked when we were alone.

He stirred his coffee vigorously. No bacon and eggs for him, unless of course he'd already eaten.

"My Aunt Lottie Bell called me yesterday with the news. I could hardly believe it. I was shocked."

"Imagine how I felt when I opened my new armoire and found a dead man inside!" I shuddered.

"I bet it was horrible. You read about this kind of thing happening in really big cities, like New York or Los Angeles. Maybe even Chicago. But Charlotte? What's the world coming to?"

"The world has gone to hell in a handbasket," I said. That is one of Mama's favorite phrases. But for her the world headed for Hades the day the first Rock Hill woman stopped wearing gloves to church.

"Killing someone, and then stuffing them into an antique armoire. That's just plain sick,'' Garland said. He took a sip of his coffee. ''Do the police have any leads? Do you know what the autopsy showed?''

I shrugged. ''Mr. Riggs, you didn't really expect me to talk about the grisly details over breakfast, did you?''

''Huh? Of course not. Actually, I'd rather talk about the furniture.''

''Yes?'' Finally I was getting somewhere.

''As you know, I was at the auction. My wife—Alma—was very upset when I came away empty-handed. We're not as loaded as Aunt Lottie Bell.''

''I'm sorry. But that's the nature of the beast, I'm afraid.''

''Yeah, well, she's been admiring that furniture for years. Ever since she married into the family. She was hoping I would give it to her for Christmas.''

''There are still almost three weeks left until Christmas,'' I said with forced cheer. ''You might find something similar down in Waxhaw.''

''Nah, it wouldn't be the same. Every time we'd go over to visit my aunt, Alma would admire the armoire. Well, not just the armoire, of course. The other pieces as well. There were five of them, weren't there?''

''Four. Besides the armoire, there was a Louis XV desk, one small Louis XV table, and a carved and gilded mirror.''

''Yes, that's right.''

''I mean, you should know. You were the one who bid against me.''

He picked up his cup and set it right down again. ''Yes, that's right, I did. Someone had to keep them in the family, you see. I just couldn't stand by and watch my Aunt Lula Mae's furniture be auctioned off like that.''

The waitress, whose name badge read Evlyn, slammed my eggs plate down in front of me. Thus alerted, I was able to intercept the plate of raisin toast. She let go of it reluctantly.

"I asked. We don't serve marmalade."

I nodded, and as soon as she was gone dug into the oblong wicker basket of jellies in front of me. In the very bottom was a marmalade. I spread it defiantly on one of the slices and left it sitting on the plate the entire meal, which, by the way, was delicious.

"So," Garland said at last, "it's time to talk, isn't it?"

"I thought we were talking," I said. While I'd eaten, he'd done a thorough job of covering the Panthers and the Hornets, and had made a brief foray into the world of golf.

"I mean business," he said. "I want you to consider an offer."

"What kind of an offer? I don't sell plants in my shop. The Den of Antiquity is strictly antiques."

I chose to interpret his grimace as a smile. "I'm not talking about plants. I'm not a wholesaler. What I want to do is to make you an offer for my aunt's furniture."

"Now? But, I mean—someone was killed in the armoire. Surely you don't want that as well."

"All of it," he said.

"Mr. Riggs, I don't understand," I said gently. "I mean, if you couldn't afford—"

He cleared his throat. "That's what I meant by an offer. If you would let me pay you in installments, I'd be willing to pay twenty percent more than your retail price."

"I see. Well, the reason I outbid you in the first place is because I have a buyer lined up for those pieces."

"Who?"

I was not prepared for his bluntness. "Well, uh, somebody down in Columbia."

Actually my buyers—a husband and wife team—lived in Belmont, North Carolina, on the northern shore of Lake Wylie. They had recently retired there from Connecticut.

They had stopped in my shop almost two months ago, liked what they had seen (thank God they didn't come to my house), and virtually given me carte blanche to shop for them. Curiously, immediately following Lula Mae's death they visited my shop again. They had the temerity to ask me to bid on her things, should they go to auction, before she was even in the ground!

"Maybe my buyer will decide against the armoire," I said. "You want me to give you a call?"

He hesitated. "Sure thing."

Then he scooped up his jacket and left, stiffing me for the entire bill.

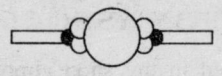

10

Call it force of habit. Before I knew it, I was on Selwyn Avenue, just a couple of blocks from my shop. I honestly couldn't remember what had motivated me to drive there. In fact, I couldn't even remember the drive. Frankly I deserved to have my license suspended for at least a couple of days.

When I realized where I was, I pulled over and parked on a side street. I closed my eyes. I did not turn the engine off. After I was through shaking—it is damn scary not knowing *why* you've done something—I had a brief argument with myself. Should I continue on down Selwyn, past my shop, or would all that yellow tape across the front door be too much for me to handle? Would stopping in to see my friends and coworkers be a help or a hindrance in my investigation? Most importantly, would there still be reporters lurking about?

The cautious side of me was winning, and I was probably just minutes away from turning around and heading back down Selwyn in the direction I'd come, when Calamity Jane tapped on my window. I can't deny that I jumped. No doubt a taller woman would have hit her head on the car ceiling.

"Hey Abigail, you all right in there?"

I rolled down my window just far enough to be polite. "I'm fine, dear. I was just resting my eyes for a minute."

"You're lucky I came along, I guess. I went to college with a girl from Virginia. Funny, but her name was Virginia. Anyway, she used to drive back home on long weekends. One day she stopped at a welcome station— just to rest her eyes, like you did—and she fell asleep. She left her car running, too. But she never woke up. You see, there was this hole in her exhaust pipe, and another hole in the floorboard, and—"

"I don't have a hole in my floorboard, dear. You wouldn't happen to know if there are still reporters hanging about, would you?"

Jane Cox, aka Calamity Jane, aka C. J., frowned. "Strange that you should mention that. I haven't been to my shop yet—I'm just now arriving—but last night a reporter with a notebook actually came to my house. To talk to *me*!"

"What? What did he ask? What did you say?"

"Oh, I didn't say anything. I never answer my door without looking through the peephole first. My Auntie Grace over in Hickory did that once, and the man pushed right past her and into the house. And then he—well—" She blushed. "He peed on her couch."

I forgot to be annoyed at her digression. "That's all he did, was pee on her couch?"

"But it wasn't Scotchguarded, you see. Auntie Grace was a very simple woman, living on a pension. It cost her almost fifty dollars to get the couch cleaned."

I nodded sympathetically. "But you're sure it was a reporter at your house last night, right?"

Her eyes widened at my naivete. "Reporters carry notebooks, don't they? The man who—well, you know—on my auntie's couch didn't carry a notebook."

"I bet you're right."

Jane Cox is new enough to our little antique community so that the gossip on her has yet to be solidified. The Rob-Bobs think she's a lesbian, Peggy Redfern thinks she's a man-eater, Gretchen thinks she's happily married and has at least one child, and dear Wynnell thinks the woman is stark raving nuts and feels sorry for her. Somewhere along the line, Wynnell is convinced, Jane Cox had a bad experience with a Yankee and just flipped out. We all agree, however, that C. J. has much improved Feathers 'N Treasures—my late Aunt Eulonia's shop—and that she is an asset to the community.

"If you're afraid you might run into reporters I could walk ahead and warn you," Jane offered generously.

"Thank you, but I've decided not to hang around. Anyway, I've got to be somewhere at ten, and I want to change my clothes first." To save time, I'd worn an old pair of pink and gray cotton sweats to meet Garland Riggs.

"This isn't an arraignment you're going to, is it?" Jane looked genuinely worried on my behalf.

There was no reason *not* to tell the woman the truth. "No, contrary to any rumors you may have heard, I have not been arrested. I have a tea party at ten. With Mrs. Lottie Bell Barras Bowman."

"Well, my, my," she said, obviously impressed.

I decided to impress her one more time. "Then after that I thought I'd run over to Belmont and see the Kefferts. They're the ones I bought the Louis XV set for. I want to see if they're still interested in it."

C. J. pointed to the passenger side of the car. "Mind if I sit down a minute? Standing too long is hard on my veins. It could lead to blood clots, you know. I read about a woman—I think she was a waitress—who had a blood clot start in her legs and then zoom up into her head. It killed her, of course. And all because she stood all day."

"You don't say." I obligingly unlocked the passenger door and motioned for her to get in. At least then I could roll my window up.

"The Kefferts, you say. Is that Rich and Terri Keffert?"

"I don't remember their first names offhand. I think she calls him Captain. You know them?"

"Captain and First Mate Keffert. Yeah, that's them. They just started attending my church. We're in the same Sunday school class. I think they're from Massachusetts."

I should have known. The Kefferts had struck me as smart people. Undoubtedly they wanted to fit into their new community as quickly as possible, and in the South the quickest way to do that is by joining a church. Here the church directories are the ties that bind the community together. That and sports, of course.

"Actually they're from Connecticut. You haven't been to their house, have you? I mean, can you give me directions?"

"Oh, you won't need directions once you get to Belmont. I haven't see the house myself, but I hear that it's awesome. It's shaped like a giant boat. Only it's made out of cement and doesn't float, of course."

"Oh really?" My Louis XV furniture in a concrete boat!

"But I'd be careful if I were you."

"You didn't perchance know someone who went down on the *Titanic*, did you?" I immediately regretted being so flippant.

"Well, yes, in a way. I mean I knew a woman named Clara, whose sister went down on the *Titanic*. You see, Clara's sister—"

"I was only kidding," I said.

She regarded me seriously. "I meant you should be careful about the Kefferts. Like I said, they just joined my church, so I don't know them that well. They could be dangerous."

I made a semi-successful attempt not to laugh. Hopefully it sounded just like a sneeze. "They're a rich, retired couple. Why should I be afraid of them?"

"They may be the killers you're looking for."

I cut off the car engine. "Excuse me?"

"Well, they had a motive, didn't they?"

I shook my head vigorously to clear it of the cobwebs that were affecting my hearing. "What?"

"Maybe they're not that rich after all. Maybe they spent all their money building that cement boat."

"So?" I asked politely.

"So maybe they thought they would get a discount on the furniture if there was a body found in it. I saw this show on TV where—"

I thanked C. J. for her company and her concern. Then I pushed her out of the car—literally—by pretending to look for a map of North Carolina in the glove compartment. And my Algebra II teacher back in high school said I didn't use my head!

Lottie Bell Barras Bowman did not answer her doorbell. After about five minutes of constant ringing—after all, she might have had a head start on *tea*—I gave up and fought my way back through the jungle and to the street. As I thrashed my way past the last aucuba bush, I nearly ran over an elegant older woman and her two Yorkshire terriers.

"May I help you?" she asked calmly.

"Uh, my name is Abigail Timberlake, and I'm here to see Mrs. Bowman," I stammered. "I've been invited to tea."

Thank God I'd actually changed out of my sweats and into a church dress. Even then I must have looked a sight.

"My name is Irma Mickley," the elegant woman said. "And these"—she pointed to the dogs—"are Rocky and Tina. We're Lottie Bell's neighbors from across the street.

We were looking out our front window when you pulled up. I guess you haven't heard.''

"Ma'am?"

"Lottie Bell is in the hospital."

"Ma'am?" The woman was going to think I was stupid as well as disheveled.

One of the dogs—Tina, I think—whimpered, and Irma Mickley bent gracefully and patted her head.

"It happened less than an hour ago. I don't know many details, just that an ambulance came and they carried her out on a stretcher. They took her to Presbyterian, I think. I heard them say something about her heart."

"I'm so sorry," I said. "I had no idea."

"Well, neither did I. I never thought it would be Lottie Bell's heart. Her liver maybe . . ." Her voice trailed off.

"Did you know her well?"

She patted the other dog, Rocky. "Well, we've been neighbors for forty some years, but we've never been *friends*. Still, it's a shock whenever someone goes, even if they are up in years like Lottie Bell."

I politely refrained from asking her if she was related to Calamity Jane. Just because someone gets wheeled off to a hospital doesn't mean they're *gone*. I thanked Irma Mickley for her information, patted Rocky and Tina obligingly, and made a beeline for Presbyterian like a bat out of hell.

The emergency room receptionist was a bucktoothed, buxom, red-haired woman named Margaret. She was a jolly gal who seemed totally out of place in such a grave setting. I had the feeling that if she had a say in the matter, she would admit the wounded and dying without first making them fill out enough paper to level a small forest. She was just the sort of person I needed to talk to.

"Hey," I said, the standard Carolina greeting.

From her smile I learned that her parents had been too poor or too cheap to buy her braces. "Hey."

"I just heard that a Lottie Bell Barras Bowman was brought in by ambulance less than an hour ago. Heart attack, I think. Can you give me more details."

"Are you a relative?"

"No, a friend."

She winked. "I'm sorry, I didn't hear you."

"She's my mother." Mama would kill me for adding twenty years to her age, but she would approve of the fact that Lottie Bell wore pearls. The Jack Daniels, however, was another story.

Margaret scanned her computer screen. She caught her breath suddenly.

"Oh, I'm so sorry. The patient you asked about has—well, she's died."

I stared stupidly at her.

"Hey, you know, I'm about to go on break. Would you like to have coffee with me?"

I snapped out of my reverie and thanked her for being a shining example of a good receptionist.

"Hey, no problemo," she said, and turned to smile at the next person in line.

Absorbed as I was in my thoughts, I can only be grateful I walked smack dab into Greg Washburn and not some poor soul with multiple contusions. Our difference in height is practically obscene, and I bumped my nose hard against his sternum.

"Pardon me," I gasped, not realizing at first who it was.

"Oh there you are!"

"Greg! Guess who was—"

He put his arms around me, and then let go quickly, as if he was ashamed to be doing so in public.

"I know," he said. "It's Mrs. Bowman."

"Yes, she died of a heart attack. It couldn't have been

more than an hour ago. I was supposed to meet her at her house for tea. It feels so weird.''

He led me over to a vacant row of seats that were partly screened by an anemic-looking schefflera.

"Sit," he ordered.

I stood. "Why are you here?"

He sat and crossed his long legs, ankle over knee. "I've been looking for you," he said.

"Me? How did you know to find me here?"

"I spoke to that doomsday woman who took over your aunt's shop. Jane what's-her-name."

"Jane Cox. We call her Calamity Jane. But she didn't know I was going to be here. She just knew about the tea."

He nodded. "Right. But when I heard over the wire that Mrs. Bowman had been brought here, I knew where to find you."

"You were worried about me?"

He patted the seat beside him, but I preferred to stand. He sighed. "Okay, Abby, have it your way. But you're not going to like this."

"Like what?"

"You sure you don't want to sit?"

My heart pounded. "It's Mama, isn't it? I knew I shouldn't have used her name in vain."

He shook his head.

"Charlie? I keep telling him not to drive so fast."

"No."

"Oh God, not Susan!"

He smiled wanly. "No. It's not your family."

"Dmitri?" The poor dear had used up at least eleven of his allotted lives.

"No. It's your shop. It was broken into last night."

I sat down hard.

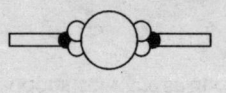

11

"My shop? The Den of Iniquity?"

He suppressed a chuckle. "That's *antiquity*, isn't it?"

"I know what it is! What happened?"

"Carter—our beat officer—noticed a strip of the tape flapping in the breeze this morning. He stopped and saw that it had been cut."

"Front or back door?"

"Front. I mean, back."

"Which is it?" I nearly shrieked.

He uncrossed his legs. "Well, both. Carter saw the tape loose in the front, but it looks like the perpetrator forced his way in through the back door, and exited through the front. Apparently that's where he was parked.

"It's likely that he—or *she*," he said with needless emphasis, "exited while it was still dark so somebody would have seen him—or *her*."

"What time did this Carter person drive by?"

"It was on his seven o'clock circuit. So within half an hour, I'd guess."

I popped up out of my seat like a tart from a toaster. "What? Y'all have known about this for two hours, and you're just now telling me?"

He motioned for me to sit down. I responded by pacing.

"Take it easy, Abby. You're not an easy lady to track down. Where were you anyway?"

"Out having breakfast with a man."

He smiled and raked a finger through that thick black hair. "Always cracking jokes. That's my Abby."

I waved a hand impatiently. "So what was the damage? What was taken? Could you tell?"

"The only damage appears to be your back door. He— or *she*—"

"Stop it!" I said.

"Yes, ma'am. Of course I don't keep track of your inventory, Abby, but I do know that something is missing."

"Oh, not that Japanese painting from the Meiji era! I knew I should have locked that in my safe. But I was showing that to a customer last Friday—"

He was shaking his head. "I don't know about a Japanese painting. What's missing is that mirror from the Barras estate auction. The one we'd impounded."

"But left in my shop." It was time to sit again. "This is crazy. Why would anyone want to steal that? I mean, it is a beautiful mirror, and quite authentic, but it isn't worth half of what that Japanese painting could bring."

"Maybe the thief likes to look at himself, or—" He bit his lip mockingly.

"First the body in the armoire," I said thinking aloud, "and now the mirror. Do you think the two are related somehow?"

Greg frowned. "Well, there's no obvious connection. But we can't rule it out. What can you tell me about the mirror?"

"It was genuine Louis XV. It was made in France— probably Paris—sometime between 1775 and 1800. The frame was hand-carved from cherry and gilded. The theme was acanthus leaves. In this case, both the workmanship and the state of preservation were good to excellent."

"I'm impressed. How much was it worth?"

"Well, that's the thing. Those four pieces were all made by the same artisan. Sort of like a set. If I sold them together—well, let's just the say the mirror by itself is worth a lot less."

"How *much*?"

"Seventy-five hundred."

He gasped. "For a goddamn mirror?"

"Wait a few more years until the turn of the century, and it will be worth a hell of a lot more. Everything will automatically have another century added to its span."

"Ourselves included."

"Don't remind me. So what are you going to do about this?"

"Well, we investigate, of course."

"Y'all better do more than that, buster. That mirror was in your safekeeping."

That seemed to amuse him. "Whew," he said, "you're five feet of pure steam."

"Four-nine, and if I were you I'd watch it, because I'm about to explode. Shouldn't you be out there lifting fingerprints, or something?"

He got up. For someone his height, it must be like unfolding an ironing board. A few squeaks and creaks, and always the danger that the thing will collapse on you before it's fully expanded.

"See you tonight. I'm off. We could take in a movie at the Towers?"

There was in fact a new Kevin Costner movie playing there that I wanted to see, but I was promised for that night. Dinner with a foot doctor named Arvin.

"Well, uh—"

"Please," Greg said, with his eyes as well as his voice.

I felt like an ice cream cone in July. Thank God he hadn't taken me seriously about Arvin.

"Sorry," I said, looking past him to the sickly schef-flera. "I promised Mama I'd meet her at church. It's

Wednesday, you know. We're having our monthly dinner. Tonight's program is a demonstration on deep fat frying your Christmas turkey. You want to come?"

It was a safe offer. I already knew that Greg takes to church like Charlie does to homework, and Susan does to housework. It would be a cold day in hell before he ever darkened a church door, and by then what would be the point?

"No thanks. Maybe tomorrow then? A movie and dinner?"

"Sounds great." It sounded a lot better than dinner with Arvin.

I excused myself to use the ladies' room so that Greg would leave first. There was a call I wanted to make.

It wasn't easy. I may as well have driven down to Rock Hill. I had to wait in line while a teenage boy mumbled interminably into the receiver. Something to do with jock itch, and didn't she (presumably his girlfriend) notice the sores you-know-where? I had just grabbed the receiver, a tissue safely covering my hand, when an enormous blond woman, quite possibly a shotputter for the German Olympic team, demanded in a heavy accent that she use the phone before I did.

"Ma'am?" I asked, bewildered.

She snatched the phone from my hand, sans tissue, and furiously punched in a long string of numbers.

"Hans!" she barked.

Hans barked something back and the woman slammed the receiver back in the cradle.

"*Ein Schwein!*"

I waited until her broad shoulders passed through the front door before trying again.

"Mama?"

"Oh Abigail, I am so glad you called. Do you think I'm being unreasonable, dear?"

"Well, I was over yesterday, after all. Some daughters don't speak to their mothers but once a week."

I could hear Mama's pearls clacking against the receiver. "Oh, I'm not talking about this call, dear. I'm talking about the club."

"Which club?" Mama belongs to at least four clubs; book, garden, bridge, and community service. And that doesn't count anything connected to church.

"The Apathia Club," she said mournfully.

"What club is that, Mama?"

"You know, it's that ultra prestigious club I've been telling you about. Anyone who is *anyone* is in it."

"I'm not."

"You don't even live in Rock Hill anymore. Louise is in it. So is Elaine Cryderman. Why don't they want me?"

"How do you know they don't want you?"

"Well, Louise invited me as her guest to one of their luncheons. They hold them at the Rock Hill Country Club, you know. Anyway, they looked me over like I was a new fall outfit at Dillard's department store, but there were no takers. Nobody asked me to join."

"Maybe they don't have any openings."

"They have three openings," she wailed. "I want desperately to join, but they won't ask me."

Having never been a club sort of person, I was at a loss as to how to comfort her. "Well, why would you want to belong to a club that didn't want you for a member?" I asked, stealing from and distorting the words of Groucho Marx.

"Oh, Abby, you just don't understand! These are *the* movers and shakers of Rock Hill."

I pictured a group of well-dressed women, Mama's age, shimmying and shaking their way through the buffet line of the Rock Hill Country Club. I had to stifle a giggle.

"I'm sorry, Mama. Maybe they plan to ask you, and

just haven't gotten around to it. Anyway, Mama, I need you to do me a big favor.''

''What sort of favor?'' Mama asked cautiously, and with good reason.

''Well, Greg might call you today looking for me, and if he does—''

''You want me to lie to him?'' My mama is every bit as bright as June Cleaver.

''I'm in a predicament, Mama. Greg asked me out, but I already have a date.''

''You're two-timing your boyfriend and you want me to help?'' Wally and Beav would never have gotten past her.

''It isn't my doing, Mama. The Rob-Bobs fixed me up with a podiatrist without asking my permission.''

''A podiatrist is a doctor, right?''

''I guess so. He calls himself Dr. Arvin Schlonecker.''

Mama did a little mental arithmetic. It didn't take long. Greg's salary, as a city investigator, versus Arvin's, taking care of tootsies. Arvin won by a big toe.

''So what do I say?'' she asked.

''Just tell him I'll be meeting you at church tonight for the turkey fry.''

''Will do—hold on, Abby. I've got another call. It might be *him*.''

Personally I don't think anyone who wears crinolines and high heels when she vacuums her drapes has any business having call waiting. Mama has yet to buy a microwave oven, for pete's sake. But I suppose it's all that social insecurity that drives her to amass all the phone paraphernalia available.

''It was just that Jumping Jane woman. She wants you to call her immediately. She said to be sure and tell you that it's very important.''

''That's Calamity Jane,'' I said.

"She jumps to conclusions, doesn't she? It's all the same."

I said good-bye to Mama and called Jane. A short line had formed behind me, but that was tough. At least they didn't have to hear mumbled conversations about jock itch.

"Hello, Feathers 'N Treasures," Jane said so smoothly that I wasn't sure if I'd reached her machine.

"Hello, Jane?"

"Abby! Thank God you called. I was getting worried. Your mother said she'd give you the message, but then I got to thinking, what if she forgot to give you the message until tomorrow? Only tomorrow, you see—"

"Jane! It's only been two minutes. What is it?"

"Yes, that. Well, that reporter came to see me again. But this time at my shop."

"And?"

"And I don't think she's a reporter, after all."

"She? Why didn't you tell me before it was a she?"

"You didn't ask, Abby. She said her name was Toxie somebody, and that she was trying to get in touch with you. Do you know her?"

"I've never met her."

"Oh, wait just a second. I wrote down something else she said."

I waited almost as long as it takes snow to melt in Charlotte. In the meantime I could hear Calamity Jane singing to herself. "Eleanor Rigby," I think it was, but terribly off-key. I was going to have to suggest Muzak to C. J. Given her voice, it would be a legitimate business expense.   •

"Oh, here it is. She said she's a niece of someone named Lula Mae. Could that be right?"

"It could be," I said patiently. "Is there a last name for this Toxie person?"

"Just a minute. I wrote that down someplace, too."

If you knew C. J., you would know that it made perfect sense to her to write my message down in fragments, on separate pieces of paper. Of course it doesn't make any sense to me, but I had no choice but to wait while she searched and sang a horrendous rendition of "There's Got to Be a Morning After."

"Here it is. It's Barras. Isn't that the name of the estate collection you bought at the auction Monday?"

"Yes, dear. Was there anything else?"

She ignored my question.

"Toxie Barras. That's an odd name, isn't it? It sounds like Toxic. You have to be careful about giving your children odd names, you know. I once lived next door to this boy named Dijon—like with the mustard? Well, folks thereabouts pronounced it 'Die-John.' That's all he ever heard, was folks telling him to die, so one day he climbed up on the town's water tower. He wasn't going to jump or anything. He just wanted to spray-paint his name up there in big letters with instructions telling everyone how to pronounce it."

I tried to interrupt her but she was on a roll.

"Anyway, he didn't get past spelling out his name when a bunch of kids from school saw him up there. They started chanting 'Die-John, Die-John, Die-John.' They didn't mean anything bad about it, of course. They were just trying to cheer him on. Well, poor Dijon took it the wrong way. He thought they were urging him to jump, and by that time he was so fed up with his name that he did jump."

"That's is the worst story I ever heard, and I don't for a minute believe it happened," I said.

"Well it did so! I was there," she said hotly.

"If you say so, dear. Did Toxie leave you a number?"

She read off Toxie's number as if she was a musician playing a series of staccato notes. "And in the future,

Abigail,'' she said tersely, ''kindly remember that I am not your answering service.''

We hung up simultaneously.

I glanced behind me after pulling another quarter out of my change purse.

''Don't even think about it,'' growled a woman with blue and yellow curlers in her hair.

''This is a public phone, dear,'' I said calmly. ''I am entitled to use it for as long as I wish. But''—I put the quarter back in my change purse—''I have decided not to make that call. The doctor said my ear infection will only get worse if I keep it pressed against the phone too long.''

I smiled warmly at her and found another phone outside the hospital.

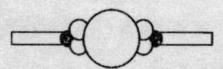

12

I should have waited to call Toxie Barras. I had no idea whether she had heard the news of her aunt's death, or how much it mattered to her. A more sensitive soul would have waited at least until the next day and offered her condolences.

Please understand that I did debate the issue briefly. However, Toxie had gone to some length to contact me, so I figured it was important enough to set convention (and good manners) aside and play it by ear. Ever since my marriage with Buford fell apart, I have become rather adept at playing things by ear. It's a wonder I can still wear earrings, given the mileage I've put on these lobes.

As it turned out, I need not have worried in the least about the propriety of calling Toxie. She had just been told of her Aunt Lottie Bell's death, but like Norma Ramsey, she sounded far from grief-stricken. Was I up to lunch, she wondered, her treat. I told her I was, if we could make it Bubba's China Gourmet. I'd been meaning to stop in and see Norma again anyway, so why not kill two birds with one stone?

"I look a little bit like Marilyn Monroe in *Gentlemen Prefer Blondes*," she said, so that I could recognize her.

"And I look like Liza Minnelli, only younger," I lied.

On the way over to Bubba's I listened to the mellow sounds of WIST 106 FM on my car radio. One of the songs they played was sung by Liza, and I tried singing along. Suffice it to say, I don't sing like her either.

Halfway to Bubba's, Ella Fitzgerald was interrupted by a weather advisory. An early winter cold front of unseasonable intensity had pushed its way down from Canada into the upper Midwest, and was dumping several feet of snow on places like Milwaukee and Chicago.

"It looks like it's headed right this way," the announcer said almost gleefully. "That's right, Charlotteans, by late tomorrow we may be seeing this year's first trace of snow. But if that low front that's down in the gulf right now keeps pushing moisture this way, we might be in for a lot more than a trace. Remember folks, you heard it here first."

I switched the radio off. Snow! There's nothing like that four-letter word to strike terror in the hearts of Carolinians. Within minutes half of WIST's listeners would be headed for the grocery stores, and like an army of ants, strip the shelves bare of bread and milk. Never mind that the snow would probably melt as soon as it hit the ground, or in a day or two at the most.

But, being a native Carolinian, I had no choice but to obey my genes and pull into the first convenience store I passed. I am not without compassion and did leave behind a half-gallon of milk that was three days past its due date and a loaf of whole wheat bread that was badly crushed (I did not mean to drop the milk on it, I swear).

We met in the parking lot of Bubba's. Toxie and I pulled in simultaneously, and it was clear by the number of bags in her backseat that she had listened to the same forecast and made a stop of her own.

She didn't, however, look remotely like Marilyn Monroe. My Aunt Marilyn looks like Marilyn Monroe—a very elderly version of course. She claims that *she* was the model upon which Norma Jean based her persona. Toxie wasn't even in the running. "Rode hard, and put away wet," Buford would have described her.

According to Purnell Purvis, Toxie was a couple of years younger than her cousins, which would put her around fifty. If wrinkles, like tree wrings, are an indication of age, Toxie was twice that. Cigarettes and too much Carolina sun had etched deep grooves into what might have once been a pretty face. It looked as if she applied her makeup with a putty trowel, perhaps in a desperate attempt to keep it from shattering. Then, as a means of distraction, Toxie had bleached and dyed her hair a preposterous shade of blond that reminded me of chrysanthemums.

Most of us have, in one way or another, felt like victims of our gene pools (being four foot nine is no picnic!), but a wise person works with what she was given. Toxie Barras had been given thunder thighs, but she was wearing either a very short skirt under that fake leopard-skin coat or nothing at all. Clearly this was one woman who would do well to *add* a few years to her age when she lied about it.

"I hope they have a smoking section," she said in a voice made husky by our state's number one cash crop.

I reluctantly informed her that all of Bubba's China Gourmet was a smoking section. However, I informed her, *she* would not be smoking during the meal.

This stopped her short. She teetered precariously on her six-inch spike heels while her torso caught up with her thighs.

"I really need to smoke while I eat," she said. To be truthful, she didn't sound nasty about it at all. Merely desperate.

"I'm sure you'll find enough secondhand smoke to meet your dietary needs," I said kindly.

She looked genuinely torn between lunch with me and a solitary pack of coffin nails. I had the feeling the nails would win, so I capitulated far more quickly than is my custom.

"Okay, you can smoke, but blow that nasty stuff away from my plate. I mean, you wouldn't like it if I farted on your food, would you?"

"Ma'am?"

"Never mind, dear."

I ushered her into the exciting world of Southern Chinese. However, much to my disappointment, Norma was off duty and not scheduled to arrive for another hour. I doubted if I could last that long in the giant ashtray that was Bubba's.

We were led to our table by the pretty young Oriental woman, Sally Lee, who was unquestionably Southern born and reared. She could stretch a vowel along with the best of us, and I began to wonder about the ethnic origins of Robert E. Lee.

"Today's specials—which are also part of the buffet— are Bubba's Beijing barbecue, Hunan hash, and egg foo young with red-eye gravy. Or you can order from the menu." She made it sound like ordering from the menu would violate some ancient Chinese taboo, perhaps endangering the lives of the kitchen workers and even their families back in China.

We chose the buffet. As we waited in line (BCG is enormously popular among south Charlotteans who love a bargain) I asked Toxie to tell me about herself. Even though many people, especially women, will hotly deny it, everyone loves to talk about themselves. It is the easiest way to validate who we are. Apparently Toxie was badly in need of validation because I got an earful.

Briefly, she was single. Had never been married, in fact. Her branch of the Barras family was dirt-poor, so she worked as a piano player and lounge singer at Rumpelstiltskin's over near Matthews. Life had not been kind to her altogether. She had had polio as a child. Had I noticed that she walked with a slight limp? I had not. Then again, what women wearing six-inch spikes *doesn't* limp? Her one saving grace was her uncanny resemblance to Marilyn Monroe. Surely I had noticed that? I lied through my teeth, but was so flustered by the experience that I accidentally bypassed Bubba's Authentic Chinese Salad Bar on my way back to the table.

"So what did you want to see me about?" I asked pleasantly, after I'd had a chance to sample a few things. (Take it from me, the Hunan hash was dry, and the egg foo young too moist—it certainly didn't need any red-eye gravy, which, incidentally, was the worst red-eye gravy I'd ever tasted. The Beijing barbecue, however, was to die for!)

Toxie had yet to touch her food, choosing instead to build a miniature log cabin out of half-smoked cigarettes in the black plastic ashtray she kept right in front of her.

"I'm interested in doing business with you," she rasped softly.

"I beg your pardon?" I had no idea what business she was in. I could only hope it wasn't fashion or cosmetics.

She smiled, revealing teeth that were the same shade of yellow as her hair.

"I want to buy some antiques from you."

"That's wonderful, dear, but as you can see, my shop is temporarily closed. That's why I'm here."

"Oh, I know that. I was hoping we could still do business. I already know what I want."

So did I, and I didn't like it one bit. "Oh, do you now?"

She nodded, and then very carefully blew a funnel of smoke over her shoulder, away from me. She had been very good about it, I'll grant her that.

"I want to buy my Aunt Lula Mae's furniture."

"I see. Sentimental childhood memories garnered from Thanksgiving and Christmas dinners no doubt?"

She frowned. Her furrows were deep enough to plant beans in. "We are not a close family. I can't remember seeing that furniture but once or twice."

"Why do you want it then?" I asked pleasantly. She certainly did not look like the kind of woman who would decorate her house with Louis XV. Frankly I didn't think she could afford it. Not on a lounge singer's salary—not unless she was getting a good deal more than I reckoned. And if that was the case, I might want to consider a career change. I may be petite, but I have been told that I posses a good set of pipes.

Toxie took a short puff from a long thin cigarette, and immediately expelled the smoke. "I've gotten interested in genealogy, you see. That furniture was my grandmothers's, and her grandmother's before her."

"And it gives you a feeling of connectedness to your past, right?"

"Right."

I could certainly understand that. I had only recently inherited a very old and very valuable piece of Venetian lace. Believe me, I would not have sold it, had I been more solvent at the time.

"And you see, Mrs. Timberlake, that furniture should never have ended up in Amy's hands."

"Because she's not of your ilk?" Calling Amy a no-account piece of white trash would be unprofessional, even though that was undoubtedly the way Toxie thought of her.

She looked startled, and accidentally let a puff of noxious fumes float into my range.

"Oh no, that has nothing to do with it. Amy's past is another story altogether. What I meant was, Amy shouldn't have gotten that furniture, because it wasn't Aunt Lula Mae's to give. She was only a Barras by marriage, you know, and her husband—my Uncle Cyrus—

was not the oldest Barras son. That was my daddy, Daniel Festus Barras.''

I waved the smoke away from my Beijing barbecue. It had to be a Bubba concoction, otherwise all the Chinese would be as pudgy as pandas.

''So you're saying that the oldest son should inherit everything?''

She finally tasted her moo goo gai grits, which had congealed to the consistency of half-cured cement. ''Delicious,'' she said, pointing to the red-eye gravy. ''No, Mrs. Timberlake, I don't think that at all. But traditionally, isn't it the oldest child who is appointed executor of the estate?''

I thought about that. I certainly hoped that would be true in the case of Mama's will. I have one sibling, a brother named Toy, who is no more responsible than a drunken monkey. He couldn't divide an orange in half equally, much less an estate.

''It makes sense to me,'' I said.

''Well, my daddy wasn't executor, I can tell you that. If he had been, he would have seen to it that each of the children inherited one piece of furniture. There were four children, and four pieces. It's really very simple.''

I shook my head. ''I'm not so sure, dear. There are four pieces, but they don't all have equal value. And as a set, they are far more valuable than individually.''

She tapped her cigarette against the ashtray impatiently. ''Like I said before, it's not their monetary value, and it's not any exotic history. It's their family connection, plain and simple. So, Mrs. Timberlake, will you sell them to me?''

''And then you will distribute them among the others?'' I asked gently.

She blew a perfect donut of smoke, but more interesting than that was the way her pursed mouth, with all its fissures, resembled a volcano.

"I'd be quite fair. You can count on that."

I smiled pleasantly. "I'm sure of that. But you see, Miss Barras, I bought that furniture for a particular customer."

She fumbled her cigarette, which fell on the floor. She put it out with the toe of her six-inch spikes.

"Who? Not that rat Garland?"

"No," I said calmly, "he bid against me at the auction. Weren't you there?"

"I had a doctor's appointment that morning. I have the big C."

"I'm so sorry!"

She pulled a fresh cigarette from her pack. "Don't be. I brought it on myself. So, who's your special customer? Not that mousy little Hattie?"

I laughed nervously. "It isn't any rodent you know, and ethically I'm not allowed to disclose their names. Not without their permission."

She seemed stunned. Too stunned to eat, certainly, and barely able to smoke. While she struggled to light up another cigarette, I made a return trip to the buffet. Much to my dismay, however, the Beijing barbecue bin was empty. I returned to my seat in a disappointed daze.

There we sat, two stunned women, one pining after old furniture, and the other after Chinese chicken. Finally I spoke.

"What did you mean earlier when you said Amy's past was 'another story altogether'? Just what is her past?"

She pushed up the sleeve of the fake leopard-skin coat and glanced at her watch. "Well, I'd love to stay and chat, but I have a new set to rehearse for tonight. I'm doing some old Doris Day favorites a la Marilyn."

She was bluffing, of course, since she hadn't yet reached for the check. I called her bluff by pocketing the check myself. It cost me a grand total of $11.43, tax and tip included.

"So," I said, "what's the story with Amy?"

"She's a thief." The three words were accompanied by billows of smoke. Toxie had abandoned any pretense of sparing me her toxic fumes.

"You mean because she stole Squire from Hattie?"

"Nonsense. That little mouse couldn't have married Squire anyway. They were cousins, for God's sake. I mean that Amy is literally a thief. She stole a car."

"As in automobile?"

"What other kind is there? When she was a teenager she stole a car in Charlotte and drove it down to Myrtle Beach."

I was taken aback. "Well, I suppose we all made dumb mistakes when we were kids. Tipped over garbage cans, that sort of thing."

"I didn't. Anyway, once a thief, always a thief, if you ask me. Frankly, I'm surprised Amy hasn't stolen back the furniture you bought. She's always been one to have her cake and eat it, too."

She stood up. "Well, it's been real, Mrs. Timberlake. If you change your mind—"

"I know where to find you," I said. "At Rumpelstiltskin's, playing the piano and singing Doris Day songs."

I hadn't meant to sound sarcastic, I really hadn't. I adore Doris Day, and *someone* has to perform in piano bars. Nonetheless, Toxie took offense at my remark and blew a final blast of smoke in my face, before wobbling off, half a foot above the floor. It took fifteen minutes for the smoke to clear enough for me to spot Norma.

"This isn't my station," Norma said. She looked bone-tired, although she had just started work. "If you sit over there, I'll try and spare a few minutes. Or do you want to eat this time?"

"How about a large order of Beijing barbecue?"

She smiled, her wad of gum tucked safely in her cheek.

"I see we're getting really authentic here. Bubba buys his sauce from an old man down in Fort Mill, South Carolina."

"Red Bailey?" His sauce was legendary throughout York and Mecklenburg counties.

She nodded. "It would be cheaper if you bought the sauce directly and made your own chicken for supper. That's what I do when I'm off."

But my mouth was craving *Bubba's* Beijing barbecue then, so I kept my order for the large platter and switched tables. What I didn't eat I'd take home in a doggie bag and Dmitri and I would polish it off in front of the TV as our supper.

I had come dangerously close to spoiling that plan, and had eaten over half the platter when Norma slipped into the booth opposite me. Her open palm was extended. The girl was absolutely right. Buying from Red Bailey directly would have been a whole lot cheaper.

"I'm not NationsBank," I said sweetly. "I'm divorced as well."

She stood up. "And I'm on duty."

I dropped a ten-dollar bill in her hand.

"Is this my tip?"

"Five more, and that's all you get."

"So what do you want to ask me this time?"

"Well, you said before that your husband—I mean your ex-husband—did odd jobs. Did he perchance ever work for an auctioneer named Purnell Purvis?"

Her molars beat a furious tattoo on that wad of gum while she considered this.

"Purnell Purvis," I repeated, and patted my purse provocatively.

"You mean that guy in Pineville?" she asked at last. "The one with the barn?"

"That's the one."

"Yeah, I think sometimes he did. Only he hated it. That

Purvis guy has two sons, both of them meaner even than Arnie. One day *he* came back from there with a black eye. It was all I could do to keep from laughing.''

It was all I could to keep from singing. Finally something that made sense. Another piece for my puzzle.

''I'd like a doggie bag,'' I said politely.

When she was gone I did a shameful thing and skipped out without paying. Bubba would undoubtedly dock her for my meal, but I had given her more than enough money to pay for it, plus a nice fat tip. Besides, now she could take the leftover chicken home.

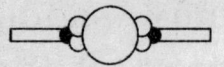

13

There are certain advantages to being slight of stature. Because Purvis's warehouse is even more cluttered than Wynnell's shop, Jimbo and Skeet didn't see me coming. By treading lightly and keeping to the shadows, I was able to sneak right up on them and catch them smoking in a little cove they had created among the packing crates. That should have startled the pee out of them, and maybe it did, but those two are masters at faked nonchalance. They pretended not to notice me and kept on puffing, no doubt hoping that I would just go away.

"Hey, fellows," I said cheerily. "How are you this afternoon?"

It was forced cheer, of course, but I'm a good actress. Just ask Buford.

Jimbo gave me a pained expression. "I ain't doing so good. Pulled my back the other day loading the truck. I was just fixing to quit and go home."

"Me, too," Skeet said, and threw his cigarette butt on the floor, where it lay smoldering, dangerously close to a packing crate. "The quitting part, I mean. Been here since six o'clock this morning."

"Well, in that case, how about I buy you both beers?"

That threw them for a loop.

"What do you want, ma'am?" Skeet said. He was a tall, skinny man, topped by a shock of unruly blond hair.

I smiled pleasantly. "I want to show my appreciation for y'all delivering that armoire yesterday. I think I forgot to tip you."

"You tipped us just fine," Jimbo said. He was short and heavy-boned, and I could see how eighty pounds might well turn him into his father.

"No, I insist," I said. "Beers on me."

"I'm religious now," Skeet said. "Don't drink no more."

I chuckled appropriately. What a hoot. The fruit of Purvis's loins pretending to be a teetotaler.

"Naw, I mean it. I'm Pentecostal. Ain't' I, Jimbo?"

"But you still smoke," I said pleasantly.

He still spat as well. "The Bible don't say nothing about smoking. Jimbo, you tell her I'm serious."

"Yup, he's serious, all right," Jimbo said. The sadness was clearly evident in his voice. "Had his head on straight though until he married Becky. But I enjoy a nice cold one from time to time."

That sounded like acceptance of my invitation. Unfortunately it was meant for *both* of them. After my close encounter with that loathsome lothario who called himself a doctor—Bobby Bowman, I mean—I wasn't about to take on a single man in some dark bar. Not even a pudgy man with a bad back.

I glanced at my watch. "Well, look at that. It's quarter to three already. I guess I don't have time for that beer after all. But I do have time for a few questions."

"I ain't got none to ask," Skeet said. He started shuffling off.

"No, no, I want to ask the questions. They won't take long, I promise."

Skeet turned and nodded in the direction of Purvis's tiny office.

"Oh, it's quite all right with your dad," I said.

" 'Cause he don't like us taking his valuable time chatting with customers."

"Well, you were both just fixing to quit for the day," I reminded them.

"That's right," Jimbo said. "So we're outta here."

"Your daddy know y'all smoke around his valuable merchandise?" I asked pleasantly.

"Ask them questions fast," Jimbo grunted. "My back's killing me."

I almost believed him. "Well—I mean, didn't y'all think that armoire was a little heavy for its size? You know, the one y'all delivered for me yesterday?"

"You're damn straight," Skeet said. "how the hell do you think Jimbo here hurt his back?" Apparently he hadn't been religious long enough to clean up his language.

"Did y'all think to look inside it?" I asked gently.

"Hey," Jimbo growled, "the police already asked us that. Like we told them, it ain't our business to look inside the merchandise."

"And anyway, it was locked," Skeet said.

I thought about that. He was right. The armoire had been locked, at least upon delivery. The key, however, had been in the door. Still, it was easy to believe that both brothers were too lazy to turn the key. Or maybe they had, but found that the eighteenth-century mechanism required too much precision for their fumbling hands.

"Why of course it was. How silly of me," I said. "Well, you didn't happen to see anyone unusual hanging around the storage room or loading dock after the auction, did you?"

They both looked at me like I was crazy.

"Monday is auction day," Skeet said. He spoke loud and slow, as one might speak to a foreigner who had only a rudimentary command of English (*and* who was hard of hearing).

"I know Monday is auction day," I said irritably. "That's when I bought the armoire."

Jimbo decided to translate for his brother. "Yeah, but he means that on Mondays there is always a bunch of strangers hanging around. People poking around here and there, wanting to get a last look at something they wished they bought but didn't. And sometimes it's just people poking. People who don't got no business being here."

"He got that right, little lady," said a third voice.

I turned. It was an obviously perturbed Purvis.

"Hey," I said amiably.

"Mrs. Timberlake—"

"That's *Ms*.," I said.

He waved a pudgy hand impatiently. "You and I do business on a regular basis. You're a good steady customer, and I like that. I know you can always pay, because you always do. But that doesn't give you a right to be bothering my boys."

I tried to disarm him with one of my more charming smiles, but I must have had some of the Beijing barbecue stuck in my teeth.

"You got any more questions to ask, Mrs. Timberlake, you ask them of me. Jimbo here is a little slow, and Skeet—you know what too much religion does for a man."

"*Daddy*," one of them said.

"Well, okay, Mr. Purvis, I do have a question. As a matter of fact, I asked it before, but you weren't inclined to answer it. Not honestly, at any rate."

"You calling me a liar, ma'am?" His pink proboscis fairly glowed.

"No, sir. Perhaps just forgetful. I forget things myself now and then, and I'm perhaps a year or two younger than you. Just yesterday, as a matter of fact—"

"Ma'am?"

I inhaled deeply, willing myself to remain calm. It isn't

easy for me to lie, even to call someone's bluff. "Norma Ramsey, Arnie's widow told me that he was working for you the day he was murdered. But you denied that when we had our little chat yesterday."

Purvis squinted at me. The afternoon sun was full in his face. It would have been a handsome face without the Pernod nose, plus the absence of a few pounds.

"I don't want any trouble, Mrs. Timberlake. I've been in business here twenty-eight years, and I've never had any trouble. Not with the police. And like I said, my boys are good boys. They won't ever amount to much, and they move slower than snakes in a bucket of ice, but they're good, honest men."

I can recognize a plea of clemency when I hear one.

"And I don't want to cause any trouble, sir."

He sighed, and I could smell fumes that were practically flammable. It was a good thing the boys had stopped smoking.

"About that Arnie Ramsey guy, he does—I mean did—do a little work for me now and then. Sometimes Jimbo's back just plumb gives out on him, and Skeet—well, before he found religion, he wasn't always so reliable.

"But Arnie wasn't working for me Monday. Come to think of it, I haven't had to use him since after Labor Day."

"That's when I found religion," Skeet said. "Me and Jimbo was fishing on the Catawba River and our boat sprung a leak."

"It didn't just spring a leak," Purvis explained. "The water was low and they hit a rock. Tore up my boat good and I just bought it in May."

Skeet waved a hand impatiently, no doubt a habit learned from his father. "Anyway, that boat filled up faster than a bathtub with both faucets turned on full. There was no way we could make it back to shore before it sank out from underneath us. Jimbo can swim some, but I can't. So I was drowning, you see, and asked God to save me. I promised that if he did, I'd start going to the first church I saw.''

"The Tabernacle of Truth and Holiness Pentecostal Church,'' Purvis said, the disdain in his voice quite evident to me. ''That's a little too much religion, if you ask me. Still, it has kept Skeet sober.''

"In for a penny, in for a pound,'' I said. ''So you didn't need Arnie after Labor Day, is that right?''

Purvis shook his head. ''Came close, though, a couple of times, because of Jimbo's back.''

"Are you sure Arnie wasn't working for you on Monday?'' I asked for the last time.

Purvis's eyes narrowed. He'd had enough of my interrogation.

"You couldn't prove it if he did,'' he snapped.

"The Lord could heal Jimbo's back if he'd let him,'' Skeet said. ''I know he could. I've seen it happen myself.''

"You don't know shit,'' Jimbo growled.

"Fuck you,'' Skeet said.

"Boys!''

Poor Purvis. No wonder he had a penchant for Pernod. It was a wonder he didn't hire someone like Arnie fulltime.

"Well, y'all have been very helpful,'' I said. ''I guess I'm going to have to dig around elsewhere for information on Arnie Ramsey.''

"I have his address,'' Purvis said, now that I no longer posed a threat. ''But it won't do you much good. I think he moved out on his wife.''

"Well, there is his girlfriend,'' Skeet said.

Jimbo nudged his brother and mumbled. Skeet didn't seem to notice.

"I don't know her real name, but they call her Kitty.

She's a waitress at the Top Half. Of course you wouldn't want to go there. Not by yourself, anyway.''

"Oh?"

"It's a titty bar," he said. The Pentecostals were going to have to work harder on their convert.

I thanked the three of them for cooperation.

"Hey, I didn't mean nothing personal," Purvis said. "Mrs. Timberlake, I hope you and I continue to do business for a long time."

"I hope so too," I said, and I meant it.

My blind date wasn't until seven, so I had plenty of time to drive over to my ex's and see how Charlie was doing. Susan was already in college, and so basically out of the house when Buford and I divorced. Charlie, however, is still living with his father, and stepmother, in the same house he grew up in. Because of that, I think the divorce has been harder on him than on Susan.

I know it isn't easy for me to drive up to the same house I'd lived in for so many years and have the door answered by someone named Tweetie Byrd Timberlake. Ironically, in the past few months, Tweetie Byrd—my silicone replacement—has begun to look up to me, almost like a big sister.

"Abby!" she cried when she saw me at the front door, and literally pulled me inside.

"Tweetie, you all right?"

She burst into tears. "No, I'm not."

I gave her a perfunctory hug at arm's length. Frankly it bothers me to have even fleeting contact with the implants that displaced me. What is it about the female mammary glands that men find so attractive? Our closest relatives, chimpanzees, don't have breast fetishes. Breasts are, after all, simply mini food factories for babies, and most men don't find babies all that interesting.

Although I haven't personally interviewed any of them,

I bet those men who live in cultures where the women go topless all the time, and come dangerously close to stepping on their own breasts, don't have a bigger-is-better attitude. But even if I allow for the average American male's obsession for that two pounds or so of fat that encase our lactose glands, what *is* so damn attractive about breasts like Tweetie's? Her silicone cones started out as petroleum, for pete's sake. Ditto for Deena, and probably Kitty.

"Oh Abby, I'm so glad to see you," Tweetie blubbered.

I didn't see how she could see anything. In a few seconds her tear ducts had turned those multiple coats of mascara into black rivulets that oozed slowly out between clumped lashes. I couldn't see her irises at all. You would think that with all Buford's money, and her penchant for plastic, Tweetie would forsake her mascara and wear a fresh pair of false lashes each day. I suppose, though, old habits die hard.

"There, there," I said and guided her to a couch that I had selected during one of the happier years of my marriage. Incidentally, it was not beige, but a cheerful blue and yellow cabbage rose chintz.

"Oh, Abby, I just don't know what to do," she sobbed.

"You can start at the beginning, dear."

"It's Carla, his secretary."

"So we've come full circle, have we?" I asked gently.

"What?" Tweetie and Jimbo are intellectual equals.

I wanted to reminded her that she had once been Buford's secretary and that not long ago I had been crying in Mama's arms about *her*—Tweetie, that is. I wanted her to realize that she had caused me the same pain Carla was causing her. But—and I know this will sound like a cop-out—what was the use? We human beings are skilled at justifying our own behavior, even when it is identical to behavior we abhor in others.

"Are you *sure*?" I asked.

"Oh, I'm positive."

"What are the signs, dear?"

"He doesn't talk to me anymore, Abby. I mean, really talk."

"What else?"

"When I tell him I love him, he says, 'Me, too'."

"Go on."

"And he never gives me presents anymore. When we first—well, once he gave me a gold, heart-shaped locket, with a tiny diamond on it."

"So that's what happened to it!" I said.

"What?"

"Never mind, dear." Buford gave me that locket shortly after we started dating in college. Even then it had a history. The miniature photograph inside had not been supplied by the jewelry company. It was Dorothy Monroe's face, the girl who sat behind me in chemistry.

"But that's not the main thing," she wailed.

"Oh?"

"Last night when we made love—"

I clamped my hands tightly against my ears.

"—he couldn't—" I still heard her say.

"Nyah, nyah, nyah, nyah, nyah," I said loudly. I wasn't being mean, I just didn't want to hear.

"—get it up—" I heard anyway.

I released my ears. "Oh, dear, you may be right after all. Tell me, has he started whistling Mozart's Piano Concerto No. 21 in C Major?"

"You mean the one that goes like this?" She gave me a mercifully brief rendition, but lived up to her name nonetheless. I have heard starlings whose tweets were more melodious than that.

I nodded. "You were probably right, dear. It could well be Carla."

"See, I told you," she bawled and virtually collapsed in my arms.

For the next half-hour I comforted the woman my husband had betrayed me with. If only my mama hadn't brought me up to be such a gracious Southern lady.

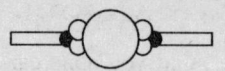

14

I don't know what got into my head, allowing Tweetie to play with my head like that. But after I chatted with Charlie, who was in a hurry to get back to school for basketball practice, I put the fate of my face into Tweetie Byrd's hands. Literally.

"One of my famous makeovers is all that stands between you and ravishing beauty," she said.

I was so astonished at her use of the word "ravishing" that I decided to give it a go.

"All right, but nothing permanent," I wisely insisted. "And please try and stick to a plausible palette. Absolutely nothing iridescent or phosphorescent."

Tweetie tittered. "Oh, you always manage to make me feel so much better, you know that?"

I hate to say it, but I had to return the compliment when I left an hour and a half later. She did a better job on my hair than Maurice, my regular stylist, and the makeup job would have made Eve Arden weep for joy. Fortunately her clothes didn't fit me, so I was able to quit while I was ahead. Not since my wedding had I looked so put together. I could only hope that Arvin Schlonecker—Bob's podiatrist—was worth having to listen to a detailed, blow by blow description of Tweetie and Buford's sex life.

He wasn't. Arvin had yet to grasp the fact that a man's brain is—at least to a woman—his sexiest organ. Not that

Arvin was stupid, mind you. One can't memorize words like "metatarsus" and the five bones it contains and not have some gray matter. But Arvin—perhaps because he was on the short side—had a complex, and obviously spent more time pumping his pecs than beefing his brain. The result was a man who bulged obscenely through his sports jacket, and upon whose neck you could have safely perched the Panthers' new stadium.

"Hey *babe*," he said when I answered the door. He was obviously vastly relieved that, even in my three-inch heels, I was shorter than he.

I was so relieved that he didn't have two heads or three eyes—at least one of the Rob-Bobs is into Picasso—that I ignored his rude greeting.

"Hey yourself," I said amiably.

I had not intended to invite him in until after dinner. He seemed to have other ideas, however, so rather than be walked over, I stepped aside. He immediately took off his jacket, presumably to give me a better look at his pecs.

"You know, we don't have to go out. Not if you'd rather stay home."

I couldn't believe my ears. Did he expect me to cook for him as soon as I was through admiring his physique?

"But I want to go out. I've been looking forward to it all day."

"Bojangles is having a special on chicken combos," he said. "And $2.99 will buy you the works."

"I took the liberty of making reservations at Cedar's Palace," I said. "In half an hour. Would you like me to drive?"

That did it. A body like his couldn't afford to be seen anywhere but behind the wheel of the car. An antique, souped-up Jaguar with more chrome than Mama's fifties-style kitchen.

The deal was that I could pick my favorite restaurant, and I had. After breakfast at Denny's, supper at Cedar's

Palace in Pineville is my favorite gastronomical event. Cedar's Palace is an upscale Lebanese/Italian restaurant (I kid you not). I go there for the Lebanese menu. The food is exquisitely prepared, the staff friendly, knowledgeable, and courteous, and the atmosphere elegant. I'm talking cloth napkins and tablecloths, and a grand piano tinkling away in the middle of the room. The prices are remarkably modest.

Arvin must have been pumping his iron in the basement of a fifties fallout shelter. He seemed to have no clue what a really good meal costs these days, or he would have seen that evening as a bargain.

"Hmm, seems to be on the high side," he mumbled.

It took a great deal of willpower, but I stifled my conditioning and did not defer by suggesting we go elsewhere.

"It's worth every bite," I said. "You'll see."

He scanned the menu again. "I suppose I could try one of the pasta dishes from the Italian side. I need a lot of carbs to bulk up, you know. The house salad looks good," he said pointedly.

I refused to take the hint and continued to study the Lebanese entrees.

"Or you could get a soup for the same price."

I silently took the Rob-Bobs' names in vain. I am a liberated woman, and don't mind at all paying for my own tab. Sometimes I even insist on it. But this was a blind date set up by my friends, and the conditions were that I chose the restaurant and that my date paid. I certainly was not going to pay to have supper with a man with no neck, and not much above it.

Tweetie, I bet, had never paid for anything in her life. Not with cash money. If Tweetie could skate through life with her wallet tucked safely in her purse, then why couldn't I for one night? This was dangerous thinking, and I am ashamed to say that I succumbed to the Tweetie

Byrd syndrome and used my feminine wiles, which Tweetie had so kindly enhanced. I fluttered my five coats of
mascara and pursed my passion-fruit lips.

"But I just *adore* Lebanese food," I purred.

"Hmm," he said, giving my side of the menu another
try. "Couscous has carbs, doesn't it?"

"Absolutely. But wait until you taste their homemade
pita, hot and fresh and from the oven. It's to die for."

"Hmm, well, I guess we could each have a side order
of couscous and split an order of pita. Unless they bring
that free with the side orders. Then we can each have our
own."

How terribly generous of him. That's one thing I have
to give Buford credit for. He was no skinflint. Not when
it came to eating in restaurants at any rate. Of course that
was all part of the good old boy milieu—trying to impress
your friends by buying enough food to choke a hog.

Fortuitously Nina, our waitress, appeared at that moment. Nina had been my waitress on several previous occasions, but always when I had Buford in tow. She had
always been polite, but rather formal. Now she seemed
genuinely pleased to see me.

"Y'all decide yet?" she asked, looking directly at me.

It was time to take the bull by the horns. "Yes, Nina.
We'll each have an order of humous for starters. Let's
see—then some nice refreshing tabouli to clear the palate.
After that, the mixed grilled kebabs with the rice pilaf—
and how about some stuffed grape leaves as well. Oh, and
then would you mind terribly wheeling the dessert cart by
for a look-see?"

"Sure thing," Nina said and left while Arvin's mouth
was still open.

"Just wait until you sink your buds into one of those
fresh pitas," I reminded him.

Arvin remained skeptical, if not horror-stricken, until
Nina returned bearing the humous and warm pitas. A few

bites, however, made him a convert. Either that or he figured I had decided to pay, since I'd done the ordering.

"So," he said, his mouth crammed with pita, "Rob and Bob say you own an antique shop."

I nodded, waiting to swallow before I answered. "It's the Den of Antiquity on Selwyn Avenue."

"Ah yes, the place that was in the paper this morning."

"Excuse me?"

"I said I read about your shop in the paper. And you, of course. Finding that dead body in the closet. It must have been terrible. I had no idea I was dating a celebrity."

I feel my throat constrict. It was a good thing I had swallowed.

"It was in the paper," he added.

"What paper?" I had been in too much of a hurry to even glance at the *Observer*. Surely if something had been in there, someone—like Mama—would have called and told me by now.

He took another large bite. Sharing a single order with him would be a sure way to diet.

"It was in the *Charlotte Observer*. It wasn't a long article or anything, and it didn't have a picture, so I didn't recognize you. Of course I should have realized that the odds are against there being more than one Abigail Timberlake in Charlotte."

"The odds are against me surviving this ordeal," I moaned. "If my ex-husband finds out, my goose is cooked."

"Why?" He asked it placidly. He reminded me of a short but muscular cow, chewing its cud.

"Well—I mean, you don't know Buford. He's not going to want his son, Charlie, to have anything to do with someone involved in a murder case."

"But you're not involved, are you? Rob and Bob didn't say anything about you being involved with murder."

"Of course *I'm* not! Not directly. But I had to go and

buy that damn suite of French furniture from the Barras estate. How was I supposed to know it came with a body?''

He unabashedly took the last pita from the basket. ''Did you say Barras estate?''

''Yeah. Do you know them?''

''Lottie Bell Barras Bowman is a patient of mine.''

''What a small world! You know, of course, she died this morning.''

''Well, I'll be damned.''

''Heart attack.''

Nina arrived with our tabouli salads and stuffed grape leaves. She took one look at the empty pita basket and the loaf in Arvin's hand, and frowned.

''Those pitas are for both of y'all,'' she said. She disappeared with the empty basket. A few seconds later she reappeared with a full basket and plunked it down on the table in front of me.

As soon as she left Arvin reached for a fresh pita. I thought of snatching the basket away from him, but instead just took one loaf and deposited it safely on my plate. It was my fault after all. I had pushed the pitas, praising them as the tastiest thing this side of Nirvana. Just as long as he kept his fingers and his fork off my plate, we could coexist until the end of the meal. But just to be on the safe side, I ate hurriedly.

''What do you want to talk about?'' he asked suddenly.

I looked up. He had polished off his tabouli and his half of the grape leaves, and was eyeing my portion hungrily.

''Do you have any hobbies?'' I asked. Having him talk wouldn't stop him from eating, but it might slow him down.

''History.''

''Oh?'' I couldn't wait to hear the history of foot medicine, or maybe how the first shoe happened to be made.

"I'm a French history buff," he said almost shyly. "I love reading anything on the subject. From the Cro-Magnon inhabitants of the Dordogne region of France to the beginning of World War II. But that's where I stop. The Vichy government pisses me off—pardon my French." He laughed. "How about you?"

"Never judge a book by its covers," Mama would say if I told her about my date with Arvin. I couldn't help but wonder how Arvin had judged me. The truth is, I am actually a very boring person, with no interests that I can think of outside my business and family.

"Antiques," I said glumly.

"Well, that's history in a way." He took the second to last pita loaf.

"Yeah, I guess."

"Of course it is. What's the oldest thing you've got in your shop?"

I had to think a minute since my inventory is always changing. "That furniture from the Barras estate. It's French, you know. Late eighteenth century."

"There you see! Imagine what has happened to that furniture since the day it was made. Who owned it, who sat in it, how it got from France to here. That's history."

"That's the furniture's history, but that's not *history* history," I said. "Authentically historical pieces are few and far between."

Lord knows, not a month goes by that I don't get a call from some hopeful person trying to sell me something they've just inherited that once belonged to Robert E. Lee or Jefferson Davis. One illiterate but very sincere young woman wanted desperately to sell me a hooped crinoline that "actually belonged to Scarlett O'Hara." I was unable to convince her that Scarlett was a fictional character. Had it not been for my rather deep regional accent, I'm sure she would have accused me of being a twentieth-century Yankee carpetbagger.

Arvin shamelessly took the remaining pita and piled it on top of the one already on his plate. If Nina saw that shameless stockpiling, she would be displeased.

"Well, you just never know," he said. "Barras is not a terribly common name, and there was a fellow by that name who was the Empress Josephine's lover at the time she met Napoleon."

"You don't say—what the heck?"

Something soft had just run up along my left calf. I threw back the tablecloth expecting to see a spider, or possibly a roach, but there was nothing there. I should have known. Cedar's Palace is not the type of place one finds vermin.

"So you see," Arvin was saying, "we have a lot in common, you and I. Antiques and history go hand in hand like—"

"What the hell?" I flipped the cloth just in time to see Arvin's right foot disappear into its shoe, like a hermit crab seeking the safety of its shell.

I stood up. "Why Arvin Schlonecker!"

"Is anything wrong?" Nina asked as she scurried up. She spied the pita pile on the podiatrist's plate. "You," she said, pointing a rather long, bony finger at him, "out of my station."

"Huh?"

"You heard me, buster. Get moving."

"I can handle this, dear," I said gratefully.

"You sure, hon?"

"Quite sure, dear." I made a mental note to personally oversee her tip.

She shook her finger again at the chagrined Arvin and stalked off muttering to herself. I sat back down.

"You know, you're a bit of a jerk," I said calmly. "And that's a real shame, because you have so much potential."

"I do?"

"You're darn tooting."

"Like what?" He seemed suddenly bashful.

"Well, you know a lot about history, and you must be a pretty good podiatrist or Bob wouldn't go to you. He's pretty picky. And, well—I guess it won't hurt to tell you this—you'd be kind of cute if you weren't all muscle."

"I would?"

"*And* if you weren't so vain," I said. "Women find vanity a real turnoff."

"They do?"

We were on a roll. "And cheapness, too. Nothing turns a woman off faster than a date who's cheap. It's in all the surveys. Pick up any women's magazine and read it for yourself."

He played with a pita piece piteously. "You have a lot of spark, Abigail. I like that. I don't suppose you'd give me another chance, huh?"

"Anything's possible," I said honestly. "But if you ask me, the real spark is in Nina. I can tell that she likes you."

She was pouring water for another customer, with her back turned to us, but Arvin sized her up. If she wore flats, and he continued to wear his lifts, they would be approximately the same height.

"You really think so?"

"Definitely. Take it from me, that woman's got the hots for you."

"Damn! In that case I've really screwed up. What the hell do I do now?"

"You can start by leaving her an enormous tip," I said, and with my help he did.

The phone was ringing when I walked in—alone and in a bit of a daze. I was a little distracted because Nina had been with us. Somehow, between the tabouli and the baklava, Arvin Schlonecker had convinced Nina to feign an upset stomach and spend the rest of the evening touring the New Heritage Festival of Lights with him. Yes, the tip was large, but not *that* large.

"Hello?" I said into the wrong end of the receiver.

"Abby? Abby, is that you?" From that distance Greg sounded like he was talking through a tin can on a string.

I flipped him right side up. "Yes, it's me. What's up?"

"Where have you been, Abby?"

"Out to eat," I said casually.

"It's nine twenty-three, Abby. Isn't that a little late to be coming home from your turkey fry?"

"It was a tough bird. It took longer than they thought."

I could almost feel Greg change his mind. He's too smart to intentionally box me in. "Who were—uh, well, I hope you had a nice time."

"I had a wonderful time," I said. "Now, why were you calling?"

"Oh, that. Well, I thought you should know that Lottie Bell Bowman did not die of a heart attack."

"A stroke then?"

"She was murdered."

I mashed the receiver tighter against my ear. "You sure? I mean, how?"

"Yes, I'm sure. It was her heart, all right. But it didn't stop on its own. Someone fed her enough tranquilizers to put an elephant to sleep."

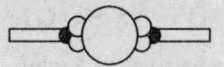

15

"**O**h my God" was all I could think to say, and I must have said it three or four times.

"Hey now, Abby, don't you be getting all upset over this. It's not like you really knew the woman."

"But I was supposed to have tea with her this morning," I wailed. "Maybe if I had, I'd be dead as well."

"Not unless you put Jack Daniels in your tea. The tranquilizer—diazepam—was mixed in with that."

"Di—what?"

"Diazepam. Valium."

"Valium? She died of a Valium overdose?"

"Mixed with the Jack Daniels, that's a deadly cocktail."

I pictured Lottie Bell Bowman happily pouring herself a glass of morning whiskey. I pictured her dead, slumped over in her expensive but appropriately shabby surroundings. I choked back a sob.

"Shit," Greg said, "you aren't crying, are you?"

"Maybe I am, and maybe I'm not. And maybe this has nothing to do with Lottie Bell's death." One of my sobs escaped.

"There, there, Abby," he said.

I know he was trying to comfort me, but he sounded lamer than a three-legged horse with stones in its shoes.

I hate sympathetic noises from others, even when they are genuine.

"How do you know it was murder?" I demanded. "Maybe Lottie Bell got tired of being lonely and packed it in."

"Maybe," Greg said, "but we checked with her doctor. She didn't have a prescription for Valium. And we checked the bottle for prints. There—"

I swallowed a lump that Arvin would have been proud of. "The prints are mine. She asked me to fetch her the bottle when I was over there. But I didn't put anything in it, Greg. I swear. I'll even bet my shop on it. And I don't have a prescription for Valium, either. You can ask my doctor, too. His number is—"

"Hold on," Greg said. I thought I heard a chuckle. "If you didn't interrupt so much, you'd learn more. What I started to say was that when we checked the bottle for prints, there weren't any. That's why we're calling it murder at this point. After all, there isn't any reason why any old lady who was trying to kill herself would attempt to cover her own tracks."

"Not unless she wanted to pin it on someone else," I said, and then wished I hadn't.

"Maybe," Greg said. There was a long pause. "Abby, would you mind if I came over?"

"When? Tonight?"

"Right now."

"Suit yourself," I said, and hoped I sounded casual.

"I'll be right over," he said. In the background I heard a large dog barking, which sounded very much like old man Crowley's Great Dane down the street.

"Where *are* you?" I asked, suddenly suspicious.

"In my car. I was just on my way—"

I hung up. I had less than two minutes to wash off Tweetie's creation and change into turkey fry duds.

I was able to exchange the black velvet cocktail dress

for a pair of gray slacks and a gray and cream wool sweater, but that's as far as I got when the doorbell rang. From the neck up I still bore the stamp of Tweetie. In my desperation I decided that confidence was my best defense and flung open the door.

Greg stared at me.

"Come in," I said. "It's getting colder by the minute."

He came in, but wouldn't take his eyes off my face.

"Coffee? Tea? Hot chocolate?" I wasn't going to offer him me until I was sure where our relationship was headed.

"Coffee," he said absently.

"Cream? Sugar?" I knew the answers—black and one sugar—but I was trying to divert his attention. It didn't work.

"Damn, but if you don't look good tonight, Abigail."

"Excuse me?"

"I mean, you look good all the time, but you look especially fine, tonight. New hairdo?"

I casually patted an hour of Tweetie's time. "Same old, same old. You want some of those soft chocolate chip cookies with your coffee?"

"Your face, too, you know? I guess that's what they mean by radiant."

"I hardly think so," I said. "This is exactly how I look every day. You just never notice."

"Then I'm a fool," he said.

Mercifully the doorbell rang.

"Not as big a fool as I," I mumbled as I went to answer it. Thanks to my ex-husband's wife I was going to have to add an hour and a half to my routine every day.

"There you are!" Calamity Jane practically shouted.

"Yes, dear, here I am." I made no move to invite her in.

"I've been trying to call you for an hour, but it's been the strangest thing. First the phone is busy, and then it just rings and rings.'' She peeked past me and saw Greg. ''And now I know why.''

I invited her in. To my knowledge, C. J. and Greg had never been formally introduced. Foolishly I wanted to impress her.

''Oh, so you're the blind date Bob Steuben arranged for Abigail. I hope you don't mind if I say so, but she got lucky.

''This girl I knew back home went on a blind date arranged by her pastor. Her *pastor*! Anyway, the guy turned out to be a serial killer. He dated college girls and then strangled them with their own pantyhose. He locked the corpses up in one of those rental storage sheds. They caught him after only five girls, because the smell got so bad. They say that if it had been the winter—''

''I am not her blind date,'' Greg said. He was staring at me. The once Wedgwood-blue eyes were now a piercing, icy blue.

''Like she said, it was Bob's idea,'' I said quickly. ''His and Rob's. They wanted to cheer me up. I couldn't just say no.''

''I said no to Deena for this evening,'' he said coldly.

I glared at C. J. and then smiled brightly at Greg. ''Well, I wouldn't even call it a date. The guy is a narcissistic foot doctor who tried to play footsies with me in a public restaurant. And for your information, he ended up going home with a waitress.''

Greg was unmoved. ''You should have been honest with me from the beginning, Abby. If we're going to see each other, we have to be absolutely up front. Some turkey fry!''

''I would have told you,'' I wailed. ''I wasn't trying to hide anything.''

''Oh Abby, isn't that a new hairdo?'' C. J. asked. I'm sure she meant to divert the conversation, but then again, we all know what the road to hell is paved with, don't we?

"Aha!" said Greg. "And you did something different to your face, too."

"Tweetie and I were just fooling around this afternoon. It was just girl stuff. It had nothing to do with Arvin."

"Arvin? Do you mean Dr. Arvin Schlonecker? That foot doctor with all those big muscles?" C. J. had clearly forgotten her job was to divert.

I glared at her again. "Yes, and he's not my type at all, is he, Jane?"

She shrugged. "I've never met the man, but my cousin Lou Anne went to see him about an ingrown toenail. She said he looked like Arnold Schwarzenegger—only shorter.

"Anyway, the next thing you know Dr. Schlonecker had removed the nail. Well, it got infected something awful, and Lou Anne had to have the entire toe removed. Of course she had that done at a hospital. But then they released her too soon, and when she was back at home she got gangrene. So it was back to the hospital for poor Lou Anne to have her leg removed, below the knee, of course. But wouldn't you know the hospital screwed up and they removed the wrong leg? Only once you get gangrene there's no stopping it, you see, so they *had* to remove the original leg as well, and now my cousin has no legs." She said it all in one breath, two at the most.

It was a horrible story, but for some perverse reason—maybe the way she told it—Greg and I burst out laughing.

She stared at us. "I don't think it's a bit funny."

We howled. We couldn't help it."

"Y'all are sick," she said.

"I'm sorry," I sputtered.

"Here!" She thrust a folded piece of paper at me. "From now on, kindly remember that I am not your gal

Friday. You are going to have to start taking your own messages, Abigail.''

I apologized again for my insensitivity, and thanked her several times for the message. C. J. stomped off into the cold night still mad at us, I'm sure.

I turned to Greg. "Feel free to follow suit. I'm too tired to fight any more tonight."

Although perhaps a bit faint, the twinkle was back in his eye. "So am I. Truce?"

"Truce! And for the record, I have absolutely no intention of seeing Arvin again. I value my legs."

He winked. "So do I. You going to open that note?"

I opened the note. It was from Amy Barras, asking me to call her as soon as possible. The word "urgent" had been underlined at the bottom. I resolved to call her first thing in the morning.

Amy didn't pick up at her home, and since I owed Mama a call I decided to kill two birds with one stone and drive down to Rock Hill. Mama often made—from scratch—biscuits for breakfast. A couple of those and some homemade peach preserves would be the perfect way to start my day. And anyway, like I said, I'd been meaning to stop in Amy's home design center for years, but had just never taken the time.

It was not my lucky day. Mama was backing out just as I was pulling in. I parked my car on the street and trotted up to her open window. She hadn't even bothered to get out.

"Mama, where are you off to so early?"

"For heaven's sake, Abigail. It's quarter after nine. It's only early yet in Alaska."

"You haven't answered my question, Mama. Where are you off to?"

Mama sighed. "If you must know, I'm going up to Charlotte, to do a little shopping."

"Shopping?" Mama never leaves Rock Hill, except to go to Pawley's Island one week a year with three of her closest friends.

She fingered her pearls nervously. "It's about time I changed my look, don't you think so, Abby?"

"It's that Apathia Club, isn't it?"

Mama nodded. "They're a very smartly dressed bunch, Abby. They don't buy their clothes at the Galleria Mall."

Mama doesn't buy her clothes at the Galleria Mall, either. She makes them. No stores I know of stock crinolines anymore.

"Mama, don't you think it's important to just be yourself? Isn't that what you always told me?"

"But I want to *belong*," she wailed.

"You do belong, Mama. You belong to me, and the kids. To church, and your friends. Even—"

"I want to belong to the Apathia Club. I want to belong so bad I can taste it."

"Mama, remember what you said to me when Marilyn McElveen wouldn't invite me to her birthday sleepover?"

"That was then, this is now," Mama said and resumed backing out, practically taking my head off.

Inside and Out—"your complete home design center"—was much more welcoming. A well-dressed woman, possibly an Apathia member, swooped down on me like a hawk on a sleeping chicken.

"What can I do for you today, honey?"

"Well, I'm here—"

"Because until December twenty-fourth we're running our 'Mrs. Santa Claus likes to decorate' special."

"You don't say. That's very nice but—"

"One of our professionally trained staff will come out to your house and assess all your decorating needs, and it's absolutely free."

"I live in Charlotte, ma'am."

"No problem."

"But ma'am—"

She trotted off, and before I could hide behind a forest of window treatments, she was back and flipping through a black vinyl notebook.

"Let's see, the nineteenth at eight A.M., or the twenty-first at six-thirty P.M. No, better make that seven."

"The twenty-first would be more convenient," I said.

I don't know why I said it. The woman undoubtedly had the power to possess souls.

"I'm afraid I have to warn you that everything I own is beige," I said.

She nodded and made a notation in the black book. "Beige is good, honey. It's much easier to start with a neutral palette and build on that."

"I want red," I said. I know the words came out of my mouth, but I had no intention of saying them.

She smiled and made another notation. "Maybe a nice subdued *deep* red?"

My lips moved of their own volition. "No, a Chinese red, with maybe just a slight touch of brown. Like Amy Barras's walls."

She shuddered. "Yes, I see. I'll put together a collection of possible accessories."

"Oh, and speaking of Amy, that's who I'm here to see. Is she in?"

Amy was indeed in. I was escorted to her office, where I had to wait for at least five minutes before Her Highness got off the phone. She did not look happy to see me.

"I didn't get your message until late last night," I said. "I tried calling you at home this morning, but there was no answer."

"Please sit," she said frostily. Despite all her plastic surgery, it was obvious her frown muscles were hard at work.

I sat in the single chair—a Biedermeier armchair—

across from her desk. She looked out at me between two mountains of paper. Either business was good or Amy liked to procrastinate. I recalled her saying she didn't need to go into the office every day, so perhaps it was the latter.

"Well, here I am," I said pleasantly.

Despite her reception, I was feeling rather good. It was the room that did that. The walls were a deep forest-green with white trim. All the furniture, including the Biedermeier, was in compatible shades of green. Perhaps I would do well to consider green instead of red.

"Yes, finally. I told Miss Cox to put 'urgent' on the note."

"She did. She even hand-delivered it. But I didn't think you wanted me calling you in the middle of the night."

"Well, maybe so. Better late than never, I guess."

"Your office is beautiful," I said honestly. "Just like your house."

She began to thaw.

"I even signed up for one of your Mrs. Santa specials."

She melted into what was surely meant to be a smile. "Who did you speak to? Carleen or Doris?"

"The lady who brought me back here. The one who doesn't like red."

"Ah, Doris. She's great with the younger generation, though. People who aren't too sure of their own taste."

I nodded agreeably. "What is it you wanted to talk to me about, Mrs. Barras?"

"Squire's aunt was murdered yesterday," she said abruptly.

"Yes, I know. I was supposed to have tea with her."

"I know who did it."

"Excuse me?"

"I know who murdered Squire's aunt."

She was waiting for me to ask who, so I obliged her.

"Hattie Ballard, that's who."

"You can't be serious. Lottie Bell was her mother."

"I'm dead serious—no pun intended. People kill their mothers all the time."

She made it sound like a natural, everyday occurrence. When I was a teenager I got really angry at Mama a couple of times, and there are times when she can still get under my skin, but I have never considered putting tranquilizers in her whiskey. Not that Mama drinks whiskey, mind you.

"Have you told the police?"

"No, because I don't have proof. I was thinking maybe you could help."

"What do you base your theory on?"

"It isn't a theory, Mrs. Timberlake. I know it for a fact."

"*How* do you know it?" I asked patiently.

"She had a motive, didn't she? I mean, Lottie Bell was the only Barras left who still had money, and Hattie, as you can clearly see, clearly doesn't. She works at a perfume counter, for chrissakes."

"Working at a perfume counter doesn't make you Lizzie Borden," I said.

She sniffed. "Hattie has a checkered past, Mrs. Timberlake. She's not as squeaky clean as she looks."

"That's what people say about you," I said gently.

"I was eighteen when I stole that car." She waved a manicured hand. "I have worked damn hard to redeem myself."

I had hit a nerve. A wise woman might have stopped there, but a wise woman wouldn't have married Buford.

"Well, you still haven't told me what's so terrible about your cousin-in-law, why she's capable of committing murder."

The plastic face contorted into a real smile. "Hattie has killed before."

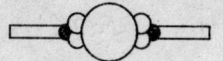

16

"Excuse me? What do you mean Hattie's a murderer?"

I'm sure it's hard to gloat when one's face is frozen, but Amy did a pretty good imitation.

"You heard me, Mrs. Timberlake. The woman is a cold-blooded killer."

"Explain, dear."

"She killed Squire."

"Your husband?"

"She killed him just as sure as you're sitting there."

"Mrs. Barras, how can you say that?" I asked wearily. It was going to be another long day.

"Because she did. You think Hattie is on the outs with the family because she married a machinist and works at Belk's, don't you?"

"That's what I was led to believe."

"Ha! That's exactly what they wanted you to believe. You fell right into their trap."

Back in college, in sophomore psychology, we called that paranoia. I wasn't going to be surprised if she told me Hattie belonged to the CIA and the FBI.

"Who are *they*, Mrs. Barras?"

The manicured hand waved impatiently. "Why, the rest of the family."

Her phone rang and she amazed me by picking it up.

She looked nervous, as if she expected the call might be bad news for her.

"It's for you," she said, thrusting the receiver at me without even speaking to the caller.

"Hello?"

"Abby, Greg. Say, I've got some good news for you."

"You've arrested Arnold Ramsey's killer!"

He laughed: "No, hold your horses. We're going to solve this case, that's a promise. In the meantime I wanted you to know that you can have your shop back."

"The furniture, too?"

"Every bit of it."

That was good news. Great news, even. Although I still didn't know what to do about the stain in the armoire.

"Greg, have you had a chance to ask your lab people about removing blood from wood?"

There was an unsettling pause. "Abby, the reason this has all taken so long is—well, someone unauthorized has already removed the stain."

I mashed the receiver into my ear. "What do you mean, 'unauthorized'?"

"Well, it wasn't you, was it?"

"Greg, you know I haven't been back to the shop."

"It wasn't us, either."

"How can that be?" I shrieked.

I could hear him tapping a pencil against his desk. "My guess is that whoever it was did it when they broke into your shop and stole the mirror. I figure stealing the mirror was just a cover, an attempt to focus our attention away from the armoire while they, uh—"

"Made their getaway?"

"No, I was going to say, while they established an alibi. Abby, this isn't a TV show with car chases, you know."

"No, it's my life," I moaned.

"We're working hard on it, Abby."

"I just might be making better progress on my own," I said curtly.

"Abby!"

I hung up. "Sorry about that," I said.

Amy shrugged. "Is everything all right?"

"Oh, fine, fine. Just boyfriend problems. I'm sure you know how that goes. Now what were we talking about?"

"Actually, I don't. As I was saying—before your phone call—Hattie Bowman Ballard killed my husband."

"How did she kill your husband? You said before that he—"

"I know what I said. And that's *how* he did it, but not why. He did it because of Hattie."

"Forgive me, Mrs. Barras, if I fail to understand. Unless it was Hattie's finger that pulled the trigger, she didn't kill him."

"Yes she did!" she shouted.

She closed her eyes and sat very still for a long time. I sat still as well. What I wanted to do was leave, but I was afraid that if I did so without permission, it would set her off again.

"You see," she said at last, her voice trembling, "Hattie was pregnant with Squire's baby."

"Oh."

"She just couldn't keep her hands off my Squire. She had to have him, and they were cousins. First cousins!"

It was not the time to tell her my redneck joke about family reunions and dating clubs. I wisely remained silent.

"Squire and I were happily married, and we would have made a go of it, despite some slight pressure from the outside."

"If it hadn't been for Hattie."

"Exactly. Well, she got pregnant, and of course she couldn't marry him, even if we had divorced—which he was *not* in favor of. One would think she would have used birth control," she said bitterly.

Again I exercised tremendous self-control and didn't remind her that men are equally responsible for such measures.

"I suppose abortion was not an option," I said, trying to move the story along.

"Not then. Not ever, for the Barrases. They're staunch Catholics, you see."

I had a hard time seeing Dr. Robert "Sex" Bowman and Toxie being staunch anything. Even we Episcopalians are generally better behaved.

"What about adoption?" I asked.

She shook her heard, amazed at my stupidity. "The Barrases don't give their children away. Besides, Hattie thought she had a solution. Ed."

"Her husband?"

"Yes. Ed was someone she knew from high school. A simple but steady kind of guy. He had always admired Hattie—God only knows why—but of course he knew she was out of his reach.

"So, you see, it was really very simple. Hattie would marry Ed and pass the baby off as his. Except that, in order for Hattie to marry Ed, she had to tell her family why she was marrying so far beneath her. Of course, society was never supposed to find out."

My tongue got the best of me. "I see. It is better to marry someone you don't love—to use him, really—than to admit you made a mistake?"

She shrugged. "I'm just telling you what happened. Do you want to hear the rest?"

"By all means."

"Well, in the beginning Squire didn't know anything about this. And it could have stayed that way, too, except that poor little Hattie just had to tell him that it was his baby she was carrying, and not Ed's. She told me, too, in front of the family."

"The little witch," I said, trying to be helpful.

She gave me odd look. "You got that right. Anyway, Squire was a very sensitive man. He knew how much this all hurt me, and he knew he couldn't stand by and see Ed Ballard raising his son. So he did what he did. Sure, he took a few liberties on the exam, and they were going to expel him, but hey, there are other professions besides being a doctor, you know. No, he wouldn't have killed himself if it hadn't been for that trouble with Hattie. So you see, it was really Hattie who did it. Her and her selfishness."

I was tempted to tell her that Squire was a wuss, a Caspar Milquetoast. That she was better off without the jerk. That just because Hattie had the hots, that was no reason for him to unzip and share the family jewels.

"And the baby?"

"Ha! Wouldn't you know but when Hattie heard about Squire she had a miscarriage. Served her right. It would have galled me something terrible to see her with Squire's baby."

At least she was honest about that. "Well, dear, this has been a very illuminating conversation, but I still don't see how it connects to Lottie Bell's death. Granted, what she did was despicable, but that doesn't mean she would kill her mother."

Amy Barras's face turned as white as the trim on her walls. "You still don't get it, do you?" she screamed. "The woman is a killer!"

I excused myself hurriedly. On my way out of the store I canceled my appointment with Doris.

"But beige is so blah," she called after me. "I was thinking we might add some cream and ecru."

I waved at her, pretending I didn't hear.

When I saw that black Jaguar parked directly in front of the Den of Antiquity, I should have just kept on driving. But—and this may surprise you—there is a bit of a confrontationist in me. When we were very little, my brother, Toy, and I shared the same room. One night, when our parents were out, and our baby-sitter, Mrs. Farewell, had fallen into one of her comalike sleeps, we distinctly heard a noise coming from our closet. Toy immediately burrowed under his covers, but I grabbed his baseball bat and flung open the closet door. Fortunately there wasn't another Arnold Ramsey, but a little white mouse, whose origins remain a mystery to this day. My point is, however, I generally prefer to meet trouble head on rather than have it tweak at my toes from under the covers.

The closest parking space I could find was on a side street, and I fairly sprinted from there to the Jaguar. Just that morning I'd noticed that my weight had crept up over the hundred-pound mark again, so I was a little out of breath when I got there. Just as I was reaching to rap on the tinted window the door opened and Dr. Robert Barras Bowman stepped out.

He was wearing his toupee this time, and while I hate to say so, looked a lot more attractive than he had the other night. He smiled, in what appeared to be a friendly gesture.

"Good morning, Mrs. Timberlake."

"Hey," I said. Then I remembered my manners. "You have my condolences on your mother's death."

"Thank you."

I was still feeling on the defensive. "Have you perchance come to see me?"

"Indeed I have. Do you mind if we talk in your shop?"

Actually I did. Not only did I not trust him, but I wanted time alone in there before I threw open my doors to the public. On the other hand, I wanted even less to be seen in public talking to that sleazoid.

"Come in." I unlocked the door as quickly as I could. Once inside I locked the door behind us. I did not turn on the lights, and I left the "Closed" sign hanging on the door. This might sound like tempting fate, but after all, I had several sharp objects in my shop, should the need arise to defend myself. The Edo period samurai sword, for instance.

"Yes, what's this about?" I asked.

"I want to let you know that my mother's funeral is this afternoon at three."

"So soon?"

"Yes, well, those were her wishes. She didn't believe in viewings. She thought they were macabre."

I had liked the lady for good reason. Displaying the empty shell of a person—all dolled up by the funeral home makeup artist—has always struck me as bizarre. I think the Jews have it right. When they die, bury them. The Russian imperial family, on the other hand, used to keep dead czars on display for as much as two weeks. Even worse, the members of the czar's immediate family were compelled, by custom, to kiss him on the lips daily. Daddy was an Episcopalian when he died, and not a czar. He was on display for a total of four hours, two hours at a stretch. Not once during that time, even though I was in the room with him, did I sneak a peek. My daddy was far away in a much happier place, not lying in a box with his jaws wired together to keep his mouth closed.

"About her funeral," I mumbled, "I really didn't—"

"Of course you didn't know her very well, but she did give you this." He handed me a small manila envelope, the kind with bubbles inside.

"She did?"

I opened the envelope and nearly dropped it. Inside was that fabulous Kashmiri sapphire ring.

"Th-there must be some mistake," I stuttered. "I only met her once."

"No mistake. She kept a copy of her will in her safe. She'd handwritten a codicil. Of course it wasn't notarized or anything, but then again, it doesn't much matter in this case, does it? Hattie's not going to want a piece of junk jewelry like that anyway.''

''B-b-but this ring—''

''—is yours,'' he said. ''Oh, St. Anne's Catholic Church on Park Road, interment immediately after.''

He left, just like that. No passes, no snide remarks, no innuendo even.

I stared at the ring. I ran to the door, switched on the lights, and stared at it again. It was every bit as beautiful as I had remembered, and every bit as valuable. I couldn't possibly accept it. It would be criminal for me to take advantage of the Barras clan, Hattie in particular, just because they were ignorant of gems.

A sudden sharp rap on the door almost made me drop the darn thing. I slipped it quickly on my ring finger. It was far too big. I put it on my middle finger and turned the stone inward. It was so big I couldn't bend my fingers all the way over to conceal it. I hid my left hand behind my back. In the meantime the rapping was incessant.

''Just a minute! Who is it?'' I demanded crossly. ''Can't you see that the sign says closed?''

''Abby, Abby, open up! It's me, Jane.''

''This isn't a good time, dear,'' I called patiently.

''Abby! Open up! This is important!''

''Not so important that it can't wait, is it?''

''It's very important. Besides which, I saw Dr. Sex come out of there. If he can—''

I flung the door open. The cowbells jangled mercilessly.

''What is it?'' I hissed, pulling her inside by one arm.

''Well, Abby, it isn't fair, you know, you talking to him and not me. You and I are friends, and I own the shop next door. That makes us almost shopmates.''

''Jane!''

''Oh, all right, Abby, but just what *were* you talking to

that man about? He gives me the creeps, you know. Did he lay a hand on you?''

"He didn't touch me.''

She gave an obvious sigh of relief. "Still, you never know what might have happened. Back home we had a sex maniac. Mortimer Graves, a mortician. That was his honest-to-God name, I kid you not. Well, old Mortimer didn't lay a hand on anyone, either. He didn't have any girlfriends that anybody knew about, or any boyfriends, either. Then one day the coroner had to exhume—''

"That's sick,'' I said, knowing full well where the story was going. "Now tell me what's so all-fired important.''

She blinked. "Oh, that. Well, Abby, you simply have to stop using me as your messenger service. I haven't got time. I have a shop to run, too, remember?''

"I remember, dear. I already apologized last night. But speaking of your shop, why aren't you there now?''

"Because I have a message to deliver, that's why.''

"Deliver away.''

"Well, it's not a verbal message. Wait right there.''

She trotted off to the front door, held it open with one outstretched leg, and pulled in a large potted camellia.

"Here's your message.''

"What the—''

"That's what I said when he gave it to me this morning.''

"Who? Is there a card?''

She shook her heard. "Naw, he said he was in a hurry and didn't have time to write one.''

I felt like shaking her whole body. "*Who* said that? Greg? The man you met last night?''

"Your boyfriend? Naw, this was some guy in a blue jacket. It had a logo of a tree on it, and some name which I forget.''

"Garland Riggs!''

"You know him?''

"Yeah, I know him. He owns a nursery."

She scratched her head and wrinkled her nose. "He didn't look like the baby type."

"I don't know that he is. He owns a plant nursery. He's trying to get me to do him a favor, and this"—I pointed to the camellia—"is his idea of a bribe."

"What's he want you to do?"

"Sell him something." She could put lit bamboo slivers under my fingernails and I wasn't going to get any more specific than that. I had already encouraged her nosiness far too much.

"Well, I'd be real careful, if I were you. I once—"

"Jane, dear," I interrupted, "I have an important favor to ask you." I didn't mean to be rude, but I had had a sudden brainstorm.

"What's that?" she asked suspiciously. "It's not about taking more of your messages, is it?"

"Absolutely not, dear. Remember that beautiful little marquetry table that was part of Lula Mae's—well, Amy's—estate sale?"

"Vaguely. I don't shop in your circles, Abigail, so I only glanced at that stuff at the preview."

"It's over here," I said. I guided her gently to where the small table reposed, a masterpiece of eighteenth-century craftsmanship.

"It's very pretty," she said. She sounded almost bored.

"Would you mind terribly keeping it for me for a few days?"

Her eyes widened. She was far from bored. "You mean it?"

"Yup. I'm taking this desk with me—" I pointed to the Louis XV desk from the Barras estate—"because I have more room. But, if you don't mind, I'd like you to keep this. *Temporarily*, of course."

"Wow! May I put it in the window? And what if someone asks to buy it, Abby?'' She was running her hand lightly around the rim. ''It isn't marked.''

''No, dear,'' I explained quickly. ''I would like you to keep it at home. If you have room, of course.'' I knew she lived in a rather small house.

She nodded, almost too eagerly. ''I am having some friends over this weekend. I hope you don't mind if I pretend this is really mine. Of course that can backfire on you, too. Once in high school—''

I picked up the small table and practically thrust it on her. ''You really must be going,'' I said. ''You have your own shop, remember? But thank you for bringing over the camellia, and thanks for baby-sitting the table, and I'm awfully sorry you were bothered.''

I opened the door with my left hand and was about to gently, but firmly, deposit her, table and all, on the sidewalk when she gasped.

''Lord have mercy! What's that?''

I whirled. If Arnold Ramsey's killer was hiding in the shop, I would have it out with him then and there.

''Where? What do you see?''

''Abby! On your hand!''

My heart was still pounding. ''Oh, you mean this?''

''Yes. Oh, Abby, it's gorgeous! What is it? One of those blue cubic zirconias?''

''Bingo.''

''I thought so. I saw them advertised on my favorite shopping channel. You know, the one where they beat a drum every tenth time they sell something? Anyway, they were only asking $19.95 for that very same ring. But it didn't look so big on TV.''

I waved my hand casually. The stone was so large, it practically took effort.

''It's gaudy,'' I said. ''Ostentatious as all get-out, but hey, it's just for fun, so what the heck.''

She was practically drooling. ''You see that ring advertised again, you call me, Abby, will you? Or, tell you what. You just go ahead and order it for me. Even if they've changed the price, I'll pay up to $39.99. Okay?''

"Will do," I said and pushed her gently out the door.

17

After some deliberation I decided to remain closed for the day. I needed time to reclaim my shop, so to speak, before I opened it to the public. Besides, I owed it to Lottie Bell now to attend her funeral that afternoon. I also owed it to the woman to find her killer. And I was convinced that her killer and Arnie Ramsey's killer were one and the same.

It occurred to me that the best way to regain emotional ownership of my shop was to start dusting at the front, by the door, and work my way to the back, where the dreaded armoire stood. I am a firm believer in dusting, and give everything in my shop at least a light once-over every week. This sets even my low-end merchandise apart from comparable items found in junk shops. Not that I have many low-end pieces, mind you, and none of them is junk.

Mine is an eclectic collection, but I am fond of virtually every piece. I only buy those things that I would be proud to put in my own home, although obviously I don't. I used to, though. But Buford didn't like "that crap" as he used to put it. Buford's idea of chic is a Lazy Boy recliner with a console on which to put the *TV Guide* and his can of beer. The remote never leaves his hand.

I ran the feather duster over an eighteenth-century Turkish pasha table, inlaid with mother-of-pearl. Some highly skilled artisan had labored intensively over that piece almost two hundred years ago. Buford would have put an ashtray on it for the cigars he smokes.

"Damn it," I said aloud, "I'm taking back my life." I peeled the tag off the pasha table and carried it to the back room of my shop. I was careful not to even glance at the armoire. Eventually my dusting would get me that far, and maybe by then I would be ready. If I wasn't— well, that would be fine, too. Part of taking back my life was learning to be kind to myself. To make the same allowances for myself that I made for others.

I was so engrossed in my work that I didn't even hear the cowbells jangling. When Wynnell spoke, I nearly jumped through the ceiling.

"Didn't mean to scare you," she said.

I gasped for breath. "How the hell did you get in? I locked the door."

"I have a key for safekeeping, remember? Abby, I stood out there and knocked for about five minutes."

"Sorry, dear. I guess I was engrossed in my own thoughts. Who's minding the store?"

"No one," she said. "I put up my sign and dashed over to see how you were doing. I didn't mean to be gone this long."

"Sorry, again. How did you know I was here?"

Wynnell laughed. "How else? Our very own town crier. She said she saw you practically having to push that sleazy Dr. Bowman out of your shop. Is that true?"

"No. He was actually well-behaved today."

"What did he want?"

"To invite me to his mother's funeral this afternoon."

"You going?"

I nodded. "She gave me this," I said, waggling my middle finger.

Wynnell stared. "Well, I'll be! One of those London blue topazes."

"Yeah," I said, "isn't it beautiful?"

There was no point in bragging about the ring. Those people knowledgeable enough to spot a perfect sapphire would appreciate it for what it was. Others would just have to appreciate it for what they thought it was.

"I brought you this," Wynnell said.

She took a package from under her arm and thrust it cheerfully at me. I took it reluctantly. My gift had not been boxed, just wrapped in used Christmas paper. A piece of yellowing tape still held part of an old name tag firmly in place. "To Burt—" it said.

"Merry Christmas, a little early." Wynnell was beaming with the joy of giving. "I thought you might need a little cheering up."

"You're a doll," I said, giving her a big hug.

"So open it." She sounded just as eager as my children had been upon bringing their elementary school art projects home.

I had no choice. I knew, without a doubt, that my gift was something Wynnell had sewn. I could feel fabric through the paper. But there was no way out. I was going to have to be the gracious Southern lady Mama raised me to be.

"Why, it's just beautiful," I said, before I'd even gotten the package halfway open.

"You're kidding. Do you really like it?"

"Yes, honest. I really—"

The package was open now, and its contents were definitely not beautiful. I had expected one of Wynnell's cockeyed creations, so I was quite surprised by the T-shirt from New Orleans depicting a naked fat woman sitting astride an alligator. "Crack kills," the caption read.

"Wynnell, I don't know quite what to say."

I held the disgusting thing out at arm's length, politely pretending to admire it. Wynnell stepped back for an admiring look of her own.

"Oh my God!" she screamed.

"What is it, dear?"

"I'll be back in a minute," she shouted and dashed out the door.

True to her word, she was back in less than sixty seconds, huffing and puffing like Buford used to do right after sex. "The T-shirt," she gasped, "was for my nephew Burt. This is for you."

She handed me a package in identical paper. The second package, however, was a bit bulkier, and the tape securing the name tag was clear. The name was mine.

I opened the second package with trepidation. As tasteless as the T-shirt was, odds were I would rather wear it in public than something Wynnell had made. Boy was I ever wrong.

"It's beautiful!" I practically screamed.

"Do you really like it?" Wynnell was beaming.

I held the teal-blue cable-knit sweater against my chest. It really was very pretty. Wynnell had done an almost professional job.

"I love it! I didn't know you could knit."

"I can't," Wynnell said. "I bought this at Carolina Place Mall. It called out your name when I walked by."

I hate feeling like an utter fool. Fortunately it is not quite yet a daily event.

"Thanks," I said, and gave her a big hug.

Wynnell's arms remained hanging at her sides, like salamis in a deli.

"I love you," I added.

Wynnell blushed. Not all women handle intimacy with facility.

"So," she said, "how are you really doing, Abigail?"

"Fine. Never been better. Well—since Tuesday, that is."

"Good, good. How was that hot date last night?"

"Not so hot. The guy was a jerk, but in the end it

turned out well for both of us. Remind me when you have time, and I'll tell you the details.''

''That'll be great.'' She seemed anxious to leave, and was edging to the door when something occurred to her. ''Abigail, have you spoken to Susan lately?''

''My daughter, Susan?''

''Yup, that's the one.''

''Well, she dropped by the house on Sunday to do her laundry, but I haven't since then. Why? What's up?''

She had her hand on the doorknob. The cowbells murmured.

''Nothing, I hope. It's just that I saw her at the mall last night, and—well, uh—''

''Spit it out, Wynnell.''

''She was with this guy, Danbo Links. He's the butcher at my neighborhood Winn-Dixie. He's got to be twice as old as her.''

''Shit,'' I said.

''And I think he's married.''

''Double shit!'' I refuse to use the ''F'' word.

''Well, that's all. Gotta be going.''

Wynnell, good friend that she was, fled as soon as she'd done her duty. Of course I immediately got on the phone. There was a real bogeyman hiding in the closet this time and his name was Danbo Links. I might not have Toy's baseball bat handy, but I had my tongue, which, I've been told, along with the pen, is mightier than a thousand swords.

''Winn-Dixie. Can I help you?'' some high school girl chirped.

''Meat department, please,'' I said crisply.

Danbo let the phone ring a half-dozen times before he picked up. He must have been busy making sausage.

''Mr. Links?'' I asked calmly.

''Yes.'' Already he sounded cautious.

''This is Abigail Timberlake, Susan's mother.''

"Yes? Can I help you?"

"I *said* I was Susan's mother. You know, the baby you were out with last night."

"Don't know what you're talking about, lady."

"Well, I guess I'll have to talk to the manager then. Can you transfer me?"

There was a long pause. "Look, I don't want any trouble. What did you say this girl's name was?"

"Susan Timberlake."

"I honestly don't know anyone by that name, ma'am. I just picked me up some girl in a bar. Said her name was Sherry. Said she was twenty-one."

"Her name is Susan, and she's nineteen. Her daddy is Buford Timberlake, the big-shot lawyer who loves putting people behind bars. And, by the way, I'm dating a cop." It was only a slight exaggeration. Buford is a divorce lawyer, and Greg an investigator, but why burden Danbo with details?

I could hear him swallow. "Yes, ma'am."

It doesn't hurt to play it safe. "One more thing, Mr. Links. I'm well aware that there is a Mrs. Links. I suggest you spend a few evenings at home with her, if you don't want her finding out. On the other hand, perhaps she could use my ex-husband's services free of charge. Do you get my point, Mr. Links?"

"Yes, ma'am!"

Thank God for Alexander Graham Bell. A hundred years ago I would have had to hitch the buckboard and spend half a day riding over to the Winn-Dixie, or its counterpart. Then Danbo Links would've taken one look at me and fed me into his meat grinder.

Of course throwing Buford's name out undoubtedly helped. His name has appeared in the *Charlotte Observer* about as many times as Ann Landers's. Unfortunately Susan wasn't going to be as easily intimidated. We could threaten to not pay her expenses at UNCC the next semester, but that would suit her fine. She hates school. She would welcome the opportunity to quit school and "get a life." That life might very well include moving in with someone like Danbo Links. She has done both before.

If Buford was in a cooperative mood, he could threaten to leave her behind when he goes to Paris. But I had the feeling that wouldn't be much of a threat, either. My daughter is geographically as well as culturally challenged. She thinks New Mexico is a country and couldn't name more than half of the other forty-nine states if her life depended on it. For sure, the world does not call to her with its siren songs. She once referred to the language of Germany as Germish. "I mean, they speak Swedish in Sweden, don't they?" she said in her defense. Susan either didn't have any morning classes or she'd decided to skip them. I would put money on the latter. She picked up on the ninth ring.

"What?"

"Susan, it's your mother. Were you asleep?"

"Of course not, Mother"—she yawned—"but what is it? I'm going to be late for class."

"Out late last night, dear?"

"I have a biology test I needed to study for."

"I have no doubt it was biology, dear, but it wasn't a test. Does the name Danbo Links mean anything to you?"

"What? Mama, I'm late for class. Can you make sense?"

"I'll cut to the chase, dear. I have it from the horse's mouth that last night you were out with a married butcher twice your age. What do you have to say to that?"

She yawned again. "He was married?"

"Susan, didn't you even know his name?"

"Yeah, Dan something. Mama, names don't mean as much to my generation as they do to yours."

"Maybe so, but Mr. Links is from my generation."

"Mama, is that all you called about? Because if it is,

you can save your breath. Dan and I broke up last night.''

''Broke up? How long were you going together?''

''I met him last night, Mama. It was a quick thing. I guess it just wasn't meant to be.''

I breathed a deep sigh of relief, but with my hand firmly covering the receiver. ''Where did you meet him?

''At his butcher shop.''

''Can it, toots,'' I said crisply. ''He doesn't own a butcher shop. He works for Winn-Dixie. Susan, when are you ever going to stop seeing me as the enemy, and start telling me the whole truth, and nothing but the truth?''

''I do tell you the truth, Mama.''

''Susan!''

''I met him at a bar, okay? Can I go now? I really am late for class.''

''No doubt you are, dear. Aren't you even going to ask me how I'm doing? Finding a body in an armoire wasn't a picnic, you know.''

She sighed, perhaps the longest and most belabored sigh in history. ''So, how are you?''

''Better, thanks. Although we still don't know who killed Arnold Ramsey and—''

''Arnie Ramsey?'' She sounded suddenly interested.

''Yes.''

''Kind of a skinny guy with yellow teeth and a tattoo of a rose on his leg?''

I hadn't seen Arnold's teeth, and I didn't want to know how high up on his leg the tattoo was. I only hoped leg wasn't a euphemism for buttocks.

''He was skinny,'' I said.

''Had a girlfriend named Norma?''

''Had a *wife* named Norma. Susan, did you know this guy?''

I could have peeled a dozen hard-boiled eggs before she got around to answering. ''Mama, promise you won't be mad?''

I promised. If she could lie, so could I. I would, however, try very hard not to let her know that I had.

"I dated Arnie for a while last summer, Mama. It didn't work out."

Thank God for small favors. "He hit you?"

"Yeah, but just one time—then I told him to get lost. Hey, how did you know?"

"Just an educated guess, dear. Sweetie, didn't you know that he was married?"

"He said he wasn't. What am I supposed to do, run an FBI check on every man I meet?"

"That's not a bad idea, dear. What if you had been with Arnold Ramsey the day he was killed?"

"Wow! I never knew a dead man before."

That wasn't true, either, but I'd give her the benefit of the doubt. She was nine when her grandfather died in a bizarre accident on Lake Wylie involving a seagull. Perhaps she'd blocked it out. Anyway, her Great Aunt Eulonia had passed on just last year. Surely she remembered that, and surely a dead *woman* counted for something.

"My point is, dear, that you could have ended up in the armoire as well."

"Holy shit! You think so?"

"Yes. Susan, what can you tell me about that creep Ramsey, besides the fact that he hit you?"

"He had dirty fingernails."

"I'm serious, Susan."

"So am I. He always had black dirt under his fingernails. Even if he hadn't hit me, I probably still would have broken it off. It was gross watching him eat fries at McDonald's."

"I bet it was."

"Look Mama, now I *have* to go, so can I?"

"Right. You looking forward to Paris, dear?"

"Is that on the ocean, Mama? Do you think I should take my bikini?"

I told her "No," "Yes," and that I loved her.

* * *

Besides the pasha table, I set aside a green velvet-covered Empire sofa with claw feet, two inlaid Napoleon chairs, both covered in green silk, and a gold brocade ottoman. With my walls painted red, my new digs would either look luxurious or like a turn-of-the-century brothel. Either way, it was going to be a welcome change from beige.

It took me three hours and no lunch to dust my way up to the armoire. I spent another fifteen dancing around it, unable to even touch it, much less open the door. Finally I touched it, first with the feather duster, and then with my hands.

"It's only a bunch of wood," I said aloud. "A very pretty and well-constructed pile of wood called an armoire. It's over two hundred years old. Now open the damn door."

The door seemed to stick a little, something I didn't remember from last time, and it opened with a creak. But once it was open, I felt a huge sense of relief. I think I had expected to see the ghostly outline of Arnold Ramsey's body slumped in there, in my mind's eye, of course. There was nothing to see but wood.

Greg was right. Every trace of blood was gone. I could almost be persuaded to believe that I had not stood in that very same spot only a few days ago, and seen Arnold Ramsey's bloody body, and the letter "B" scrawled on the back wall. But that illusion would only work if I viewed the armoire through squinted eyes.

With both eyes open, however, it was obvious to me where the blood had been. The back wall of the armoire had been scraped, perhaps with a coarse sandpaper. One thing for sure, the piece was no longer as valuable as it was the day I made my winning bid.

Suddenly I realized that I was no longer feeling squeamish about the armoire, and I was definitely not afraid. I was mad as hell.

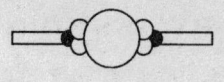

18

I have a terrible confession to make, but I know I'm not alone in this. The best way for me to relieve tension is to get on the road and burn some rubber. That, and you know what, but I didn't have a *who* to do *what* with—at least not handy. Which is not to say that I eschew the safest sex of all, just not in my shop. C. J. might come poking around and get the wrong idea. You know how she is with jumping to conclusions. I can't imagine anything more embarrassing than having a SWAT team break into my shop to rescue me from my own ecstasy.

So I chose to burn rubber. Please don't get me wrong. I am a responsible speeder in every way. I don't drive while under the influence, I slow down for school zones, and I never cut in front of people who are old enough to have seen me in diapers. What's more, I am a good driver who drives a safe and reliable car.

Some of my friends—Wynnell, for instance—think that all laws are meant to be obeyed equally, that we can't just pick and choose which ones we want to ignore. Well, I think that there are a few of us exceptional drivers out there who are quite capable of driving well above the speed limit, and that the spirit of the law does not intend to inhibit us. I know, to you folks out there who aren't quite as adept behind the wheel, this sounds like rationalizing. So be it.

I made it to Belmont without getting a single ticket. I'm sure that siren I heard briefly behind me was intended for someone else. At any rate, C. J. was absolutely right. One doesn't need directions to find the Kefferts' "boat house." I was at least three blocks away when I spotted the Connecticut flag flying from the mast.

It has been my observation that there is a rough correlation between exterior building materials and income levels. Neighborhoods where wooden and vinyl siding predominate tend toward the low- to middle-income end. Brick houses proliferate in middle- to upper-income neighborhoods. It's when you start to see a lot of stucco that you can be certain money no longer just speaks, it shouts.

The Kefferts' "boat house," which was not cement after all, but stucco, floated in a sea of stucco houses. I'd seen the *Queen Mary* once on a trip to California, and while I suppose the Kefferts' ship is smaller, it is every bit as impressive. I felt like I needed to have a ticket in my hand just to ring the doorbell.

"Is Mr. or Mrs. Keffert here?" I asked politely of the uniformed maid.

"Who is inquiring?"

"Abigail Timberlake, owner of the Den of Antiquity."

"I'm Mrs. Keffert. Permission to come aboard."

I looked at the uniform again. Of course maids don't wear gold buttons embossed with anchors. And I suppose few maids wear white, but it was an honest mistake nonetheless. I didn't notice the bibbed cap until much later.

Mrs. Keffert—or First Mate Keffert, as she liked to be called, led me to the starboard side of the house and into the main deck salon. I gasped. It wasn't the size of the room that threw me, but the eclectic collection of curios the Kefferts had amassed through their life's voyage together. There was a real, but stuffed, polar bear rearing up on its hind legs, several assorted suits of armor, a pair of very large and thankfully very old elephant tusks, an exquisite *uchikake*—a Japanese wedding over-kimono (worn by a life-size mannequin)—an almost life-size olivewood cross bearing an olivewood Jesus, and thirteen mounted gnu heads. Here and there was the odd piece of furniture; a rare floor model Bavarian cuckoo clock, a nineteenth-century English fainting couch, a maroon Naugahyde armchair, an Italian rococo settee with two matching chairs, and what I can best describe as a throne. It was an intricately carved chair, probably Chinese rosewood, but had been gilded to within an inch of its life.

"No deck chairs?" I asked pleasantly.

Surprisingly she laughed. "We keep them midships in our private quarters. I wanted you to see this room, where I plan to put the Louis XV things I'm buying from you."

I forced a smile. "They're essentially bedroom things, ma'am. They might look a little out of place here."

"Oh nonsense," she said. "Have a seat."

"May I?" I pointed to the throne.

"Please, be my guest. We just won't tell the captain. It's a real throne, you know. We picked it up on our latest trip to the Orient. It's from a minor Asian kingdom that was swallowed up by China and incorporated in one of the western provinces. The king had to abdicate."

The Chinese throne was not nearly as comfortable as it was beautiful. His Majesty was probably relieved to not have to sit on it anymore. I'm sure he had hemorrhoids.

"Ma'am, you do know about the slight misfortune I had with the armoire," I said.

She sat forward in her Naugahyde chair. "Oh, yes! Isn't it exciting? We're just tickled pink."

"Excuse me?" I was beginning to think Wynnell was right about Yankees. They were an eccentric lot with a bizarre sense of humor—at least if they were all like First Mate Keffert.

"Oh, I don't mean we're tickled that poor Mr. Ramsey was murdered," she said quickly. "What I'm trying to say is that whenever possible, we like our things to have a bit of history behind them."

I nodded. "Like that Naugahyde chair."

"It belonged to Elvis," she said, just as serious as a librarian with a headache. "That's where he sat to eat his late night snacks."

I was dying to ask her about the almost life-size Jesus and the thirteen gnu heads, but I had business to conduct.

"So you still want to buy the set?"

"Oh, yes."

"*Including* the armoire?"

"It is still available, isn't it?" she asked. She sounded anxious. "You haven't sold it behind our backs, have you?"

"No, ma'am, but it can no longer be classified as being in excellent condition."

"You mean, there's blood?" Her face lit up, possibly with hope.

"There was some blood, but somebody—probably the person who killed Mr. Ramsey—scraped it all away. So you see, it's been marked up."

"How much are you marking it up?"

"No ma'am, I'm not marking up the price. I'm talking about marks on the back inside wall of the armoire. Where the blood used to be."

"How visible are they?"

I'd had enough of the macabre. "Not very," I lied. "In fact, I'd have to say that without a magnifying glass, you couldn't even tell they were there."

Her face fell. "Well, a deal is a deal though, right? We did ask you to buy the pieces for us, so we'll take them anyway."

I squirmed on my royal perch. I was going to have to do some fancy lying to get out of this one. Too bad I didn't have Susan along to use as a resource.

"Yes, but I forgot about covenant number nineteen of

the Selwyn Avenue Antique Dealers Association.''

''What does that have to do with this?''

''Why, everything. You see, we're not allowed to sell anything which has been involved in a misdemeanor for a period of thirty days. And murder is definitely a misdemeanor.''

''That's silly,'' she had the nerve to say. ''I never heard of such a thing. You're holding out for more money, aren't you?''

I hopped off the throne and fidgeted discretely with a wedgie. ''No ma'am. I'm terribly sorry about this, but I can't sell it yet.''

''But *if* you could, how much would you ask for the armoire alone?''

I named a ridiculously high figure just to get her off my back.

She took off her first mate's cap, brushed a lock of gray hair off her forehead, and replaced it. ''All right then. But I expect a call from you in a month's time. The captain and I want those pieces. And remember, a deal is a deal.''

''I remember,'' I said, at least two of my fingers crossed behind my back.

''Shake?''

''Excuse me?''

She thrust out a diamond-encrusted hand. I was tempted to thrust out my monstrous sapphire, but wisely refrained.

''Ma'am, it's not like we really had a deal. I mean, that's why I'm here. If it was a *deal*, then I wouldn't have bothered to check. I would have just shipped the pieces to you, and sent you a bill.''

''You're reneging, aren't you?''

''Let's just say I'm confused.''

''About what?''

''About why you want those pieces so bad. Frankly, Mrs. Keffert, it seems a little strange to me.''

She whipped off the hat and began turning it through

her hands. "The captain's not going to like this one bit."

"I'm sorry, but that's the way it is."

She tossed the cap at the Naugahyde chair. It missed, and landed on a hammered silver aardvark.

"Then I guess I'll have to tell you the truth."

I stepped away from a suit of armor that was wielding a wicked-looking battle-ax. If her version of the truth staggered me, I didn't want to step backward into that.

"Shoot."

"You see, the captain really wants those pieces because they once belonged to his family."

I gaped, but I didn't stagger. As far as I knew, Lottie Bell Barras Bowman had three siblings: Lula Mae's husband, Cyrus; Toxie's father, Daniel; and Garland Riggs's mother, Mimi.

"I beg your pardon. You mean his mother was a Barras?"

"His great-grandmother. His father was a second cousin to the late Mrs. Bowman. The captain was her second cousin, once-removed."

"The one whose funeral is in less than two hours?"

"Yes. The captain's great-grandmother fell in love with a Yankee soldier whose unit was occupying her house. After the Civil War they married, but her family and friends wouldn't accept him, so they moved up north."

A likely story—to somebody born yesterday. It was probably plain old carpetbagger blood, which would explain a lot. At least that's what Wynnell would say.

I rubbed a thumb against the giant sapphire. "I knew Lottie Bell Barras Bowman, but she never mentioned having a Yankee cousin living in Belmont."

"Do your cousins come up much in conversation?" she asked coolly.

I come from a small family, but not a particularly close family. I have only five cousins: one in Charleston, two in Raleigh, and three in Portland, Oregon. They are never mentioned in casual conversation, and I'd have to think first before I told you their names. I don't know their children's names—my first cousins once-removed.

"But you are in touch with the family?"

She stared at me, and I could feel her evaluating me. I should have saved her the trouble and told her I wasn't worthy of her trust. I'm all for keeping secrets, but if anything she told me would point a finger at Lottie Bell's, and Arnie's, killer, I would sing like a canary with a megaphone.

She swept her gaze around the salon, taking in the doors in particular. Apparently the captain was nowhere to be seen.

"We have never met any of the Southern branch of the Barrases. We were waiting until we got everything here shipshape." She chirped a few times, in what I think was supposed to be laughter. "We've been told that some Southerners are very suspicious of Northern transplants."

"Not me," I said. "Moving down here is proof of your intelligence. Do you plan to go to the funeral? Because you could meet the family there. I could introduce you."

"You are very kind, Mrs. Timberlake, but I'll have to talk this over with the captain. I don't think he had planned on going."

"Maybe that's just as well. No offense, Mrs. Keffert— I mean, First Mate Keffert—but your husband's cousins are not among the nicest people in Charlotte. In fact, they might give you a bad impression."

She seemed perversely pleased by my bad news. "Oh, really? Well, maybe we'll make it a point of being there."

I glanced pointedly at my watch. "Well, you don't have much time to decide. Do you know where St. Anne's Catholic Church is?"

"Is that on Park Road?"

I nodded and edged toward the door I'd entered. "That day you came into my shop and asked me to bid on Lula

Mae's estate . . . why didn't you just go to the sale yourself? It was open to the public. You would have saved on my commission.''

''We had plans for that day,'' she said. ''They couldn't be changed.''

There was something about the way she said it that made me shudder. Mama says that a goose walking over your grave on the day you attend a funeral is a sure sign of bad luck. Thirteen gnu heads staring down at me through glass eyeballs weren't going to help in the luck department, either. I said a hasty good-bye and jumped ship faster than a rat on a burning schooner.

I have a dark gray polyester/cotton blend dress with three-quarter sleeves that is my designated funeral dress. I wear it to all funerals, no matter what the season, and funerals are the only time I wear it. I know, nowadays, folks think it's all right to wear anything to funerals, but Mama and I don't agree. We feel the same way about weddings. Mama, however, takes it one step further. She has ''Sunday only'' dresses. Frankly, I think that's bordering on the eccentric.

At any rate, it should have taken me only fifteen minutes or so to slip out of my jeans and sweatshirt, into my funeral dress; out of my high-tops, and into black heels; rub off some of my lipstick and run a comb through my hair. Like I said, on a regular day I can be funeralized in fifteen minutes, but on that day, try as I might, I couldn't find my funeral dress. I *always* hang it on the extreme left side of the closet, right up against the wall. Today it wasn't there. I knew it wasn't at the cleaners, because I wash it myself, and it wasn't in the bathroom laundry basket, either. I checked three times.

I called Mama.

''Oh Abby, you're a mind reader, you know that? I was just going to call you.''

"Mama, you didn't happen to borrow my funeral dress, did you?"

She laughed. "Why would I do that, dear? I have my own. Besides, I don't have any funerals to attend anytime soon. Knock on wood."

"Well, it's missing, Mama. I just thought maybe it was over at your place. Maybe I wore it to a funeral and left it there, or something."

"You want me to look?" Mama asked. She did, after all, realize the importance of a proper funeral dress.

I toyed wildly with fate. "No, don't bother. I've got a black skirt and blouse set I can wear. Thanks, anyway."

"Aren't you even going to ask why I almost called you?"

I glanced at my watch. The blouse was silk and would need a quick touchup with a cool iron. I was definitely going to be late.

"Can you make it quick, Mama?"

"Abby, how you talk to your dear, sweet mama! Did you make it quick, dear, when you were born? I don't think so. First you were ten days overdue, and then when you did finally decide to come—"

"I know, Mama. I took thirty-six hours of excruciating labor to get here. I do want to hear what you've got to say, it's just that I'm already late for the funeral."

Mama sighed while she weighed the relative pleasures of a short but immediate version of her tale, or a much longer, but delayed one. Immediacy won out.

"Diane just called. She had lunch today with some of the girls from Apathia. She thinks there's a good chance I'll get voted in at their next meeting." She couldn't have sounded happier if she'd just won the New York State Lottery.

"That's great, Mama. Congratulations." And then, being a mama myself, I felt compelled to follow with a little advice. "But don't get your hopes up too high. Sometimes the obvious doesn't always happen."

"Oh Abby," Mama whined, sounding for all the world like a preached-at teenager.

"I'm just being realistic, Mama."

"You're always so negative, Abby. And speaking of negative, that Calamity Jane woman called again. She wants you to call her back immediately. She says it's urgent."

"Yeah? Well, you know her. A hangnail is urgent."

"She sounded really upset, Abby."

I said good-bye to Mama, but did not return C. J.'s call. Whatever it was could wait until after Lottie Bell's funeral. I had more important things to do, like iron my black silk blouse.

When I got out the ironing board I found my funeral dress in a ball on the floor of the laundry room closet. There was a huge stain across the bodice. I had forgotten that the last funeral I'd attended had been followed by a rather wild supper. Hopefully, Lottie Bell's funeral wouldn't be the same.

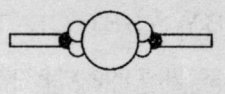

19

I t was a full house. If Lottie Bell had been a bit of a local celebrity in life, she was a full-blown star in death. There is nothing like a murdered society maven to pack them in. As it turned out, I was only a few minutes late, but still, there wasn't enough room for a sardine in slid oil to slide in anywhere. The ushers, apparently all contemporaries of the deceased, kept shaking their heads and muttering admonitions against tardiness. A few, however, were probably not shaking their heads at me, but had merely nodded off to sleep. It was downright hot in that church with the heat turned on and such a big crowd.

Finally, after many failed attempts to breach the pews, I had to take a seat in the least desirable section of any church—the front row. Fortunately I had chosen the left side of the church, the side opposite the mourners. Next to the side aisle sat a nattily dressed couple, with at least six inches of space between them.

"Excuse me," I whispered, "would y'all mind scooting together just a touch so I can sit down? I'm a very dear friend of the deceased."

"Mrs. Timberlake?"

I stared at the woman. She looked familiar, but I couldn't place her.

"Have we met?" I asked calmly. I have been thrown

out of a few weddings in my time, but I had yet to be ejected from a funeral.

"Of course, silly. I'm First Mate Keffert, and this is the captain."

I stared harder. She was right about who she was. However—and this is what threw me off—she was now wearing an elegant navy wool suit, with a matching wide-brimmed hat, trimmed with a wide black ribbon and large black bow. The captain, who was a tall, broad-shouldered man, was wearing an expensively cut charcoal-gray suit, a white dress shirt, and a plain black silk tie. There was nothing maritime about them at all.

"It's me," I confessed. "Do you mind if I join you?"

She whispered something quickly to her husband and turned back to me with a smile. "Be our guest. We've never been to a Catholic funeral, you know, and were not quite sure what to do."

That was the understatement of the year. As an Episcopalian I can bluff my way through a Catholic service, but not so the Kefferts, who, they informed me, were lapsed Presbyterians. They sat, stood, and knelt at all the wrong places, which really isn't such a big deal unless you are a large man like the captain and sitting in the front row, in front of a bunch of other non-Catholics.

I tried whispering succinct instructions, but they either didn't hear, or blissfully ignored them. Frankly I think the captain enjoyed causing bedlam behind him. Eventually he was bobbing up and down like a felt puppy in a car rear window. By the sound of things behind us, there wasn't a Catholic in the bunch.

"You're supposed to sit now," I hissed at one point.

The captain stood up, along with half the congregation. The first mate was more obedient.

"What is he trying to prove?" I asked.

She shrugged. "That's just the captain for you. Say, you still willing to introduce us to the family afterward?"

"If you don't get thrown out first, dear. *Now* is when we stand."

We stood, while the captain and his bunch sat. It was then that I saw Greg, on the other side of the church, talking to Dr. Bowman. After a few seconds the doctor clearly became quite agitated, and when Greg left, he followed him out.

"What was that all about do you think?" the first mate asked. She is one of those people who can't quite manage a true whisper.

"I don't know, but that was your husband's second cousin, Dr. Robert Bowman."

"He's cute."

"Not him. The cute one was Investigator Washburn."

"Oh?" She said something to her husband, who turned to look at the two departing men. A sea of heads followed in his wake.

Before I sat back down I glanced over at the bereaved family. Greg was conferring with Hattie Ballard, who was shooting daggers my way. Surely she didn't think I had put the man up to such rude behavior. Hattie left with Greg, but returned a few minutes later. Her face was porcelain-white. As for her brother, the sleazy Dr. Bowman, he never did return to his seat.

It was toward the end of the Mass, as the last of the handful of practicing Catholics there were straggling up for Holy Communion, that I felt someone lightly touch my left shoulder. I looked up to see Greg, his blue eyes very serious. He nodded almost imperceptibly, but I knew exactly what he wanted. I slipped out of the pew and tiptoed up the aisle behind him, to the back of the church. Unseen, we ducked past a sleeping usher and into the narthex.

"What is it, Greg?"

He sighed. "This could have waited, I guess, but I

wanted you to hear it from me, not"—he gestured toward the sanctuary—"from the crowd."

"Mama?" I asked. "The kids?"

He smiled tiredly. "No, this doesn't have anything to do with you directly. It has to do with Mrs. Lottie Bell Barras Bowman."

That damn goose walked over my grave for the second time that day. "She is dead, isn't she? I mean, if she isn't, then who is in that coffin?"

His smile broadened. "You have almost as much imagination as your friend C. J. Mrs. Barras is undoubtedly in that coffin, although I haven't personally checked. It's her house I'm talking about. It's on fire."

"What?"

"Hopefully it's out now, but about twenty minutes ago the call came through. An anonymous tip."

"So that's what you were talking to Dr. Bowman and Hattie about."

"Yeah, I hated to disturb them during the funeral, but the procession is scheduled to drive past her house. I didn't want them to be surprised by fire trucks or whatever."

"I get your point. You don't think it was deliberate, do you? Like arson?"

"Who knows. We'll have to wait and see what the fire chief says. Unofficially though, it seems a little odd to me that someone's house would burn down the day they were buried. It's not like she was there to leave a cigarette burning or knock over a lamp."

I shook my head. "It could have old wiring that finally gave out during a power surge. That happened to Mama once. She was cooking dinner—" I stopped. "I do sound like C.J., don't I?"

We both laughed.

"You want to ride with me to the cemetery?" he asked.

"Well, I, uh—"

"It's snowing, and you don't like driving in the snow."

"It is?"

I rushed over and pushed open one of the heavy wooden doors. Clumps of wet snow, the size and shape of popcorn kernels, were falling heavily to the ground. Fortunately they melted as soon as they hit the sidewalk and street beyond. Even the grass seemed too warm to warrant more than scattered wisps of slush. Still, given the general hysteria that any frozen precipitation arouses in us Carolinians, I preferred not to be behind the wheel. Not that close to rush hour.

"Okay," I said, just as the inner doors opened and the casket containing Lottie Bell Barras Bowman came bearing down on me.

Either Lottie Bell's friends were all fair-weather friends, or they were incapable of following in a procession. By the time we got to the cemetery, there were only a handful of cars trailing the hearse. At the grave side I counted only eleven people I didn't know. To be fair, I will have to mention that the popcorn had changed to pea-size pellets and was coming down at a fast rate, fast enough to start sticking on the grass. In Charlotte that is genuine panic time. No doubt the grocery stores would be filled with people stripping the shelves bare of bread and milk. Tomorrow when the snow had melted and it was sixty degrees, thrifty housewives would be busy baking bread pudding. Every five years or so we do get a genuine snowstorm, but seldom does it last long enough for the average household to run out of perishable staples. Still, a tradition is a tradition.

Much to my surprise, Captain and First Mate Keffert were there, and they latched on to me like magnets to a steel plate. We stood apart from the family, outside the small tent that sheltered the grave site and a small knot of people. It didn't matter much, since the wind drove the snow under the tent roof. We were all cold, stamping our feet and wiping our noses futilely on soggy shreds of tissue.

"You call this snow?" The first mate was wearing a topcoat, but she wore it unbuttoned. "Back in Connecticut this would barely count as a flurry."

I smiled tolerantly. "I'm glad I don't have to put up with Connecticut winters then."

"Well, they're not that bad," she said defensively. She sounded homesick. "Connecticut is not like Maine or New Hampshire. So are you going to introduce us to the handsome young man you're with?"

I introduced them to Greg, who charmed them—at least her—with his good looks and his good manners. I had filled him in on my visit to Belmont during our drive to the cemetery. He had been both very surprised and very interested to know that they were Barras kin.

"How long have you been in the area," he asked, "and what brought you here?" He made it sound very casual.

"Two years," the captain said. "I retired from the yacht-building business about four years ago. My wife and I looked around the entire country and decided that Charlotte was hands down the best place to retire."

"Not Hilton Head, or someplace on the coast?" Greg asked.

"Naw, too many tourists. We wanted a place where we could belong, feel like we were part of a permanent community. Besides, we've got Lake Wylie."

I suddenly felt sorry for the pair of them. Living in a monstrous stucco boat was not going to speed up the process. I wondered if they had made any friends yet. According to C.J. they had at least joined a church.

"So you've never met your relatives," Greg said just as casually.

The captain flushed. "Well, there's no time like the present, is there?" he said heartily.

Personally I would rather not meet a long-lost cousin at Mama's funeral, but then again I expect to be devastated when she dies. The Barras bunch, on the other hand, seemed to be taking their grief in stride. Dr. Bowman had rejoined the mourners, and I had observed him conferring briefly with each of them. To a soul, they looked sullen, rather than sad.

Courtesy dictated that we postpone the family reunion until after the interment, perhaps sneak it in as part of our condolences offered on our way from the grave site. Unfortunately the weather decided to be rude. A sudden gust of wind, and the tent sheltering the grave collapsed. I could see it happening as if it were in slow motion. The gust caught the back flaps first, straining to uproot the aluminum poles, which it did. Then the entire tent bulged like a hot air balloon before collapsing, the poles splayed out like the legs of a fallen colt. Everyone managed to get from underneath the tent before it came down, except for Lottie Bell, of course.

"Oh my God," I heard Toxie rasp, "it's a goddam omen!"

"Shut up," someone said. I think it was Garland.

When the tent collapsed Hattie had scrambled in our direction, and she seemed to notice us now for the first time. She strode up to our little group.

"You," she said wagging a gloved finger at me, "what are you doing here?"

"I came to pay my respects to your mother," I said. "I owe her a lot."

I rubbed my thumb appreciatively against the Kashmiri sapphire. It wouldn't fit in my glove, so I kept my hand in my pocket.

"And just what it is you owe Mama?"

"Well—"

"You have my sympathy, ma'am," Greg said, gallantly stepping forward.

"Yes, you have my deepest sympathy," I said. It sounded dumb repeating Greg's words, but I never know what to say at funerals, even under the best of circumstances.

"I don't need your sympathy," she snapped. The clipped tip of her nose was bright red, but whether from the cold or emotion, it was hard to tell.

I smiled, and my teeth got stung with sleet pellets. "This is Cap—I mean, Mr. and Mrs. Keffert. They're distant cousins of yours, actually. All the way from Connecticut."

Hattie put her hands on her hips. "So, the roaches are coming out of the woodwork already."

I was stunned. "I beg your pardon?"

"You heard me. Well, I have news for all of you. Mama's will mentions only Robert and me. Fifty-fifty. As for you, Mrs. Timberlake, there isn't going to be an estate sale—"

She burst into tears and turned away. The four of us stood there, speechless, like mute penguins—two with their coats buttoned, two not. The snow stung our eyes and whipped our hair. We would all have been better off fleeing with Lottie Bell's other fair-weather friends.

"What did she say to you?"

I turned, startled.

Amy Barras was dressed in a fur coat and hat—beaver, I think. Real animal skins, nothing spun out of petroleum-derived threads. The coat came down below the tops of her hand-crafted leather boots. Clearly her business was doing very well. She certainly didn't need my patronage.

"Hey Amy. I'm sorry about your aunt," I said.

The other three chorused similar greetings.

"Yeah, thanks. You know how I felt about her, of

course. Still, one needs to do the right thing in public, doesn't one?''

"I guess one does," I said.

I introduced her to the Kefferts. She seemed neither surprised nor offended by their presence. She shook their hands with her buttery soft lambskin gloves, delved into her buttery soft purse, and extracted a little gold case containing her business cards. The gloves were so flexible, she was able to open the tiny hasp and extract a card without removing her gloves. She handed one to them.

"My shop is down in Rock Hill," she said. "We do entire living spaces, inside and out. No construction work, but we do have a landscaper in our employ."

"Their house is already shipshape," I said wickedly.

"Our house is shaped like a boat," the first mate said.

"A schooner," the captain corrected her.

Amy was ready for anything. "We got in some lovely drapery material with a nautical theme. It's a little on the informal side of course, but it would be perfect for a child's room."

"We don't have any children," the captain said.

"Or grandchildren, of course" the first mate added. "We're just two officers without a crew."

The buttery purse yielded a silk pouch containing tissues and Amy delicately dabbed at her remodeled nose. It may have been sentiment that necessitated the act, or just the cold. I was dying to be back home, soaking in a hot bubble bath, with Dmitri balanced on the rim of the tub, batting gingerly at the bubbles.

"Well," I said, giving Greg's arm a quick squeeze, "I really have to be going. Can you give me a ride back to the church?"

"We can do that," the first mate said. "We have to drive right by there anyway."

"So do I," Greg said. Bless him.

"You sure? It's on our way."

"Positive," Greg said.

The Kefferts said good-bye. At some point they had buttoned their coats, but not before they had begun to turn into Popsicles. The poor captain's lips had turned blue, and he was shaking like a three-legged washing machine on the spin cycle. Perhaps their Yankee blood had started to thin.

"We'll stay in touch," the first mate said. Even though her teeth were chattering, it sounded like an order.

Amy didn't budge. "You want to check on Lottie Bell's house, don't you?" she asked Greg.

"Ma'am—"

"The fire," she said. "Don't play dumb with me, Investigator Washburn."

"Ma'am?"

"I know what's going on. I saw you take Robert and Hattie aside, and I saw the fire trucks in front of her house. You want to see what's left of her house, don't you? You want to see if Lottie Bell's little secret gets buried with her, so to speak."

My frozen ears stood at attention. So did Greg's.

"What secret is that?" he asked.

"I told you not to play dumb with me. It's too damn cold and I don't have the time."

"But I'm not playing dumb, Mrs. Barras."

She sniffed. "Then you're not exactly Columbo, are you?"

"No ma'am, I'm not." Greg had managed to sound enough like Columbo for me to pick up on it, but apparently Amy had not.

She sniffed again. "Columbo would know that it's not the damn furniture everyone is after, or Lottie Bell, or her house—but a secret that goes with the furniture."

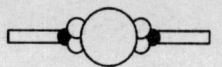

20

Trust me, if you stand gaping in a snowstorm you're guaranteed to collect a mouthful of flakes. I'm sure Greg did, as well. In the meantime, Amy seemed to be enjoying her little power trip.

I spit out some snow. "But you told me there was nothing special about that furniture's history."

A stranger might have interpreted her smile as a smirk. I chose to think of it as collagen contracting in the cold.

"I'm not the fool you think I am, Miss Timberlake. Believe me, if there was anything about that furniture that made it especially valuable, I wouldn't have sold it at a Pineville auction. I would have had it shipped to New York or London. You do think I got a good price for it, don't you?"

"Excellent," I said quickly. "But apparently the rest of the gang, doesn't. Am I correct?"

The buttery gloves fumbled in the depths of the buttery purse for an interminable length of time. I thought sure she was going to extract something of interest. Her hand, however, came out empty.

"Do you have a spare tissue?" she asked. "Leave it to Robert and Hattie to bury their mama on such a nasty day. Thanks to them I've got a cold."

"A cold requires an incubation period," I said. "Besides, they're caused by a virus, *not* the temperature."

She gave me an icy stare. "No tissues, dear?"

"That's right." I hadn't even bothered to check my purse, which is always crammed with tissues and enough other hygiene-related sundries to stock a Russian pharmacy.

"Here, you can have this." Greg gallantly handed her his handkerchief. I could only hope it had been previously used.

"Thanks." She blew long and hard.

"What is it the others believe?" Greg asked calmly.

She honked a few more times, sounding not unlike the geese in her own backyard. "The stories seem to be different in each family."

Greg nodded. "People remember things differently and pass on their own versions. It happens all the time."

"Exactly. Squire's mother—men don't care about such things, you know—said that her mother-in-law told her that the furniture once belonged to Napoleon. That it was sent with him on his exile to Elba. But of course that's silly, and even Miss Timberlake can tell you why."

Greg looked expectantly at me. I wisely refrained from kicking Amy on her ostrich-leather shins.

"Because the furniture is Louis XV, not Empire," I said. "It was made at least fifty years before Napoleon's exile."

"So you see," she crowed triumphantly, "it's all nonsense. And you should hear some of the other stories—Napoleon's initials carved inside the armoire. Ha!"

"Ha, indeed," I said bitterly. "The only initial inside that thing was written in blood. Late twentieth-century blood."

"Achoo!" That's exactly how her sneeze sounded. I wouldn't have been surprised if her cough went "Cough, cough."

"Bless you," Greg said.

"And get this, the biggest lalapalooza of them all—

that hidden somewhere in those fancy French pieces is a document, in Napoleon's own hand, deeding one hundred hectares of land to a man named Barras and/or his descendants.''

"What is a hectare?" Greg asked.

"Ten thousand square meters, or approximately 2.47 acres," I said. I couldn't help it if I accidentally sounded smug. "The parcel of land in question is roughly two hundred and forty-seven acres."

"Yes, but this land was supposedly located on the outskirts of Paris. It is supposed to be worth millions. And I mean dollars, not francs."

Greg whistled.

"Of course it's all a bunch of nonsense. Everyone with an ounce of Barras blood has gone over those pieces a million times, but of course there's been nothing to show for it. I guess some legends die hard."

"It's too bad that people have to die, because some legends won't," I said.

I'm sure she tried to frown at me, but the cold wouldn't permit it. As consolation she blew her nose, and then tried to return the handkerchief to Greg. He wisely and politely refused to accept it.

"You keep it," he said. "You may need it again before you get where you're going."

"Tanks," she said, looking at him intently. She didn't even glance my way. "Hab a pweasant ebening."

She turned slowly and walked away, deliberately thrusting her hips from side to side with each step. Those beavers hadn't seen that much action since their dam-building days.

I don't care if she was coming down with a cold, and we were standing in near-blizzard conditions in a cemetery. That was a come-on if I ever heard one. Why is it that we women can hear come-ons issued by other women, but the men in our lives act deafer than posts?

"She's sicker than a dog, but she still wants your body," I said. "Go figure."

Greg laughed and put his arm around me.

"She may not look it, but she's fifty-six," I said. "She's too old for you."

"Age isn't a number. It's how young one feels inside that counts."

"That's a cliché, which in this case isn't true. That woman's soul was old when Methuselah was a child. Besides, if she looked twenty years older, instead of younger, than she is, we wouldn't be having this stupid conversation."

He slid his arm off my shoulder. "You're jealous, aren't you?"

"You have got to be kidding."

"Come on, admit it." He put his arm back on my shoulder.

I slid out from underneath his arm. "That woman's a walking computer chip. She had to hurry home before her face would crack. What do you think it is I'm jealous of?"

"Jealousy does not become you," he said pompously.

"Go f— yourself," I said, and generations of polite Southern ancestors turned over in their graves.

Greg did not drive me back to the church. By sprinting, which meant a great deal of slipping and sliding, I was able to catch up with the captain and his mate. They were delighted to give me a lift, they said, and then they proceeded to pump me all the way to the church on my relationship with Greg. It was not a subject I wanted to discuss and told them so. After telling them that rather gently several times, I finally became emphatic. I didn't mind walking the last two blocks to the church.

Like I said, I am a skilled driver, and despite the intense concentration required to keep my car on the road, I managed to listen to the radio at the same time. The weather news wasn't good. This was supposed to be the worst snowstorm to hit the Carolinas this early in the season in a hundred years. Of course for the last ten or fifteen years, every bit of weather that comes our way seems to be hailed as the worst of the century, so I was not surprised. I was surprised to hear that even as far south as Hilton Head, where my Aunt Marilyn lives, they were experiencing snow flurries.

The first thing I did when I got inside was to call both children to see if they were safe. They were. Then I called Mama. Ditto for her.

"Are *you* all right, Abby?" She sounded two decibels away from hysterical.

"I'm fine, Mama."

"You sure?"

"Yes, Mama. Why the third degree?"

"Well, that Jane woman called again, asking why you hadn't called her back. Then she went on to intimate that maybe you had been in an accident because of the snow. She said that a cousin of hers—a Norman somebody—had driven off the road in a snowstorm up North—Ohio or someplace, and they didn't find him for three weeks. He was dead of course, and field mice had managed to squeeze through the air vents and had eaten his eyeballs. Do you think that could be true?"

"I don't know, but my eyes are just fine. And if C. J. calls again, you tell her I'll call her back tomorrow, if at all."

Mama wasn't through yet. Did I know that the latest forecast was predicting an almost unheard-of eight inches, and that a few flurries had been spotted in greater Jacksonville, Florida? I had not. This was terrible, Mama said. The Apathia membership committee was supposed to meet tomorrow morning to decide her fate. Even if Rock Hill didn't get another flake, there was no way the ladies were going to drive all the way out to the Rock Hill Country Club to cast their votes.

"Can't they do it over the phone?" I asked patiently.

Mama gasped. She continues to be surprised by my gaucheness.

"Abby! That's *not* how things are done."

I told Mama not to worry. The longer the vote was delayed, the more time she had to impress upon them that she was exactly the kind of member the club wanted. No, needed, in fact.

"What do you mean?" she demanded.

"How is your tread?"

"Excuse me?"

"On your tires, Mama. Are they fairly new?"

"Abby!" she wailed. "My only chance for happiness is falling apart in a snowstorm, and you want to talk tires?"

I tried not to laugh. "Mama, what I'm suggesting is that tomorrow, *after* the roads are clear, you call up some of the more nervous ones and offer to go to the store for them. They'll love you forever."

"They'll see right through me," Mama said, and hung up.

There is nothing like a good hot soak to give me perspective on the world in general and my life in particular. If I was a writer, I think I would do all my plotting in the tub. So soak I would, but I wanted an uninterrupted soak, one that I decided to terminate. So before entering my inner sanctum, I turned off all the lights but the bathroom, and unplugged the bedroom phone.

Ever since that first time I had sex with Buford, I've been a big believer in the philosophy that more is better. Since I adore Mystic Gardenia bubble bath, I poured twice the recommended amount of it into my tub and filled it with water as hot as I could stand it. That's almost hot enough to cook a lobster, and certainly hot enough to make most people look like cooked lobsters. Then I put on my favorite Mozart CD, the one with Piano Concerto No. 21 in C Major.

Next I fixed myself a mug of hot chocolate. The mug I habitually use is ceramic, and can take the heat, but it was originally intended as a beer stein. There is no point in dragging myself, sloshing, out of the tub for refills.

The last thing I did was call Dmitri. Gardenias do for Dmitri what catnip does for most felines. Often there is no need to call him. As always, he hopped up on the rim of the tub, sniffed vigorously at the foam, and then settled down to drowse in a semi-intoxicated state of bliss while I soaked and pondered. As long as I took care not to get him wet, he would remain supine and purring on the rim until the tub drained.

I soaked, sipped, and pondered. I spoke my thoughts aloud to Dmitri, who responded periodically by squinting his eyes and purring louder. I'm not weird about animals. I don't cootchy-coo them and talk to them in baby talk. I don't dress Dmitri up in human clothes and pretend that he's anything other than a cat. A big yellow male cat that looks a little bit like TV's Morris, only not quite as handsome. Still, I'd swear there are times when Dmitri understands every word I'm saying, and there are times, even, when he seems to offer me his opinions.

"I wish I'd never bought those damn things," I said.

Dmitri purred comfortingly.

"I wish I'd never laid eyes on that damn furniture, or that damn family. I wish that whole damn Barras bunch would get lost in the damn blizzard."

Dmitri squinted.

"Okay, so I don't. Not really. But you can bet your bippy that it's one of them who killed Arnie Ramsey and Lottie Bell too, I bet. And it could be any one of them. I wouldn't put it past the sleazoid, or Hattie, to kill their own mama.

"Of course, it's not likely that one of the women killed Arnie and stuffed him in the armoire. I'm not a sexist, Dmitri, you know that, but Arnie's skull was cracked. Would a woman be strong enough to do that?"

Dmitri purred louder.

"You're right. The autopsy showed that Arnie had *two* blows to the head. The one to the left cheekbone just breaking the skin, the one to the back of the head definitely fatal. Maybe Hattie, or Toxie, or even Amy hit him in the face with something, and he staggered backward and hit his head hard on something else. That could have happened, I bet."

Dmitri purred louder.

"Now we just have to figure out who did it. Hmmm. Hattie is the poorest, or would that be Toxie? Hattie might not make a whole lot selling perfume at Belk's, but she has a husband who works. Toxie, on the other hand, doesn't. And I doubt if a lounge singer makes that much—not unless she's really good, and who the hell has heard of Toxie?"

Dmitri squinted.

"Okay, so I shouldn't be catty—oops, sorry dear, but I'd have to vote Toxie as the poorest. At least based on her income."

Dmitri's green eyes opened wider.

"Of course wealth is a relative thing. I'm sure Garland Riggs isn't exactly rolling in dough, and even that creepy old Dr. Sex might be having financial problems. Wasn't he sued by some of the patients he exposed himself to?"

Dmitri stood up, stretched, and lay down again, his eyes half-closed.

"It could even be Amy! Sure she has money—at least she says she does—but greed can know no bounds. Well, at least I read that someplace. Anyway, D., maybe Amy—

or any of those women—had second thoughts after the auction, after it was too late, and went into the storeroom for one last final check. Maybe Arnie surprised her, whoever she was, and she panicked and let him have it. Perhaps with her purse.''

Dmitri opened his eyes wide. He didn't seem to think so. "What do you know? You're just a cat. You can't even decide if you want in or out half the time. And you're worse than a chicken about crossing the street. You've already used eight of your lives just doing that.''

Dmitri's eyes became mere slits and he stopped purring. I was tempted to splash some water on him.

"What's the matter? Can't you take a joke?''

Dmitri stood up, stretched, yawned with his tongue curled in an arc, and hopped down to the floor. Without as much as a backward glance he trotted out the door, his tail held high like that of a warthog.

"And you're as dumb as a dog!'' I yelled after him. I threw my shampoo bottle at the door, knocking it closed.

I turned the hot water on with my toes. The bath was becoming tepid. It could no longer poach eggs.

"Well, where were we?'' I said to myself. "Oh yes, we were busy lining up suspects. And while we're at it, we may as well throw Norma's name into the ring. She clearly hated Arnie, and his murder might have had nothing to do with the Barras family at all.

"Come to think of it, it could even have been Purvis or one of his two boys. Maybe they had some kind of a disagreement that got out of hand. It would be real dumb of Purvis, and not like him, to ship me a body in an item that he sold to me in a public auction, but maybe the Pernod clouded his judgment. As for his two sons, Jimbo and Skeet, hell I wouldn't put it past them to send ice cream by parcel post.

"Oops, I almost forgot! Why not the captain and his mate? Sure, they're newcomers to the scene, but that doesn't mean they haven't been playing backstage behind the scenes. For all I know, they were at that damn auction. What I need now is a picture of them to show around. But hell, that shouldn't be too hard. All I have to do is pay them another visit, and ask them to pose in front of their silly boat house. I'm sure they'll be more than happy to oblige. The first thing tomorrow, if this blizzard—''

The lights went off.

''Shit,'' I said. I think I said it several times. I probably said a few more words that were bad enough to make Mama blush.

It wasn't just the lights going out that were causing me to swear like a trucker. For one thing, I burned my toes on the hot water while trying to turn off the faucet in the dark. Then when I hopped up on one leg—to hold my burned foot out of the water—I slipped, thanks to my excessive use of bubble bath. Fortunately I was able to grab the towel bar in time to prevent me from going down all the way, but unfortunately, I somehow managed to dislodge my towel. So there I was, standing on one foot, stark naked, and in the dark.

Of course I have more than one towel, but the others I keep in a bathroom closet opposite the tub. As I was trying to get out of the tub, still on one foot, I knocked my ceramic mug into the tub. Thankfully the cocoa had long been finished, or I would have had even another reason to swear. At any rate, the heavy mug filled with water and settled to the bottom of the tub with a heavy thunk, just grazing my big toe.

Just as I opened my mouth to swear I heard Dmitri yowl, like he does when I accidentally step on his tail. A second later there was the sound of splintering wood.

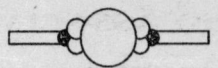

21

I knew there was someone in the house with me, but I didn't want to believe it. How much more vulnerable can one get than to be naked, in the dark, with a scalded foot? I may as well have hung a sign around my neck that read *Pacifist, Come and Get Me*. Except that I am anything but a pacifist. My very first serious boyfriend, Wayne, taught me that the meek shall inherit a backhand across the mouth. It was a lesson I had to be taught only once. That was back in the days when Lucite purses were all the rage. After Wayne hit me, he got to feel my pocketbook up side his head. It was a lesson he had to be taught only once.

I didn't have a Lucite purse handy. In fact, there wasn't anything throwable within reach except the bottle of Mystic Gardenia bubble bath and a half-empty bottle of Suave Shampoo Plus. I decided on the bubble bath. It was fuller. As I was hopping over to get it, I stubbed my toe on the ceramic beer stein.

"Eureka!" I whispered. As far as I was concerned it was the most important bathtub discovery in history.

Armed, I felt better. Which is not to say that my heart wasn't trying to force its way through my mouth, or that the knee on my uninjured appendage didn't threaten to buckle a thousand times. But I would go down fighting, and if I could somehow harness and use all the resentment for Buford I'd stored up through the years, I had a fighting chance.

Even if the intruder had a gun, I still had a chance. That was the most important thing I learned from that self-defense class I took the previous winter. Only a small percentage of bullets hit their mark, and of those that do, only a small percentage *kill*. If someone ever tries to force you into a car at gunpoint, run like hell. You at least have a chance *if* you run. Otherwise they might shoot you in the car, with the gun pressed right up against your temple. Your chances of that bullet missing are much slimmer.

Unfortunately my bathroom has only one door. In effect it was a big car, but it was big enough that I could feint and dodge a little. I certainly was not going to stand there like a target with a bull's-eye pasted on my forehead.

Feeling around in the tub, I scooped up the mug and scrambled out of the tub, sloshing water everywhere. I hobbled directly to the door. Even though it was still dark in there, and my bathroom has no window, I could discern the door by a pencil-thin line of faint light that seemed to pulsate. Obviously the intruder was bobbing a flashlight around.

I pushed the lock button in the door handle. It was silent, but I would have welcomed the click from a dead bolt. I should have taken a clue from watching *Psycho*. It had been on TV just the month before. If I got out of this jam alive I was either going to have a dead bolt installed on every door of the house, or buy eight Doberman pinschers.

I considered my options. I could stand naked by the door, holding my mug aloft, prepared to crash it down on the head of whoever decided to burst through the door. I could hide in the closet along with the towels. I could climb back in the tub and pretend that I had slipped and drowned.

I chose the first option, but decided to get dressed first.

Unfortunately I had left my bathrobe hanging on a hook on the back of my bedroom door. I had no clean clothes in the bathroom at all, but I had *lots* of dirty clothes. An entire hamper full. The past week had been far too stressful and event-filled for me to even consider doing laundry.

While I was sifting through my options, my uninvited visitor was busily and noisily vandalizing my bedroom. There was the distinct sound of more glass breaking, and the sickening—at least to an antique dealer—sound of splintering wood. I could also hear a few grunts and some heavy breathing. The latter were sounds occasionally heard in my bedroom, but not while I was out of the room.

I dressed. I started by putting on the first thing I touched—that day's bra. Then my panties. When the third item I pulled out of the basket inexplicably turned out to be panties as well, I put them on anyway. Might as well make certain vulnerable spots hard to get to, just in case my nocturnal visitor turned out to be a rapist. My funeral outfit I'd hung, but yesterday's jeans and sweatshirt were next, followed by a pair of warm cotton socks. I automatically put on both socks. As I was putting on the second sock, I realized to my surprise that my scalded foot no longer hurt.

Since there was nothing else to do, except listen to the vandalism over the pounding of my heart, I continued to dress. Why not? Perhaps several layers of clothing would help soften the impact, or even deflect a bullet that came my way. They would certainly help keep me warm if I had to make a dash for the outside without a chance to grab my coat.

I was clumsily trying to button my third top, when I became suddenly and acutely aware that some of the heavy breathing was just on the other side of the door, mere inches away. I froze, my fingers still on a button. I couldn't see the doorknob turn, but I could hear it turn, and then catch against the lock. The heavy breathing momentarily stopped. Then I heard the knob turn again, this time with more pressure applied to it. I also heard what sounded like a shoulder hit the door.

"Yes, I'm in here you goddamn creep!" I screamed, "and I have a double-barreled shotgun aimed right at your guts."

It just came out. I hadn't planned to say it. Trust me, I wouldn't have planned to say something so inane. I mean, who would believe that your average woman keeps a loaded shotgun in her *bathroom*? A handgun, perhaps, but a shotgun?

The intruder believed me, that's who. There were a few seconds of what I took for stunned silence, and then it sounded like a herd of buffalo went racing from the room. A few seconds more and I heard the distant sound of a door slam, probably my kitchen door.

I slumped to the floor, my back against the wall. The shakes started slowly, like a passing chill, but before I knew it I was vibrating faster than the paint mixer at Home Depot. My teeth were chattering so hard I was in danger of knocking loose my caps.

"Breathe deeply," they always say in the movies, but they are just acting. What do they know about breathing deeply when your upper and lower jaws are slamming into each other with the force of pistons, and your stomach has been tied into a knot and pulled halfway up your throat?

It must have taken me five minutes to get enough self-control to stand again. But that was only the beginning. What should I do next? What if the intruder I'd so obviously frightened had recovered from his or her fear first, and had silently returned to the scene of the crime? Or what if there were two intruders, and one had noisily fled as part of a ruse? What if the partner in crime was just on the other side of the door, waiting for me with a far deadlier weapon than a ceramic beer stein?

It's quite possible I would have stood there, holding that beer mug in my hand, for the better part of the night, had not dear sweet Dmitri come to my rescue. No, he did not dial 911—although if a pet could be trained to do so, Dmitri would be a likely candidate. What my hairball hero did was to demand his supper in a loud and plaintive voice. I knew then that my unwanted visitor had skedaddled for sure. Food for Dmitri is a very private thing. I opened the door.

I keep a flashlight on my night table, but before I got even to my bed I began stepping on wooden splinters. Thank God I was wearing three pairs of socks.

"Oh shit," I said. I knew immediately that the wood had come from the Louis XV desk I had taken home for safekeeping.

My eyes were becoming accustomed to the dark now and there was enough light coming through the bedroom window, reflecting off the snow, for me to discern a portion of that exquisite frame lying on the floor in front of me. I swore vengeance on whoever did such a horrible thing and to his or her descendants for the seventh generation.

I decided not to risk stepping on any more of the glass to get to my bedroom phone, even though it was on the other side of my bed. With Dmitri still complaining loudly, I forged ahead through the living room and into the kitchen to use the wall phone there. Please give me no credit for bravery on that account. As long as Dmitri kept wrapping himself around my legs, I was in far more danger of tripping over Dmitri than anything else—that, and slipping on the kitchen linoleum. I could feel puddles of water through my layers of socks. Apparently the intruder had forgotten to wipe his feet.

There was a dial tone.

"Thank you, Lord," I whispered.

I dialed 911 and gave them the particulars. They promised to send someone out immediately, but cautioned that it could take as long as twenty minutes, due to the current road conditions. Without giving it a second thought, I dialed Greg.

"Hello?" he said after only the second ring.

"Greg—"

"Abby! Is anything wrong?" Our quarrel was clearly a thing of the past.

I took my first really deep breath since the bathtub. "Yes, there's a lot wrong, actually. I was—"

"I'll be right over," he said, and hung up.

Greg lives at least twenty minutes away—on a good day—so I wasn't going to just stand there and twiddle my thumbs until somebody showed up. Fortunately I keep a second flashlight in the kitchen. Keeping Dmitri with me as a test—like a caged canary in a coal mine—I went into the laundry room and inspected the circuit breakers.

To my horror, but not to my surprise, a quick sweep of the flashlight confirmed what I had suspected. The snowstorm was not responsible for my "power failure." Someone had tripped all the switches.

Greg was true to his word. It couldn't have been more than fifteen minutes, sixteen at the most, when he pulled up. By then I was sitting in the living room, just inside the front door, holding two flashlights and a nine iron. Every light in the house was on, and I was wearing shoes. I was ready for fight or flight, whatever circumstances demanded.

Greg hugged me without hesitation the second I opened the door. "Abby."

"Thanks for coming," I mumbled, my lips squashed against his chest. "I bet Santa is pissed at you. You must have borrowed his sleigh."

"It's stopped snowing, Abby, and I would have been

here sooner if it hadn't been for that damn salt truck that just wouldn't pull over.''

"Anyway, thanks.''

I pulled him aside. I had to start my story three times, because he kept insisting it wasn't the beginning, and then even once I was allowed to continue, I was interrupted more than the mother of a three-year-old. Perhaps I should have written it all down while I was waiting and just handed it to him.

"Why didn't you lock the bathroom door?'' he demanded.

"Do you, when you take a bath?'' I asked, trying to remain calm.

"We're not talking about *me*,'' he said with typical male obstinacy. "And why the hell didn't you have a bathrobe in the room with you?''

"You don't even sleep in pajamas,'' I snapped.

We were getting nowhere fast. He sighed. I sighed.

"I appreciate your coming,'' I said, "and your concern, but I'm afraid this isn't going to work.''

He stared at me with those incredibly blue eyes. "Look, it's hard for me to be professional about this. It's—''

"Then maybe you should just sit with me here, and we'll wait until the professionals arrive,'' I said coolly.

To my surprise a smiled tugged at the corners of his mouth. "Abby, I was about to say that it's hard for me to be professional with you when I care so much.''

"I beg your pardon?'' I had heard him very well indeed.

It took a little special effort for him to repeat it, a fact for which I gave him full credit.

"Thanks,'' I said. I hoped it sounded nonchalant.

He shook his head. "No, I don't think you get it. I *really* care about you, Abby. I love you.''

I could hardly believe my ears. My close encounter had truly moved him. The Croats and the Serbs were welcome to settle their differences in my bedroom, if that's what it took to get a declaration like that from Greg. The Arabs and Israelis too. Heck, might as well throw in the Irish.

"I love you, too," I was quick to say. None of that ditto stuff on such a momentous occasion.

"I want us to get married, Abby."

I refrained from jiggling a pinky tip in my ears to check for wax deposits. Clearly I had major buildup. He couldn't possibly have said what I thought I heard.

"Excuse me?"

He smiled, his eyes and his mouth. "You heard me. I said I wanted us to get married."

"Is that a proposal?"

He shook his head, causing my heart to do a belly flop into my stomach. While my ticker was floundering about in my gastric juices he got down on one knee and took both my hands in his.

"Will you marry me, Abigail Louise Timberlake, nee Wiggins?"

"No," I said quietly.

His eyes spoke louder than his lips ever could.

"Greg, I love you. I mean that. But I don't love you enough to marry you—at least not right now."

I averted my eyes while he got off the floor. "I guess I made a damn fool of myself then."

I lightly touched his arm. I could feel his muscles stiffen.

"No," I said. "You didn't make a fool of yourself. You endeared yourself to me forever."

He stood up, towering over me. "Hell, I don't want to be endeared. I want to marry you, Abigail. What have I done wrong now?"

I stood up, equalizing our height difference by a fraction. "It's not anything you did, although"—I couldn't help but say—"your flirting with anyone who pees sitting down doesn't help. But it's not really that. It's *me*. I'm not over Buford yet. I'm not ready to commit to marriage.''

He raked his fingers through that thick head of black hair. "Will you ever be?"

I shrugged. "I don't know. When I am, you'll be the first to know."

"Like I give a damn," he said.

From that point on he had no trouble being professional.

The 911 team knew Greg. They also knew that something was up between us because they kept exchanging knowing glances. Outside of that, they, too, were very professional.

"The perpetrator came through the back door, ma'am," the one named Jim said.

"No shit Sherlock," I said, but being a Southern lady, I said it so softly he couldn't hear.

"Apparently you forgot to lock your door, ma'am, because there's no sign of forced entry."

Greg gave me an I-told-you-so look, and I tried not to grin foolishly.

"I was late for a funeral this afternoon," I said. "What else can you tell me?"

"That the perpetrator was a female."

That surprised me. "Shoe or boot prints, eh?"

Jim held up a cigarette butt. "We found this lying in the heel of one of the boot prints. It hasn't been stepped on. Apparently she left just about the time it stopped snowing."

"How do you know it was a she?" I asked.

To his credit, Jim did not smirk. "I know that is an assumption, ma'am, but this cigarette butt has lipstick on it."

So it did.

Maybe it was time to call C. J. after all.

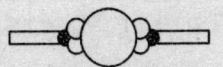

22

Despite our little misunderstanding, I fully expected Greg to ask me if he could spend the night. But he denied me the opportunity to refuse him, and left even before the 911 team. I had no intention of spending the night alone, however, and called my faithful buddies, the Rob-Bobs.

"Sure thing," Bob boomed. "We'd be happy to have you. You have dinner yet?"

"Stuffed," I lied.

"Well, you can watch us eat then. I made Japanese tonight. You ever have *unagi*?"

"I can't say that I have."

"It's grilled eel. Basted with soy sauce and sweet sake. It's supposed to be grilled over hot coals, but it's damn cold outside, and Rob won't let me bring the grill into the kitchen. I'm going to have to broil it in the oven."

Rob got on the line. "I know that year-round barbecuing is a Carolina thing, but how did this Yankee from New York get hooked?"

"Toledo," Bob reminded him. "And I'm a Charlottean now."

"Anyway," Rob said, "you're more than welcome to stay with us. But besides that, is there anything we can do?"

"No. Like what?"

"Anything. Like talk to what's-his-name for you. You know, the good-looking stud who's probably gay and just doesn't know it yet."

I laughed. "I don't think so, dear. Or else he deserves an Academy Award. I'll be fine, really. Anyway, it's my fault."

"Don't say that," Bob practically bellowed. "He's the one who's demanding it be either feast or famine. Ah, speaking of feasting, I have to go now. The eels are calling me."

He got off the line, but Rob stayed on. There was a long pause.

"Hurry, Abby," Rob whispered. "I don't want to eat those damn eels any more than you do. I'm going to need some moral support at the very least."

I promised to be right there, and then I remembered C. J. She kept coming back to plague my thoughts, like unfinished homework. Maybe she would, or maybe she wouldn't, have any light to shed on my chainsmoking nocturnal visitor. Either way, it was time to call her and get it over with.

It took her nine rings to answer. Not everyone uses an answering machine. And ever since I read—in Ann Landers, I think—that one should wait ten rings before hanging up, that's exactly what I do. I know from personal experience just how frustrating it can be to interrupt one's bodily functions just to talk to a dial tone.

"Huh?" C. J. said. She had been sleeping.

"C. J., it's me, Abigail."

"Do you know what time it is, Abigail?"

"Quarter after seven," I said. "Do I win a prize?"

"Very funny. I was asleep, you know. I had a hard day."

"C. J., you're twenty-three years old, for pete's sake. You should be out partying. Meeting guys."

"I don't party," C. J. said somberly. "Especially on

days when I have to do somebody else's job along with mine."

"I'm sorry about the phone calls. Who was it this time?"

"I'm talking about waiting on your customers. I had to close my shop to open yours with that key you gave me. You might have cost me a very important sale."

"What on earth are you talking about?"

She clucked her impatience. "That man the Kefferts sent over to pick up the armoire."

I wanted to reach through the receiver and grab her shoulders. Maybe if I gave her a good shake she would awaken to make some sense. It occurred to me that she might have been drinking. That would certainly explain her early bedtime.

"C. J., dear, have you been sipping the sauce?"

"What?"

"Hitting the bottle. You know, drinking."

"I beg your pardon, Abigail! I'll have you know that I'm a Christian."

How stupid of me to forget that some non-Episcopalians eschew alcohol. Perhaps some Episcopalians as well.

"Well, you just aren't making sense, dear. Nobody picked up the armoire because I haven't sold it to anyone. And as for the Kefferts, they were with me at the funeral this afternoon. You must be mistaken."

"What?" Her pique had turned to alarm.

I repeated myself.

"Oh no," C. J. moaned. "The same thing happened to my Uncle Delbert and Auntie Nina. Only with them it was an expensive car. You see—"

"Damn it, C. J.! Spare me the family reminiscences and cut to the chase. What *happened?* To my armoire?"

"He assured me it was all right," she said. She sounded close to tears. "He mentioned your name several times.

Said you had told the Kefferts that they could buy the armoire after all, and that he had been sent to pick it up. He had a check with their name on it, and everything.''

"Check? For what amount?"

"Twenty-five thousand dollars," she said.

I took a deep breath. If the Kefferts were going to cheat me out of an armoire, I guess it wasn't so bad if they paid for it through the nose. The first mate had met my offhand figure, and added an extra five. Nice touch.

"What did you do with the check, C. J.?"

"It's right here. I brought it home with me. You aren't mad?"

"Hell yes, I'm mad. But what's done is done, I guess. Did you remember to write up a bill of sale?"

"Un-hunh. I brought that home, too. Just in case."

"Good girl," I said. "Now tell me, C. J., what does this man who works for the Kefferts look like?"

"Just regular."

"What do you mean, 'just regular'? He's not a grade of gas, is he?"

"Uh—no. I mean he had sort of brown hair and was sort of normal tall. I don't remember what color his eyes were, if that's what you're going to ask me next. I guess someone your age might think he was sort of cute."

"How old was he?"

"Pretty old."

I prayed for patience. To someone C. J.'s age, anyone old enough to remember Donny Osmond was old.

"How old is 'pretty old,' dear? As old as I am, or older?"

"Uh . . . older, I guess. Kind of really old. Maybe as old as my dad."

"How old is that?"

"Forty-five."

C. J.'s dad was three years younger than I. I didn't know whether to thank her for thinking I didn't look "kind of really old" or wring her neck for thinking forty-five fell in that category. I decided to merely hope that she aged badly and looked like a prune by the time she was thirty.

"So somebody you don't know from Adam shows up and hands you a check, and you let them cart off the most valuable thing in my shop?"

"They said it was all right," she whined. "And there is the check. Personally, Abigail, I think that's a lot of money for that piece."

I mumbled something about that not being the point.

C. J. decided it was time to distract me. "Oh, but there was a phone call for you, too, Abigail. I'm not an answering service, you know."

"Who from, dear?"

"Somebody named Riggs. Gorman, or something like that."

"That's Garland, dear. What did he say?"

"That you should call him back. That it was very important."

"Was it *urgent*?" I asked.

"Huh?" Sarcasm, like youth, is wasted on the young.

I called Garland at the nursery, but even after ten rings there was no answer. I would have thought he would still be open, selling Christmas trees, or whatever it is nurseries do that time of the year.

The Kefferts were the next scheduled victims of my index finger. The first mate picked up after the first ring. I took a deep breath, willing myself to sound calm. Vexed, but calm.

"This is Abigail Timberlake. I think we have something to discuss."

"It was the captain's idea," she said quickly. "Would you like to speak to him?"

"No, you'll do just fine, dear, since you were obviously a part of it, too."

"I'm only the first mate, remember?"

"Don't give me that sexist nonsense, Mrs. Keffert. You were obviously in on it. I made it very clear that I didn't want to sell just yet."

"But you named a price."

"Yes, an exorbitant price, I want you to know."

I waited for that to sink in. If it did, she didn't do me the courtesy of acknowledging that it had.

"So who was the errand boy that did your dirty deed?"

"That was August. He does our yard work. But he just did what the captain asked him to do, Mrs. Timberlake."

"I'm sure. And so did you. It has a certain Germanic ring, doesn't it? You realize, of course, that what you— the captain—did is illegal. I could have him arrested for fraud."

I could hear her gulp. It was a satisfying sound, one I would play back in my head after I had banked the twenty-five-thousand-dollar check.

"However, I have decided not to press charges," I said magnanimously.

Her sigh of relief was louder than her gulp. "Thank you, Mrs. Timberlake."

"But I do have one word of advice."

"Yes?" she asked eagerly.

"Mutiny."

"Pardon me?"

"I said 'mutiny.' You and this August fellow should mutiny. Tie up the captain and lock him in the brig. Then you and August can sail off into the sunset together. From what I heard, someone your age might find him 'sort of cute.'"

"Mrs. Timberlake!"

I rang off.

* * *

"So, how was the eel?"

I had arrived later than I had hoped, and apparently eel is better not left waiting.

"Delicious," Rob said.

"Bullshit," Bob brayed. "You only ate one bite."

"I ate two."

"Well, you win some and lose some. Tomorrow night it's going to be *ika toh uni*."

"What's that?" I asked pleasantly.

"Squid with sea urchin roe," Bob said. He made it sound like a dish fit for a king. Neptune, I guess.

Rob blanched. "Uh—I prefer not to eat anything with suction cups."

"This is squid, not octopus. The suction cups are very small. And besides you like squid. You raved about my calamari."

"I don't suppose steak is ever going to be on the menu?"

"Now, now, you know red meat is bad for you." Bob added one last dish to the collection piled in his arms.

"Lean ground beef then. One hamburger, broiled, once a week. That's not so bad."

Bob mumbled something about not having his efforts appreciated by the philistines among us, and scurried off to the kitchen.

"I love him dearly," Bob whispered as soon as the door swung shut, "but I've got to get my hands on some good old-fashioned American food. You didn't happen to sneak a hamburger in with you, did you?"

"No." I hung my head in shame and pointed to my overnight bag. "But I will confess to swinging by Dunkin' Donuts on my way over here. I lied about eating supper. I was going to eat them tonight after y'all were in bed."

"I'll give you two bucks a donut plus father as many children as you want. You have any cream-filled?"

It was quite an offer coming from Rob. Hurriedly I put my coat back on, and he his, and we sneaked out onto the balcony to gorge on donuts while the grumbling gourmet washed the dishes. I supposed we should have helped him—Rob should have, at any rate—but our stomachs were demanding precedence.

Besides, it was too beautiful out there to even contemplate exchanging the balcony for a steamy kitchen. I am not a fan of cold weather, but not only had the snow stopped, but the moon was out, almost full. Native Carolinians both, neither Rob nor I had had many chances to observe moonlight on snow, and before Christmas yet.

"It's gorgeous," I said, my mouth full.

"Takes your breath away," Rob said.

"Isn't it funny how life is such a mixture of, well—"

"The hideous and the sublime."

"Exactly."

"This is definitely sublime."

"Arnie's body in the armoire was hideous. So was that break-in tonight. If there wasn't a sublime every now and then, I'd plumb give up."

"I know what you mean."

We were both silent for a minutes, the only sound our chewing, and a sporadic drip coming from a corner of the balcony above. As we might have expected, the early snow was not going to stick around for long.

"Abby," Rob said suddenly, "I suppose it would be redundant if I told you to be careful."

"Yes, but I appreciate it. And I am careful." Yeah, right. So careful I hadn't bothered to lock the back door.

"I mean, *real* careful," Rob said, his words muffled by a wad of donut. "Don't trust anyone until this whole thing is resolved."

"Well, I have to trust some people. Like Mama and my children. And Greg. And even you and Rob." I laughed nervously. "I can trust you guys, can't I?"

He finished chewing slowly and swallowed. "Yes, you can trust us, but nobody else."

"Well, I certainly can't trust any of the Barras clan, that's for sure. And that includes the Captain and Tennille."

He honored me with a short but forced laugh. "I mean *anybody* else, Abby. Like Purnell Purvis, for instance. Or that waitress Norma you told me about."

I chewed on that for a while myself. "You're scaring me, Rob."

He put his left hand, the sugarless one, on my shoulder. "I mean to, Abby. It's a scary world out there. A lot of wolves in sheep's clothing."

"Well, I can certainly trust Wynnell—she's practically my best friend, and doesn't have a thing to gain by any of this. And I'm sure I can trust C. J., too."

"Can you?"

I could feel that old goose revving up, ready to run over my grave again. "What do you mean?"

"What do you really know about her?"

"Well . . . she's just a kid, Rob. And she doesn't have a drop of Barras blood that I know of."

"And?"

"And what? You mean because she keeps calling me all the time with urgent messages, and sold that armoire to—wait a minute! You don't think she was in on something with the Kefferts, do you?"

"You never know," Rob said quietly. "That's my point."

The sliding glass door to the patio opened then and Bob stepped out bearing a tray with three steaming mugs.

"Don't bother to hide the contraband," he said. "I can smell a jelly-filled donut a mile away. In Toledo I lived just around the corner from a bakery. So confess all your sins and help yourself to something hot to wash down all that fat and sugar."

Rob and I obediently took our mugs. "What is this?" I asked pleasantly. It didn't smell like coffee, tea, or hot chocolate."

"Try it, you'll like it," Bob coaxed.

To prove we were good sports, and feeling guilty about the donuts, Bob and I sipped simultaneously. Just as simultaneously we spit out the hot broth.

"It's mizo," Bob boomed, beaming in the moonlight. "Japanese fish stock soup."

We shooed him from the deck and rinsed our mouths out with what little snow remained on the railing. In five minutes he was back.

"This time it's tea," he said.

There was no sugar or cream on the tray, but my fingers and my mouth were cold from the snow. I took a mug and sipped greedily. *One* greedy sip. The concoction was definitely not tea.

"What the hell is this?" Rob said, his handsome face twisted in a grimace.

"Tea," Bob said. "Japanese green tea. It's supposed to taste like that."

We banished him from the deck until all the donuts were gone and our extremities numb. Then we made him fix us some hot chocolate.

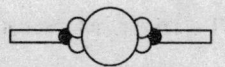

23

Rob and Bob have a well-appointed guest room, and I would have slept very soundly on the authentic Queen Anne bed, but I woke up about three o'clock in a sweat. Now, I know I am forty-eight years old and waking up in a sweat is something to be expected, but this one was different. This sweat was preceded by a dream in which C. J., her face at least ten times its normal size, was looming over me.

"To market, to market to buy a fat pig," she kept saying. She was holding a machete in her huge right hand.

"But I'm not a pig!" Although my mouth seemed to be working, my lips definitely moving, no sound was coming out.

After a few minutes the giantess C. J. got tired of playing the market game and exchanged the machete for a sledge hammer.

"For your table, Lisa," she grunted, raising the sledge hammer over her head.

"I'm not Lisa!" I screamed. That time my vocal cords worked. I woke up.

I lay there on the Queen Anne bed, panting, the covers thrown off. Apparently the Rob-Bobs were capable of sleeping through a hurricane, or else they were simply being discreet. Perhaps, in their optimism, they thought I had somehow managed to sneak in a lover.

At any rate, it was impossible for me to go back to sleep after that. Mama firmly believes that all dreams have some meaning, and that if we could learn to interpret them correctly, we would understand ourselves much better. In her mind, dream interpretation equals mental health. She keeps a notebook by her bed and jots down everything she remembers dreaming. She has done this on a regular basis ever since Daddy died.

I am not sure, however, that this discipline of hers has led to greater self-awareness. Perhaps I'm being too judgmental, but how self-aware can a woman be who lives in a time warp? Please don't get me wrong, my dear mama isn't psychotic by any means. I just don't think that cleaning one's house in pearls and crinolines is a sign of good mental health.

Still, there was undoubtedly something to be learned from my dream, if only that I shouldn't eat three jelly-filled donuts and two glazed ones that close to bedtime. I lay there awake for almost an hour, alternately trying to interrupt my nightmare and to block out the sound of Bob snoring. I assumed it was Bob. The snores were bass, and loud enough to wake the dead clear over in Ashville. It was a good thing Bob had moved south and not to Colorado, where he might have found himself responsible for starting a number of avalanches.

Another one of Mama's pearls of wisdom is that things come to us when our hands are open. There may well be some truth in this. Just as I was giving up on both interpreting my dream *and* a good night's sleep, a bizarre interpretation occurred to me. What if C. J. hadn't been saying "market," but "*marquetry*." One of the four Louis XV pieces displayed excellent marquetry, and that was the small table.

But what then did marquetry have to do with a pig? And why had she called me Lisa? Perhaps the pig was just something my brain had used to complete the "market" phrase, to have it somehow make sense to me. After all, that particular nursery rhyme was one I would recite almost daily to the children after their baths when they were little, while drying off their toes with a big fluffy towel. As for the Lisa part, my middle name is Louise, which sounds similar, but did C. J. know that?

"But wait a minute," I said aloud. "It's not about what C. J. knows, but what I know."

And then it hit me, not like a ton of bricks, but like a ton of Mama's homemade pound cakes—which she insists on baking from scratch, when any grocery store sells much better ones, and at a fraction of the cost.

"*Liseuse*!" I shouted. "*Table liseuse*!"

Seconds later there was a rap at the door, and Rob stuck his head in.

"You all right, Abby?"

"I got it!" I turned on the bedside lamp and jumped out of bed before remembering that I was wearing one of my shorter flannel nightgowns and that it had a tendency to creep up,

Rob discreetly averted his eyes while I jerked the darn thing down. No harm done.

"I'm fine," I shrieked, and pranced over to him and gave him a big hug.

It was at that moment that fate decreed Bob should appear on the scene. A lesser man might have felt threatened by what he saw. The prancing and hugging had hiked up my ornery gown again.

Bob barely blinked. "What's up?"

Rob had the presence of mind to peel me off him. I was too excited to think straight.

"Our little Abby seems to have had an epiphany," he said calmly, much to his credit.

"Yes!" My brain was starting to kick in, in high gear, so I pranced over to Bob and gave him a hug as well. Let him chew on that, if he still had any doubts.

"What is it?" Rob said. "What's going on in that pumpkin head of yours?"

I released Bob. Rob is, after all, the more jealous of the two.

"My pumpkin head has just thought—in my sleep, mind you—of the most likely place for the document to be hidden!"

"What document?" Bob asked. His brain was obviously still playing catchup.

"The document that has turned the Barras bunch into bloodthirsty bludgeoning burglars."

"Stop alliterating and elucidate," Rob said.

"Maybe over tea," Bob suggested sensibly.

Rob and I groaned.

"Real tea. American tea—English, whatever. The kind you can put cream and sugar in. Or lemon, if you like."

We cautiously agreed.

"So you see," I said, over a cup of real tea, "the marquetry table that I gave C. J. to keep for me might be more than it appears."

"Not a *table liseuse*?" Bob boomed.

"Exactly."

"I don't get it," Rob said.

I wasn't surprised. There is too much about the antique business for any one person to know everything. That is why any antique dealer worth his salt will have a shelf full of up-to-date reference books, and enough humility to call in an expert from time to time. I certainly would not have known about *table liseuse* had I not combed through some period reference books in preparation for the estate sale. Even then, I had no reason to suspect that the marquetry table was anything than what it appeared to be.

"A *table liseuse* is a small mechanical table of the latter part of the Louis XV period," I said, trying not to sound pompous. "These tables often have well-concealed panels that open to reveal secret compartments. More often than not the compartment contains a stand that unfolds, and upon which you can prop a book.''

"And I can't think of a better way to conceal one of those compartments than with marquetry!" Bob bellowed. "Abigail, you're a genius!"

I shrugged modestly. "We don't know yet if it is a *table liseuse*. And even if it is, the compartment might be empty."

"Hmmm," Rob said ominously. "Hmmm."

"What?"

He flashed me what I suppose was meant to be a reassuring smile. It came across stiff and foreboding.

"Who did you say was keeping the table for you?"

It hit me like two tons of Mama's pound cakes. "My God," I moaned. "You really think it's her?"

Rob's steady stare was his answer.

"Well, I don't," Bob said, putting an arm around my shoulders. "If C. J. had this table, and access to its secret, there was no reason for her to kill again. This Ramsey guy, maybe, but not Lottie Bell."

I swallowed hard. "I gave it to her *after* Lottie Bell was murdered."

"And she is young and strong," Rob said. "I could see her stuffing a body into an armoire."

"Y'all are getting carried away," Bob said. It was the first time I'd heard him say the word "y'all," and it brought a smile to my lips despite the gravity of our conversation.

"Well, there's one way to settle this matter once and for all. I'm going to march straight over there and give that damn table a thorough examination, like I should have done in the very beginning."

Rob's stare had turned to blankness. "What does that prove? Either you find a hidden compartment or you don't. If there's anything of value in it, do you think she's just going to leave it there?''

"Besides," Bob said, "if she has already offed two people, what makes you think she's going to stop at a third?''

" 'Offed'? What is that? Toledo tough talk? But, you're right," I said. "We'll all go over there together.''

Rob grabbed me by both shoulders. "Whoa! This sounds like a matter for the police. Or that boyfriend of yours.''

"He's not my boyfriend.''

"Ex-boyfriend, whatever. My point is, this is definitely not something three amateurs should be messing with.''

"I agree," Bob said. He glanced at the kitchen clock. "It's only twenty to four. What do you say we try to get some sleep. We can call your detective in the morning. Nothing is going to change significantly between now and then.''

"But—''

"Nighty-night," Rob said. He kissed the top of my head, like I was his baby sister.

"And don't you do anything foolish," Bob said. He patted my cheek.

They could not be dissuaded from crawling back under their warm covers in the middle of the night. What kind of friends were these? I wanted friends who were willing to risk hearth and home, to leave no stone unturned in our mutual quest for justice. Pulling a feather-filled comforter over their heads was not what I had in mind.

"Nighty-night," I said cooperatively.

I had long since learned from my kids the importance of feigning compliance before defiance, so I trotted off to the guest room like a good little girl. About twenty minutes later when Bob's loud snores gave the all-clear sign, I dressed and slipped silently down the hall and out the front door. The Rob-Bobs had a lot to learn about raising children.

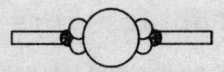

24

The streets were as deserted as church is the Sunday after Christmas. No doubt sensible people were still in bed and/or had listened to the weather forecast. The partially melted snow had refrozen during the night, turning Charlotte into the world's largest skating arena.

" 'Twas two weeks before Christmas and all through the streets, not a creature was stirring without wearing cleats," I chanted as I skillfully steered my car out of its third spin.

If you relax, I discovered, and do exactly what they teach you in drivers education about turning into the skid—even though it sounds unnatural—it isn't all that bad. Provided you aren't driving very fast to begin with, and the streets are deserted. I at least had the desertion part in my favor, and was able to make it to C. J.'s without any injury to my car, and only minor injury to the garbage bin some lazy homeowner had neglected to bring in.

I may be impetuous, but I am not stupid. I've seen my fair share of crime movies. I knew it would be risking life and limb to just charge into C. J.'s house and accuse her of two murders. But I also knew—thanks to Hollywood—that people are all the time getting away with serious crimes, simply by driving away in the middle of the night. If I wasn't going to sleep anymore anyway, it surely didn't hurt if I kept an eye on C. J. until dawn when we called the police.

C. J. lives in a modest, two-bedroom rental house. She claims to eschew apartments because she likes her privacy. If you knew C. J., however, you would probably draw the same conclusion I have, which is that it is the apartment owners who eschew C. J. and her quirky ways. At any rate, I circled her block twice, awakening only two dogs, who were apparently too cold to howl for more than a few seconds. I finally parked on the street, three houses down on the left, as you face her house. From where I sat I could see the corner of her carport, her car reassuringly inside. There was not much else to see. The drapes were drawn in front of the scaled-down picture window, presumably as a precaution against the cold.

It was rather exciting being on my first stakeout, almost fun, except that I had woefully neglected to bring any of the amenities that scriptwriters provided for their detectives. A huge thermos of cafe au lait and another half-dozen donuts would have hit the spot. A couple of feather ticks—like the one my erstwhile friends were snuggling under—would have been most welcome as well. It was too risky to let the car idle in order to keep the heat going, and far too cold to just sit there.

After about five minutes I began to fear that unless I moved around a little, I was going to spend my Christmas holidays as a Popsicle. My choices were to abandon my stakeout or rev up my internal furnace by getting a little exercise, like maybe a casual stroll past C. J.'s house.

It wasn't easy closing the car door behind me without making a sound, but it was virtually impossible to walk on the sidewalk that led past C. J.'s house. She and her slovenly neighbors ought to be sued for shirking their snow and slush removal. The sidewalk was solid ice. I was forced to walk across the fronts of the narrow lawns on crunchy, frozen snow. You can bet I avoided the bare spots where the neighborhood's dogs had contributed to snow melt earlier when temperatures were warmer.

I knew C. J. didn't have a dog, and her immediate neighbors didn't seem to, either, so I saw no harm in cutting deeper into her lawn for a closer inspection of her house. Of course I took precautions. There is a sporadic but overgrown hedge that lines the driveway and the street side of the walk from the driveway to the front door. Being short has its occasional advantages and I was able to dart—as much as frozen snow allows that—from clump to clump and crouch behind them, without being seen from her house. Of course the house across the street was another matter, but since its front yard was in far worse shape than C. J.'s, it seemed obvious to me that the owner was not the early-rising type.

I think I would have stopped short of going all the way to her front door if I hadn't seen that faint crack of light. Not coming from underneath the door, but along the side of it. C. J.'s front door was ajar.

I froze. Almost literally. That's how long I crouched there. Perhaps C. J. was on her way out, and had just popped back in to get her car keys or something else she'd forgotten. Perhaps she had been keeping track of me all along, and the open door was a part of her surveillance. Or maybe it was a trap.

When my toes had become totally numb, and my nose was running faster than an Olympic sprinter, I concluded that Jane Cox had not forgotten her car keys and gone back in after them. And given the fact that the front door had a little window at the top, she was probably not watching me through the crack. Either she had forgotten to close the door behind her the night before, or something was seriously amiss.

I would have bet good money on the latter. Any woman who owns her own antique shop at age twenty-three, and rubs shoulders with mature adults on a daily basis—not to mention one who had probably offed two people—is not likely to forget to lock up at night. But if something was amiss . . .

"Oh no," I moaned. "What if it's not Jane. What if I've been stupidly standing by while whoever it really is offs Jane?"

The thought made me sick. In the time it takes a teenage girl to fall out of love, I found myself switching sides. Jane the probable aggressor was now Jane the possible victim. Jane the aggressor had been almost too easy to believe. Jane the victim broke my heart. Poor girl, first orphaned, and now this.

"Now what?" I asked myself. Mumbling aloud under stress is, I believe, a genetic trait. At least in my family. Answering one's own question is as well.

"Now you go straight back to your car and drive like a bat out of hell to the nearest public phone," I said.

My feet ignored their mistress and headed up along the driveway, closer to the walk that led to the house. If I knew them, they were going to propel me right up to that front door and beyond. There was simply nothing I could do about it.

I pushed the front door open slowly, trying to ignore the widening gap of light that could surely be seen by anyone in the house across the street, *if* they happened to be looking out the window. Perhaps at this point it was better to get the neighbors involved. Let them call the police.

My feet forced me inside. The light, which I wanted to gather up in my arms and push back into the house, was coming from a single small lamp on an end table by the couch. The house was utterly silent, not a fridge humming, nor a furnace purring. It was as if I had caught the house between breaths.

"Jane?" I whispered.

Silence.

"Jane?"

The furnace kicked in then and answered me with a roar. I jumped almost high enough to see what St. Peter wears under his skirt.

"Damn it!" I said. "You're such a little coward, Abigail. There's obviously nobody here but you and your shadow, and you almost left it behind. Now get a grip on yourself."

Having chastised myself, I closed the front door and turned on the overhead living room light. For a twenty-three-year-old, C. J. had rather sophisticated taste. The room was done up in Federal style, most of it used reproductions I would wager, but here and there I saw something that might be the real thing.

It wasn't too bad going through the house, as long as I could turn on an overhead light in each room first. Fortunately the house was just old enough that virtually every room had a light fixture smack dab in the middle of the ceiling. Those squared, etched glare plates in some, globes in others.

The kitchen was country, the real stuff. Outside of that and the living room, everything else appeared to be early garage sale. Apparently C. J. couldn't afford to decorate with her own stock. Not many dealers can. The garage sale stuff was tastefully arranged, however. I'll grant her that.

I called her name in every room, but there was no answer. Understandably I did not check the closets, or under the beds. Fortunately the shower was glazed glass, and half-open. There did not appear to be a body stashed in the tub.

I returned to C. J.'s bedroom and picked up the phone receiver. I glanced at my watch. It was only five-fifteen. Too early to call Greg without a legitimate excuse, and breaking and entering on my part—well, I had found the door open, so breaking couldn't be added to my list of sins. Still, Greg would be pissed, and who could blame him? To be roused by a phone call from an on-again, off-again girlfriend at that ungodly hour would be more than enough reason. In fact he might be so pissed at me that he would run straight to the already half-filled arms of Hooter. I decided to call anyway.

C. J.'s bedside phone was one of those complicated jobs attached to an answering machine, the kind that makes Mama think all Japanese engineers are the devil's spawn. It even had a feature that allows you to see the number of the last person who called. Out of curiosity—not nosiness—I pushed that button. In for a penny, in for a pound, I told myself and dialed the number displayed.

"You have reached Broken Tree Nursery," Garland Riggs said. "We value you as a customer. At the tone, please leave your name, number, and a brief message. We will return your call as soon as possible."

I hung up.

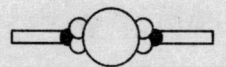

25

I immediately dialed Greg. After the fourth ring his machine picked up. I felt as if I had been slapped. How did he expect me to call and apologize, or otherwise worm myself back into his life? His indifference to what was supposed to be our mutual angst galled me. Not only did he look like a store mannequin, but he had just as much sentiment. Either that or he was busy boffing Hooter, to use a crude term I picked up from Buford. Either way, our relationship was clearly over.

"Up yours," I screamed into his machine. It is too damn hard to be a Southern lady at five in the morning.

Knowing she is a thrifty person, I turned out all the lights in C. J.'s house. Then I turned them all back on. It had suddenly occurred to me that I had not seen head or tail of the marquetry table. I searched the house thoroughly, more confident this time, even managing quick peeks into the closets. The marquetry table would not have fit under her bed. Ditto for C. J. Two pieces of the puzzle were definitely missing.

I didn't bother to sneak out. I closed the front door firmly behind me and used the walk to the driveway like any normal human being. That, at least, C. J. had bothered to salt.

I suppose my intentions were to search her car, but I never got that far. I happened to glance down the driveway, and in the waning moonlight the two wide tire marks in the snow stood out in bold relief. I should have noticed them on way in. They were definitely not made by C. J.'s tiny Festiva. They looked like the tire marks of a truck, one of those pickups with the monster tires. Garland's?

But of course! It wasn't a bloody "B" that Arnie was trying to scrawl in the armoire, but an "R." An "R," of which the left leg dripped down, partially closing it off and making it look like a "B." How stupid could I be, not to have seen that possibility from the beginning?

And C. J., always bothering me, always trying to distract me with her bizarre stories. The captain and his first mate, indeed. It was more like Garland and C. J.

So that was it! C. J. and Garland were in on this together. That's why he kept sending messages through her. Perhaps they were even lovers. Garland was married, I knew, to someone named Alma. But what difference did that make in today's world? And so what if he was old enough to be C. J.'s father? Ask Mia Farrow that one.

Now the two of them (Garland and C. J., not Mia) had run off in such a big hurry that they hadn't even bothered to close C. J.'s door. Of course I didn't have proof yet— not the kind you could take to the police—but at least I knew where to look next.

I dashed back inside and pressed redial for the second time. Greg's machine answered again. Surely there was a law against public investigators making themselves unavailable while they frolicked and fornicated with femme fatales. Especially if the public investigator in question had given you his private phone number, and had in exchange taken your heart.

The Rob-Bobs didn't answer, either. I guess I shouldn't have been surprised. They sometimes get nasty calls at odd hours from people who have nothing better to do than to harass those who were dealt cards from a different deck.

"This is Abby," I said to their machine. "I'm fine. You were half-right, Rob. I mean about C. J. She *is* in on this, but she's not acting alone. Don't worry—she's not going to get away with this, I can tell you that. And neither is he. I'm headed for Broke—"

The machine cut me off, just like that. I thought about calling back, but decided I had told them enough, perhaps even too much. Besides, I really didn't have a minute to spare, not if I wanted to get over to Broken Tree Nursery before the trail got cold.

It took me forty-five minutes to make what should have been a twenty-minute trip. But I arrived safely, without any dings or dents to my car, or to anyone else's, for that matter. It was still dark at that hour, but already a smattering of headlights could be seen, creeping slowly along the frozen roads.

Broken Tree Nursery is on the southeast side of Charlotte, south of Pineville even, and it straddles the state line. Garland, or whoever does his menial labor, can stand in North Carolina while he prunes a shrub in South Carolina. Until only a year or so ago the area around Broken Tree Nursery was farmland, peaches mainly, with the odd cotton field here and there.

But Charlotte is growing faster than a fourteen-year-old boy, and Greater Charlotte now threatens to spill over into South Carolina. The land all around Garland's nursery is being converted from productive farmland into upper-middle-class subdivisions. A few of the subdivisions are prestigious enough to be predominantly stucco. If Garland really wanted to make a killing, it seemed to me, he would sell his nursery to local developers, instead of chasing after some mythical French fortune.

The nursery was dark when I arrived. The moon had set, and as Buford would say, it was blacker than a well digger's ass. The subdivisions that bordered Garland's property were still under construction and not yet inhabited. Except for a handful of light on in Laurel Oak Plantation, the newly completed subdivision across the road, and the occasional car pulling out of its handsome wrought-iron gates, it might as well all have still been farmland.

I pulled off the highway and into the parking lot, dousing my lights the second my tires crunched on the gravel. I braked and shut off the car, remaining in the warmth of my car a few minutes while my eyes adjusted as well as they could.

The first thing I looked for, and the first thing I saw, was Garland Riggs's pickup with the ridiculous oversize tires. I couldn't read the writing on the side, but that bizarre broken tree stood out like a beacon. It may as well have had a spotlight trained on it.

I am not blessed with particularly good night vision, but my eyes are overall very healthy, and soon I was able to make out, quite clearly, the various buildings and sheds that comprise the nursery complex. Between them and the blacker outline of the manmade forest were the stock fields. I was already vaguely familiar with the layout because I had driven by Broken Tree Nursery many times. Although I have a fairly keen interest in gardening, I had never bothered to stop in. Not with Kmart, Lowe's, and Home Depot to choose from.

My shoes made almost as much noise on the gravel as my car had made. At least I didn't sound as loud as an engine, if you discount the almost deafening thump of my heart. I had no choice but to crunch my way over to the pickup.

I felt its hood, and my heart pounded harder. The metal beneath my hand was still warm. Garland had been at C. J.'s. The two of them were undoubtedly inside the main building now, emptying the cash register, or whatever it is lovers do as they prepare for a life on the road as fugitives. Why they would do whatever it was in the dark was beyond me. But then so is murder. Evil people thrive in darkness. That's what the Bible says—even the version we Episcopalians use.

There was no point in me hanging around longer. I had passed an all-night CoGo market not a quarter-mile down the road. Undoubtedly they had a phone I could use. I would make one last call to Greg, and then call the police. The *real* police. The police who weren't busy humping Hooter. Then I would park just inside the entrance of Laurel Oak Plantation and keep an eagle eye on the suspects. It would be starting to get light soon.

But first there was one thing I wanted to do to confirm my suspicions. Just to make double sure that I was right. A quick peek inside the double cab, and I would have my proof. C. J. was not the type of girl who would run off without taking at least a pair of clean underwear and her toothbrush. There had to be luggage of some sort stashed back there, perhaps even my marquetry table.

To say that I hopped nimbly up on the running board would be an exaggeration. Truthfully, I've mounted horses with more ease. I was making my third assault on the monster, and had finally made a purchase, when I felt myself lifted off the running board—literally—just as surely as if a giant owl had swooped down, grabbed me in its talons, and was carrying me off to its nest to eat for breakfast.

"What the—"

"You nosy little bitch," the owl snarled.

"Garland!"

He set me down, but kept one fist knotted around the collar of my coat. Next time I did any snooping I was going to wear the damn thing unbuttoned. You never know when you might want to slip out of your coat and run for your life.

"I-I was just driving by," I said stupidly, "and decided

to stop in and thank you personally for the lovely camellia.''

He laughed. "So you're a nosy, *stupid* little bitch."

I couldn't argue with that. "Well, a gal's gotta try to save her own neck, right?''

"You're in it up to your neck. I'm afraid there's no saving you.''

"C. J.!''

She may have been his accomplice all along, but on some level we were friends. I didn't think C. J. would have it in her to see me offed as well. Perhaps I could take some sort of special vow of silence. I would be willing to do that, you know. Wouldn't you? I mean, what is so wrong about sealing your lips on evil, if it means saving your life? I know that sounds terrible, but when the Grim Reaper has you by the collar, you might reconsider your position. The only trouble was, I didn't think someone as hardened as Garland was going to fall for that.

"C. J.!'' I called again.

Garland laughed, and then hoisted me up by the collar, like I was a kitten, and he a mother cat. He swung me forward so that my nose bumped the rear window of the double cab.

"See that?''

For a few seconds I didn't see anything but the stars in my head. Then I saw C. J. lying there on the backseat, all trussed up like a Christmas turkey. She had her hands tied behind her back. Her feet were bound together, and her legs were bent at the knee, and tied in that position. There was a gray swath of duct tape across her mouth. Her eyes were closed.

"You goddamn, goddamn, goddamn—'' I said. I was too stunned to say anything worse.

Garland pushed my face into the glass. The stars all came out again, along with a few planets. I took a short nap.

When I awoke, I, too, was trussed like a Christmas turkey, only my legs were not tied behind me. I was propped on the front seat of the cab, beside Garland. My mouth wasn't taped, and I had one hell of a headache.

I felt for my ring. The idiot had let it be. It wasn't worth half of Paris, but it was worth a good sight more than all four Barras pieces combined. I groaned, as much from relief as from pain.

"It's about time," he said. "I didn't want to kill you without an explanation. It's more fun that way."

"Maybe for you." I groaned again.

"That Arnie guy died without an explanation, damn son of a bitch."

"So, you killed him, too. I knew it!"

"He had no business hanging around the warehouse—"

"He worked for Purvis," I snapped. "Of course Purvis made my job a little more difficult by denying he was there that day. But who can blame him? Why borrow trouble?"

Garland grunted. "Hell, Arnie did. All I wanted was a good look at that damn mirror, and he started asking too many questions, and for your information, girlie, I didn't mean to kill him. I just decked him, and he hit his head going down."

"So, you stuffed him in my armoire!"

He laughed. "It was mighty convenient. Then the next morning I called the cops."

"That was you? Well, at least Arnie left a clue with his own blood."

"I scraped that blood off when I paid your shop a little visit and lifted the mirror. Your precious clue, for what it was worth, is gone."

"Gone, yes, but not forgotten. *Everyone* saw it," I lied.

"Bullshit. You're the only one who figured it out, and you came alone. That little secret will die with you."

"Like Lottie Bell's did with her? Is that why you burned her house down? To cover your tracks."

He laughed again. "Better safe than sorry. Anyway, thanks to your friend there"—he pointed to C. J.—"I did solve the Barras family mystery."

"Bullshit."

His reaction to my use of the swear word was remarkably calm.

"It was in that little table, not the mirror. I would have smashed the fucker to smithereens, like I did the desk, but C. J. found it for me."

"That figures."

"Oh, she wasn't very cooperative. She might not get a chance to wake up before she buys the farm." He laughed.

"Well, so you're a rich man now, are you, Garland?"

"Bitch!" he said angrily.

I waited. We were driving through the entrance of a new subdivision. One of the yet unoccupied ones behind Garland's nursery. Magnolia Manor, this huge sign said, in stucco-on-stucco relief. At least I was in the stucco subdivision. It's not much of a comfort, but if you have to die, you may as well die in an upscale neighborhood.

Garland pounded the steering wheel with one of his hamlike fists. "I'm not rich. You don't get rich in the nursery business. Not when you have record heat one year, and record cold the next."

"Then sell it and quit whining," I snapped. "You don't get sympathy from me—and get to kill me—all in the same night."

He glanced at me, surprised at my cheek.

"But I don't own this fucking business by myself. My wife owns half of it, and she won't let us sell." He jabbed the air with a sausage finger. "There! I could be living in a house like that if we sold out to developers."

"Well, you've got your Paris property now, or whatever was hidden in that table, haven't you?''

He pounded the steering wheel so hard I thought he would break it. Actually I hoped he would break it, and puncture an artery on a jagged edge. I am not yet the good Christian I intend to be.

''All I've got is shit. A fucking bill.''

''I didn't bill you, buster,'' I said through gritted teeth. ''You stole that table from C. J.'s house, remember?''

''Ha! Not a bill from you, but from some damn furniture company.''

''No sympathy,'' I reminded him.

His laugh then was almost pleasant, like we were out for a joyride instead of on our way to my funeral.

''The bill, Miss Timberlake, was made out to a man named Barras. Apparently he was an eighteenth-century ancestor of mine. It was a bill for that table and the other pieces.''

''You're kidding!''

''There was a letter as well.''

''Oh?''

''Yes. A letter from a Monsieur Laurier, a Paris furnituremaker. Apparently Josephine—who was not yet married to Napoleon, and who was living with my ancestor—was buying expensive furniture and charging it to her host. When the bill came, she hid it in the table. She did the same thing with the letter demanding payment.''

''Y'all were deadbeats even then,'' I said.

''Barras was my ancestor,'' he snarled, ''not Josephine.''

We rode in silence for a minute, turning first left and then right on the deserted streets. The sky was beginning to lighten. The stucco mansions were assuming shades of gray.

''Aren't those letters at least worth something?'' He sounded pathetic.

''A couple hundred each, maybe, *if* you found the right

buyer. Not nearly enough to trade your life for.''

He spit, but his window was closed. ''Goddamn! See what you made me do?''

''I didn't make you do anything, dear,'' I said, mimicking the sweet sarcasm Susan uses. ''You did it to yourself.''

''Shut up!''

I was on a roll. ''Were those your cigarette butts the police found, dear? If so, that shade of lipstick does nothing for you.''

''Huh?''

''Do you prefer lethal injection or the chair?'' I asked. Certain death—mine—brought with it a surprising amount of freedom.

''I'm not the one who is buying it, girlie. You are. Only you don't get a choice. You and your friend back there are buying the farm right now—or what's left of it.'' He laughed.

''You'll never get away with it, asshole. People know where I am. I called for help before I came out here. Even if you do kill us, they'll trace it to you.''

''Yeah, right. You're lying, girlie. But even if you aren't, they'll never find you. Last week I signed a contract to plant one dozen big magnolia trees back here. Not container size, but great big ones. Field dug trees. They're all bundled in burlap and sitting back here waiting to be put in the ground. Magnolias for Magnolia Manor.

''Yesterday morning I finished digging the last hole. Twelve of them. As big as craters. So you see, y'all's graves are already dug. Y'all will be Magnolia manure, in a manner of speaking.'' He didn't laugh.

We came to a sudden stop at the back end of the development. Garland immediately jumped down and undid a heavy metal chain, which was as thick as my wrist. Obviously the man knew where he was going.

Still I closed my eyes when Garland got back in the

car and drove right through what appeared to be the back of a long but very narrow house. Although bound, I braced myself for a crash as best I could. When there was none, I twisted my head around for a backward look.

"Well, I'll be!" I couldn't help but say.

It wasn't a house we'd driven through, but a facade worthy of a Disney feature. It was a two-dimensional Tara in stucco. Magnolia Manor, it said in free-standing letters set on the grassy slope that banked toward the "house." Six huge spotlights, as big as washtubs, were trained on the letters, but unfortunately they had yet to be turned on. On either side of the make-believe mansion, the grassy bank continued for a hundred or more feet, and that's where the magnolias were to be planted.

"When it's all done, this is going to be the main entrance," Garland said. He sounded proud, as if he was in charge of the entire development, not just the landscaping. "There's going to be a country club across the road there, and the builders decided to compete for attention. The country club is going to be so exclusive that even Arnold Palmer has to go on a waiting list."

"Maybe my mama will apply if the Apathia Club doesn't take her," I said.

He gave me a strange look. I realized I could see the whites of his eyes. It was definitely getting on toward dawn and my foretold demise. He seemed to read my mind.

"No more time to waste, girlie. Which side do you want to be planted on? Right or left, take your pick. Just tell me where you want to go."

"Up yours," I said.

He chuckled and got down from the cab. A few seconds later he was hauling me out like a sack of flour, and throwing me over his left shoulder. He held me in place with both hands.

"I decided to plant you on the left. You'll get a better

view of the country club. The clubhouse is going to be over there.''

''Where?''

He pointed with his right hand. Fat lot of good it did me, since I was facing the other way, toward the Tara monstrosity.

''Where?''

The stupid man jabbed the air with that sausage finger. Apparently he thought I had eyes in the back of my head. He could think I had horns, too, if he wanted, because his very stupidity presented me with a chance to get away.

It wasn't much of a chance, but I knew it was all I was going to get. Kicking and twisting at the same time, I managed to wiggle out of his grasp and off his shoulder. I slid backward. As my left hand moved past his face, I twisted to the left, bringing the Kashmiri sapphire in contact with his cheek, starting at the corner of his mouth and continuing to the ear.

He screamed, a long agonizing howl, like a wolf caught in a steel claw trap. Both hands flew to his face, and I hit the ground, harder than a sack of flour. For the second time that morning, I passed out.

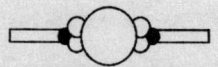

26

When I woke up, it was in the ICU of Mercy Hospital South. Mama was hovering over me like a hummingbird on a hibiscus.

Trust me, regaining consciousness is not like what they show in the movies. I didn't wake up suddenly and ask, "Where am I?" It was a gradual process, my consciousness flickering on and off like a light bulb on a bad circuit. But every time it flickered on, there was Mama. Although Mama is taller than I am, she still doesn't scrape five feet, so hovering over a hospital bed was no easy task for her.

Other faces hovered as well, and as the light bulb stayed on longer, I began to focus and sort them out. I saw Susan several times, and Charlie at least once. I thought I saw dear Wynnell, although that might have been an orderly who didn't bother to shave. As for those periodic flashes of intense blue, they were undoubtedly Greg's eyes. Nurse Beasely told me later that she would gladly trade places with the lowliest of Candy Stripers if she could have a boyfriend like Greg. Was he really taken? she wondered. I assured her that he was, and to punish her pushed my call button a few more times than was absolutely necessary.

Little by little my family and friends pieced together for me a rather ragged version of my rescue, which was about as fractured as my skull. "Subdural hematoma," the doctors said. A hairline fracture, which had caused two small blood vessels to burst in my brain. Fortunately the bleeding stopped spontaneously, and since no surgery was required, I was released from the hospital in just over a week.

It wasn't until Christmas Day, however, that I got the full, unabridged story of the events that led up to my nicked noggin. Mama and I were having Christmas dinner with the Rob-Bobs since Susan and Charlie were off in Paris with Buford and the Tweetie Byrd. The Rob-Bobs, bless them, had been kind enough to invite Greg as well.

The fact that Rob is Jewish apparently has little effect on the way they celebrate Christmas. The place was decked out as lavishly as the Biltmore Estate, only on a smaller scale, of course. They had not held back on the food either, and the gilded Regency groaned under the weight. The beaming Bob had clearly outdone himself.

''Roast suckling pig,'' he said as he placed a pewter platter the size of a surfboard in the middle of the table.

We stared in disbelief at the centerpiece. It was indeed a pig—small, granted, but a whole pig with an apple stuck in its mouth. The pitiful creature had undoubtedly been shaved, but otherwise was gruesomely intact. It had tiny hooves that looked as if they were made of burned plastic, ragged ears that were charred along the edges, and a three-inch tail. Mercifully, Bob had replaced the piglet's eyes with stuffed green olives.

The pheasant under glass was real as well, as were its feathers. Ditto for the individual servings of quail *en brochette*. It was clear from the start that this was going to be another one of those meals where the food earned mileage on the plate, but never actually touched the lips.

I allowed myself to envy Tweetie for a moment. Although she had to put up with Buford—who sort of resembled the suckling pig—she was probably enjoying a Le Big Mac at EuroDisney with my kids.

Mama gaped at the graphic display of medieval food. A true Southern lady, she has the ability to comment on any situation and make it sound like a compliment.

"It's all so incredible," she said.

Bob beamed.

"He does have a way with food," Rob agreed. A Southern gentleman, he shared Mama's ability.

We were all chatty that meal. What better way to avoid eating? Even Bob, who actually ate, did his fair share of talking.

"It was Garland's cousin Toxie, you know, who left behind those cigarette butts."

"You don't say! Not Amy? She had the cold. I thought she might have caught it skulking around outside."

"No, it was Toxie all right," Rob said. "We went down to her club last night and talked to her. Man, can she ever sing."

"You're kidding!"

"Almost as good as Liza," Bob said. "But enough about her." He raised his wineglass. "To Abby," he said. "May she have more lives than her cat, Dmitri."

"Here, here," everyone chorused.

"And to Bob," Rob said, "who wields a shovel as well as he does a spatula."

Mama laid down an empty fork. "Excuse me?"

"It's time we told her," Bob said, sounding as proud as a mother hen. He looked at Greg.

Greg cleared his throat. "Well, when Abby called that morning, I, uh, was otherwise occupied."

My heart sank. "Not with that bimbo Bambi!"

Greg smiled weakly. "Her name is Deena, and she's not a bimbo. But no, I wasn't with her."

"Then where were you?" Mama is nothing if not protective of me.

Greg swallowed hard and glared at Rob. "I was in the hospital myself."

"What?" Since food had yet to pass my lips, swallowing was no problem for me.

"I had a—well, I skidded off the road," Greg said miserably. "I was on my way over to see you and hit an ice patch."

"A likely story," Mama snapped.

It isn't right to kick one's mother under the table, but I couldn't help myself.

I stared at Greg. "Were you hurt?"

"Naw, just a few bumps and bruises, but she insisted on keeping me overnight."

"Who is *she*?" Mama was at it again. "Silicone Sally?"

Greg glared. "You must be referring to Deena, Mrs. Wiggins, and that's not who I mean. The she I'm talking about is the doctor."

Rob waved his hands, presumably to get our attention, but maybe to dispel the bad vibes that were piling up faster than the bones on Bob's plate.

"Anyway," Rob said, "the hero is Bob. You see, he was—well, you tell them, Bob. And don't be modest about it."

Bob grinned and had the grace to blush. Modesty becomes some men.

"Well, I got up earlier than usual that morning, despite the time we went to bed." He turned to me. "I was going to bake you some cinnamon rolls. From scratch. When I walked by the guest room the door was open and it was empty. I thought of waking up Rob, but he can be a bear when he hasn't had his eight hours."

Rob nodded. "A grizzly."

"I had a hunch that you had gone over to C. J.'s to search the—the—"

"*Table liseuse.*"

"Yeah. So I called there. First it was busy, then nobody answered."

"I must have just left."

"Yes. But C. J. should have answered, unless something had happened to her."

I recoiled in my chair. "You thought I killed her?"

Everyone laughed, albeit nervously. Bob blushed scarlet.

"That's not what I meant. But you might have been provoked into something and found yourself in deeper water than you'd planned."

"Abby's a good swimmer," Mama said loyally.

"Mama, please. Go on, Bob."

"Well, there's not much to tell. I drove over to C. J.'s and just as I turned the corner, there you were, driving off. So I followed you."

"Why didn't you follow faster?" I didn't mean to sound so sharp. But even with my insurance, the week in the hospital had cost me a pretty penny.

"I followed as fast as I could, Abby, but you drive like a bat out of hell." He glanced at Mama. "Pardon the language."

"Pardoned," Mama said. "Please go on."

"Yes, well, I lost you on South Boulevard, and was about to give up when I remembered you said Garland Riggs owned the Broken Tree Nursery, and that it was somewhere down near Pineville. So then I drove around trying to find a phone book and—"

"You drove around looking for a phone book?" I nearly yelled.

Okay, what else was the poor man supposed to do? He wasn't from the area. I couldn't expect him to just know where Broken Tree Nursery was. But it scared the dickens out of me to think that Southern Bell Yellow Pages was the only thing that had prevented me from becoming compost down in Magnolia Manor.

"Hey, hey, Abby," Rob said, and rightly so.

"Sorry, Bob," I hastened to apologize. "I really am grateful. You are my hero. Now please go on."

Bob smiled graciously. "Well, there isn't much else to tell. I got to the nursery and found your empty car. There wasn't anything else for me to do but follow the monstrous tracks of that ridiculous pickup of his."

"That and conk him over the head with a shovel," Rob said proudly.

The doorbell rang and my unassuming hero sprang to answer it. In a minute he returned, with both C. J. and Wynnell in tow.

"We pulled up at exactly the same time," C. J. gushed. "Imagine that! I read a book once where—"

"Merry Christmas!" Wynnell said. Bless her soul.

"Merry Christmas," we chorused.

"Here." Wynnell thrust a package at me before C. J. could open her mouth again. "Open it, dear."

Against my better judgment I tore into my gift just to shut C. J. up. It worked for a few minutes. Perhaps in a former life Wynnell wrapped mummies for a living, or manufactured chastity belts. Even Houdini would be slowed by her efforts.

"Ooh," I heard Mama gasp as I ripped away the last sheet of Santa Claus paper.

"Ooh," the others chorused.

I stared silently at the gift my thoughtful friend had made with her own two blessed hands. The lime-green corduroy jumper with purple patch pockets and yellow buttons the size and shape of egg yolks was truly beyond intelligible words.

"I felt kind of bad, having given you that store-bought sweater before. I mean, you could have *died*, Abigail."

I gave Wynnell a big hug. I hadn't realized the woman felt so strongly about me. But if the tears that drenched my back were any indication, she was the best friend I ever had.

"Thank you," I said, on the verge of tears myself.

"Ahem," Greg said and tapped on his water glass.

I released Wynnell and gratefully gave Greg my attention.

"I have a present for Abby, too," he said and pulled a little black velvet box out of his right pants pocket.

"Uh-oh," Mama muttered.

Greg cleared his throat. "Abby, I—"

"Later," I mouthed. I wasn't about to be proposed to in front of a room full of people.

He didn't notice my desperate attempt to stop him. "I want you to know—"

"Please, not now. Not here," I whispered, as if no one else could hear me.

But Greg was determined. Wynnell may as well have tried to stop Yankees from spilling across the Carolina border. I held my breath, helpless to save both Greg and me a lot of embarrassment.

"—I appreciate your help in nabbing Garland Riggs. In fact, the entire department is very grateful. So we got you this."

He opened the little black box and held it out to me. Inside was a small but exquisite gold charm in the shape of a cat.

I exhaled loudly, for all the world sounding like a punctured tire. But I couldn't help it, given the bizarre mixture of relief and disappointment I felt.

"And for you," Greg said, turning to Bob, "the department has unanimously declared you Citizen of the Week. Anytime you want to ride along with us in our civilian program, you just let me know. But no hands-on stuff again."

Everyone laughed. Bob blushed.

"Thanks," he said. But I suspected he would rather have the gold cat charm.

"My cousin Elmo went on a ride with the Shelby police once," Jane said, "but he wasn't exactly an invited guest. You see, he'd been reaching under a police car to retrieve a quarter he'd dropped when—"

"Shut up," Mama said gently.

"Shut up," we chorused, and a merry Christmas was had by all.